RAVE REVIEWS FROM THE MYSTERY WORLD FOR RANDALL HICKS' DEBUT NOVEL, *THE BABY GAME*

"Hicks's breezy mystery debut introduces Toby Dillon, an adoption attorney who has seemingly stumbled his way into a lifestyle unusual for an attorney but which suits him perfectly. The result is extremely satisfying as Hicks's facile prose converts technical expertise into a solidly entertaining mystery debut."

—*Alfred Hitchcock Mystery Magazine*

"One of the most engaging first novels I've read this year."

—*Mystery News*

"Hicks has a wonderful voice and his writing is filled with humorous moments that offset the seriousness of what is going on perfectly. He has a unique style that while similar to others is truly his own. A terrific debut, and I look forward to next year's *Baby Crimes*. I would strongly recommend this book."

—*CrimeSpree* Magazine

"A romp for anyone who loves to laugh. A sequel would be very much appreciated."

—*Deadly Pleasures* Magazine

"What a delightful debut! Hicks, a noted adoption attorney, has a great voice and a way with telling a mystery story. . . I couldn't stop reading even if I'd wanted to."

—Confessions of an Idiosyncratic Mind
(SarahWeinman.com)

"A light and tasty treat. . . An engrossing mystery."

—*Mystery Scene* Magazine

"Randall Hicks has the three vital ingredients for mega success: great narrative, humor and style. This has the making of a great series. It's smart, sassy and with a streak of compassion. Best of all, Hicks has that rarest of all qualities, he's even better on your second reading."

—Ken Bruen (Shamus Award winning author of *The Guards* and *The Dramatist*)

"An exciting action-packed thriller. . . an exhilarating story line."

—Amazon.com (#1 reviewer)

"The plot developed by Hicks is a convoluted one, with tantalizing clues dropped along the way, plus a sentimental touch woven into the ending. . . A well-told tale peopled with sympathetic characters."

—I Love A Mystery Newsletter (IloveAMysteryNewsletter.com)

FOR MORE REVIEWS AND INFORMATION
PLEASE VISIT TOBYDILLON.COM
OR BABYCRIMES.COM

ALSO BY RANDALL HICKS

Fiction

The Baby Game

Nonfiction

Adoption: The Essential Guide to
Adopting Quickly and Safely

Adopting in America:
How to Adopt within One Year

Adopting in California:
How To Adopt within One Year

FOR YOUNG READERS

Adoption Stories for Young Children

BABY
CRIMES

Randall Hicks

$\mathcal{W}$

W O R D S L I N G E R　　P R E S S

San Diego, California

BABY CRIMES. Copyright © 2007 by Randall B. Hicks. All rights reserved. No part of this book may be used or reproduced in any manner without written permission, except in the case of brief quotations embodied in critical reviews or articles. Printed in the U.S.A. For information, contact WordSlinger Press (WordSlingerPress.com), 9921 Carmel Mountain Rd, Suite 335, San Diego, CA 92129. WordSlinger Press books are distributed by SCB Distributors, 15608 S. New Century Drive, Gardena, CA 90248 (scbdistributors.com).

Cover by Sosebee Design NYC

Library of Congress Cataloging-in-Publication Data

Hicks, Randall, 1956-
  Baby Crimes / Randall Hicks. -- 1st ed.
    p. cm.
  Summary: "A mystery novel featuring adoption attorney, Toby Dillon. A wealthy couple is being blackmailed due to the illegal adoption of their daughter sixteen years ago. They seek Toby's help to legitimize their adoption and discover who knows their secret. The case turns deadly when suspects start turning up dead" – Provided by publisher.
  ISBN-13: 978-0-9794430-0-8 (trade pbk. : alk. paper)
  ISBN-10: 0-9794430-0-8 (trade pbk. : alk. paper)
    1. Adoption—Corrupt practices—Fiction. 2. Extortion—Fiction. I
    Title.
  PS3608.1285B32 2007
  813'.6–dc22
                                                    2007012717
First Edition

10 9 8 7 6 5 4 3 2 1

H

To Ken Bruen
for his support and encouragement:

A great writer,
an inspiration,
my friend across the sea.

Gra go mor

There's more to life than increasing its speed.

—Mahatma Gandhi

Acknowledgments

Many people provided their help and encouragement—something writers can never get enough of—and I'd like to thank them here:

To the people every writer needs: advance readers to give blunt advice on making a book the best it can be. My thanks to writers Barbara Seranella (I really miss you, Barbara, heaven is richer for your presence), Brian Wiprud (my fellow fashion walker) and Ken Bruen (Mr. Rock and Roll of noir); mystery enthusiasts Maggie Mary Mason (Reacher Creature and mystery savant), Emily Bronstein (my favorite "con" pal), Maddy Van Hertbruggen (my first mystery confidante), Jack Quick (reading more books daily than humanly possible), Yvette Banek (whose mystery knowledge is only exceeded by her own artistic talents); and family members Angela, Ryan, Hailey, Bob and Carolyn Hicks.

To Lynn Orcutt, for giving me a plot twist as we stood on the steps of the luxurious Diplomat II.

To the many people who either went out of their way to support my debut mystery, *The Baby Game*, or perform some random act of kindness to which they may have given little thought, but meant a lot to me: Stacy Alesi, Sarah Weinman, Barbara Franchi, Janet Rudolph, Joan Hansen, Beth Feydn, Luci Zahray and Lee Child.

To Dr. Joan Elkins for help with all medical questions.

To the San Diego County Sheriff's crime lab staff. No, I wasn't asking those questions because I was planning to kill someone and try to get away with it.

To Captain William Solberg for the boating advice, even when I chose to ignore some of it out of literary stubbornness.

To my editor, Bill East, for his hard work, and continuing the tradition of picking up the tab for our celebratory lunch at *Subway*. I hope you get it covered on your expense account, big spender.

BABY CRIMES

1

"IT'S NOT LIKE we *stole* our daughter. We just. . ."

The female side of the white bread Bonnie and Clyde duo sitting in front of me faltered and her husband picked it up. He did look a bit like a young Warren Beatty. Lucky bastard.

"We just didn't adopt her in the traditional way," he said, flashing me a TV teeth smile, followed by a wink that said "we're pals." They'd strolled into my office thirty minutes ago like Grand Marshals in a parade, missing only the "Don't hate us because we're beautiful" banner preceding them.

The *she* we were discussing was my tennis student, Lynn. Of course, they likely thought of her as their daughter. And they also likely preferred the names Nevin and Catherine Handley to Bonnie and Clyde. He was a millionaire fifty times over, a retired-at-forty-something dot-comer, and was just elected as a county supervisor on a "giving back to the people" platform. Officials like mayors and senators got the glory, but supervisors had the power, each one of San Diego County's five supervisors dividing up a section of the county as their own private fiefdom.

When Lynn's mother had called me yesterday to ask to chat privately before Lynn's lesson, I'd assumed it was to discuss tennis. Lynn had quickly risen to the number four ranking in the 16-and-under category in California and I'd guessed they were moving her to a big name coach. I wouldn't have blamed them, but it turned out they weren't here to see me as a coach.

The thing is, I wear two hats. By day I'm an attorney, specializing in adoptions, at least as much as one can specialize when you've been an attorney for all of eighteen months. By, well, the rest of the day, I'm a tennis pro. Assistant tennis pro, actually. The operative word being *assistant*, denoting as much importance as when used in the title "Assistant Manager at McDonalds." At age thirty-three I just had fewer pimples.

At the moment we were sitting in my office, the former storage room of the Pro Shop of the Coral Canyon Country Club, now the domain of Toby Dillon, Esq. I never quite got what the word Esquire had to do with being an attorney, but then there's a lot I can never figure out about my own profession.

"Do you mind if we back up a step?" I asked, picking up my legal pad. This was intended to make me look more lawyerly, and to mitigate the fact I was wearing shorts and a t-shirt emblazoned with "WILSON: Get extra fuzz on *your* balls."

Nevin gave me a magnanimous nod and surreptitiously glanced at his watch. I guess straightening out your daughter's adoption mess had time limits.

"Okay," I recapped. "Sixteen years ago the two of you were newly married, didn't have much money and were just starting your own computer software business."

Nevin shot me the teeth again. "You know what they say,

Toby. The first million's always the hardest." Thank goodness he didn't forget the wink at the end. He used it like punctuation.

"Right. A girl was working for you—"

"Melanie," Catherine interjected. "Melanie Dubravado. She was a sweet girl. I really don't think we're going to have any trouble."

"Uh huh. And when she got pregnant and told you she wasn't ready to be a mom, you agreed to adopt the baby."

Fear of a wink, or the teeth, kept my eyes on my legal pad and I pressed on.

"But Melanie didn't have any health insurance, and you did, so you had her check into the hospital," I looked up at Catherine. "Under *your* name."

She nodded and didn't look the least bit embarrassed. "It wasn't just about the insurance, Toby. It just seemed so unnecessary to have to go to an adoption agency and go through a home study, like something was *wrong* with us. Imagine."

They shared a chuckle over that and I stole a glance to see if they were winking at each other.

"So Melanie," I plowed ahead, "gave birth *as if she were you*. And she listed her husband—meaning your husband—Nevin, as the father."

Catherine nodded. "Well, of course. Who else would we put? He's my husband."

Who indeed, I thought. "But he's not the biological father, any more than you're the biological mother. Right?"

"Yes."

"So Melanie checks out of the hospital, gives you the baby— Lynn—and because everyone thinks it was you who gave birth, you end up with a birth certificate naming you as the legal mother and father. Just like if you gave birth to her yourself."

Nevin cleared his throat. "So you see, Toby, it's already legal, really. We just need you to go back and dot the i's and cross the t's. You know, do whatever it is you adoption people do."

You adoption people, huh. Well, Mister i-dotter and t-crosser, think again. My eyes went to my tennis racquet leaning against the wall and I wondered what kind of sound it would make if I hit them on the head with it. But ever the soul of discretion, and not wanting to risk breaking my strings on their pointed heads, I decided to hold off on that option.

Somehow, these two bozos had managed the perfect fraudulent adoption. I'd have been impressed if I weren't so disgusted. I didn't particularly care about what consequences they were facing; they deserved their headache. My fears were for Lynn. The adage of kids paying for the sins of their parents was too true, too often.

In a traditional adoption, the birth mother signs a consent to the adoption after the baby is born, and the adoptive parents go through a six month home study. When everything's approved, a court grants the adoption. Later, the adoptive parents receive an amended birth certificate naming them as the biological parents and naming the child as they'd like. They skipped a few steps. Actually, all of them.

"Okay," I said. "The first problem I see is you defrauded your insurance company. That's a crime, of course. A felony, actually. Then you falsified a birth certificate. There's probably a conspiracy charge in there too as the three of you were planning this together. You've had a child in your custody who's not legally yours, without a foster care license. Child-abduction charges are a possibility since although Melanie gave you Lynn voluntarily, we don't know if the birth father agreed. That's four crimes, and we haven't even got to the adoption yet."

I looked up to see how they were handling this so far, but both looked unconcerned. I plowed ahead.

"You don't have a consent to adoption by the birth mother, and you don't know where she is, or if she'll consent even if we find her. You don't have a consent from the birth father, and you're not even sure who he is to try to get it. You never did a home study. You never filed anything with the court. You. . ." I gave up. "You've got a big mess is what you've got."

Nice legal summation there, Toby. The good old *big mess* diagnosis.

"So you're saying. . ." Catherine's face took on an expression designed to show concern, but clearly a practiced one that wouldn't cause facial wrinkles.

"What he's saying, honey," Nevin said, reaching into his jacket pocket, "is that this is going to take some work." He had a check pre-written and slid it onto my desk. A glance told me it was for $20,000, or roughly half my yearly income. He'd left the recipient name blank, maybe so I could decide between "Toby Dillon" or "Soul for Sale."

I ignored the check. "Can I ask why you even want to try to fix this? I mean, Lynn will be eighteen in a couple years. Do you realize all the things that could go wrong for you? There's always the possibility they could take Lynn away from you, although that seems unlikely. Or that you could go to jail. And the criminal charges would be public, so everyone would know what you did."

They just looked at me, unconcerned. Then it hit me.

"Wait a minute. You've already *been* to an attorney, haven't you?"

Of course. They weren't about to place all their trust in the hands of some part-time, squeeze-in-a-law-practice-around-tennis-games lawyer, no matter how righteous his topspin forehand may be. Which brought up, why were they here at all? Nevin managed to keep his teeth under control and gave me his sincere face.

"Toby, no offense, but people like us don't go to jail. Our *crime* was giving a child a wonderful home. A life no one can fault. Insurance companies can be reimbursed. We were young and made a mistake. No one benefits from disrupting our family."

What I just heard sounded more like an attorney's closing argument.

"And that's who speaking?" I asked.

Nevin seemed a bit put out I didn't accept the words as his but shrugged and answered. "Anton West."

Yep, that figured. West was one of the top criminal attorneys in the state. Five grand just for a consult.

"And let me guess," I said. "He's already brokered a deal for you with the D.A., so you know you'll come out fine on this. And no press guaranteed too."

He spread his hands. "You do things right, Toby, and everybody wins."

Yeah, when everybody's rich that is. I had no problem with the rich and beautiful getting favors. I'd just like to see the people sweating under them get a break or two. It was for those kinds of people that I became a lawyer.

"So why are you here? You don't need me."

Nevin leaned forward, moving in to close the sale. "Can I be honest?"

Sure, like you know how. "Yes, please."

"We're here because we know you care about Lynn. And she's nuts about you. We know because of that no one's going to work harder to get the adoption part of this worked out."

He reached out and took his wife's hand, the gesture holding all the sincerity of Geraldo Rivera holding an orphaned baby on camera after an earthquake.

"Plus, adoption is all you do, Toby," he went on. "What big law firm is going to know how to handle these birth parents? To find them, and get them to cooperate? Do you think some five hundred dollar an hour suit is going to know how to approach them? You're young. You're. . . different."

He didn't actually make *different* sound like a compliment, but I let it slide.

I had to admit he had me pegged, about Lynn anyway. If it weren't for her, I'd have kicked them out within minutes of sticking their rhinoplastied noses in my door.

He knew he had me and pulled out a pen. "How do you want me to make out the check?"

But he wasn't the only one who could play games. Last week the club's head tennis pro had given me the assignment of raising money for a free summer tennis camp for all the lower income kids in town. I thought since it had been my idea I shouldn't be saddled with begging for donations too. I was the idea man, after all. We needed only five grand, but thanks to Nevin, suddenly it was looking like an annual event.

"Make it out to the Boys and Girls Club of Fallbrook."

His head jerked up.

"Hey," I said pointedly. "You may have the criminal side of this all worked out, but at some point we're still going to have to get this approved by an adoption judge. And the judge who has the adoption calendar plays here. Don't you think it's going to look good if he sees your face on the banner reading "Tennis Camp sponsored by Nevin Handley, County Supervisor?""

Nevin's crap-o-meter was alerting him, but either he ignored it, or I was a better liar than I thought. Actually, I had seen Judge

Bornman here once, although it was in the club's restaurant, not on the courts. So it wasn't a complete fib.

Nevin smiled and filled in the check. As he handed it to me, I was waiting, waiting, waiting…

Then yes! *The wink.* And a real guy-to-guy, "you are my special friend" wink, too. It suddenly hit me that's why I hadn't made my first million. No winking!

"I like the way you think, Toby."

"Thanks. And you can make out a check to me for one thousand. That'll be for twenty hours at fifty an hour." I reached in my drawer for a couple retainer forms.

"Fifty?" His look said that no self-respecting lawyer charged only fifty dollars an hour.

"Fifty," was all I said back, though.

He was the kind of guy who assumed he got more if he paid more, while I felt guilty getting more than I felt I deserved. So in some screwy way, I felt I'd just won a little battle by getting paid less. Besides, who in society decided lawyers should make triple what teachers, cops and firemen did? I mean, it's not like they had some world-shattering impressive skill, like a perfectly disguised backhand drop shot or anything.

Nevin glanced over the retainer before signing both copies, then passed them to Catherine, who signed without a glance. I signed them as well—meaning for better or worse, I was now their attorney. I gave Nevin their copy. As he took it they started to get up to leave. I thought we had more to cover, but maybe their high breeding could no longer tolerate their shoes' contact with my Astroturf carpeting, and they needed the reassurance of the distressed oak planking and fine Berber awaiting them at home. I wanted to ask at least one more question, though.

"You still didn't tell me why, after all these years, you want to try to make the adoption legal. There's so much to risk."

Nevin put his copy of my retainer in his jacket pocket, maybe so it would be out of my reach and I couldn't grab it back.

For once his confidence seemed to sag and he took a second to answer. "Oh, didn't we tell you? The thing is. . ."

He decided to focus on picking imaginary lint off his slacks and let the words trail off.

Catherine finished for him. "We're being blackmailed."

The word hung in the air for a moment.

"About the adoption?" I asked. Actually, I should have said *the lack of one.*

They both nodded.

Now it was making sense. Here was the motivation for setting the adoption straight. Do it before it possibly became public and got even more complicated. Unlike judges and District Attorneys, a blackmailer wasn't intimidated by their wealth and power. The saddest part of all this was that Lynn's welfare was evidently just a by-product. The issue was damage control.

"And you think the blackmailer is Melanie."

"Who else could it be?" Nevin said. " No one else knew."

She did seem the most likely suspect. Her, or someone she told.

"How much is she asking for?"

Nevin again seemed at a loss for words and he looked to Catherine.

"She's not asking for money," she said.

And I thought this case couldn't get any stranger.

"Then what is she asking for?"

Nevin found his voice, confusion masked with an indignant snort.

"Justice! Can you believe it? She wants *justice.*"

He looked to Catherine, both completely lost in the concept of the word as it applied to them.

"What the hell does *that* mean?" he asked.

I wasn't exactly sure, but it sounded like someone was planning to teach them.

2

I GULPED THE fresh air outside my office with the same gratitude of a deep sea diver rising on an empty tank. Maybe it wasn't
so much the air itself as the fact I was no longer sharing it with
the Parents of the Year.

We'd agreed I'd go by their house tomorrow, when Lynn was
at school. They had the blackmail notes in their safe, as well as
Melanie's old employment records, and information I could use
to find her.

I wasn't sure if my anger was more for what they'd done, or
for making me privy to their secret, a secret their own daughter
didn't know. Well, almost daughter. I knew one thing: I wasn't
going to lose a friend over this. Lynn was more than a student to
me.

I could hear Lynn's booming serves as I got closer. The courts
were about six hundred yards from my office, nestled between
two fairways on the front nine and hidden behind a thick bank of

eucalyptus and blood red bougainvilleas. Coral Canyon was one of San Diego County's top golf courses, and the Spanish style bungalows ringing the course gave it a nice Mediterranean flair. The course was one of the primary draws of our little town of Fallbrook. The other being the hundred-plus square miles of rolling hills covered with avocado groves and hilltop peeks of the Pacific fifteen miles away.

While most people paid big bucks for country club living, I got to stay at Coral Canyon twenty-four hours a day, gratis. When I'd got back from a three-year Peace Corps stint in Nepal, I had no money, no job and four years of college with no discernable major or learned skill. What I did have was the uncanny ability to smack a tennis ball like few could do.

I'd been a court rat throughout high school and college, and helped the club pro, Lars, with his clinics from time to time. So he created a part-time job for me: Assistant Tennis Pro. That was seven years ago. There was no salary, but in exchange I got a small apartment right next to the courts. It was kind of a no-lose proposition for the club, since everyone who rented it complained about being awakened by the crack-of-dawn hardcore tennis players who wanted to sneak in a couple of sets before work.

My job was to blow the courts off every day at sunrise and fill in for Lars when needed. Mainly though, I was supposed to do what I'd always done—hang around the courts and hit with any of the club members or guests who needed a partner. And it didn't hurt if they left the courts feeling a bit better about their game.

When I passed the bar exam last year, Lars feared I'd turn the grunt work back over to him and trade my racquet for a tie, so he convinced the Pro Shop to give up their storage room to keep me on the premises. My potential clients had to wend their way past a cardboard cutout of Tiger Woods, and displays of overpriced putters, but this seemed a small price to pay.

Some lawyers may have looked at wiping pigeon poop off the tennis courts as beneath them, but I considered myself the lucky one in the deal. Ritzy country club. Free apartment. Free office. Unlimited tennis and golf. Plus, recently one of the club's more remote swimming pools had been taken over by a contingent of French women who decreed it bathing suit optional. My hair was getting lighter every day due to the extra chlorine exposure. Of course, *I* was just there for the swimming.

Lynn was at our usual court, the most distant of the six. She saw me the minute I opened the gate and ran toward me with the abandon of a five-year old seeing Santa.

"They're *not* making me get a new coach, Toby, are they? Tell me they're not!"

"No, no new coach. You're stuck with me."

"Yeeessss." She gave me a quick hug. "I told them I'd quit if they made me switch."

We fell in step as we walked back to her court. Over the years a few people had asked if we were brother and sister. We did share the same fair skin, but thanks to a daily coating of SPF 30 we managed to keep our year-round tans. Her hair was straight and blond, while mine was wavy with an odd mix of intertwining rivers of brown and blond. We also shared the same strokes. Why wouldn't we; she learned them from me.

"You know, Lynn, I'm not what's making you a great player. It's all you."

"So *you* say."

For Lynn, something had clicked a year ago. On the court anyway. A shy, friendless kid stepped inside the lines and suddenly had such ferocity you'd swear demons were chasing her. Dr. Phil might be alarmed by the jarring transition, but I could only admire the tennis.

"I'm all warmed up," she said. "How about five miles a game?"

"What? You only want to drive five miles today?"

"Ha!" She pushed me toward my side of the net with her racquet. "You'll pay for that comment."

Lynn had her learner's permit, and like any sixteen-year-old was anxious to get her license. I found it hard to believe, but her parents had two limousines. No regular cars. So out of the four hours she spent at the club each day, lately we'd been driving for an hour or so. Can't expect a kid to learn on a hundred-foot-long Lincoln.

We rallied for a few minutes to let us get our strokes down then settled into a game. She'd get five miles behind the wheel for every game she won. Thanks to a serve as fast as some top level men, she could usually take one game a set off me, meaning she got about fifteen miles of drive time after three sets. I took the first set 6-0 and she wasn't too happy about it. We grabbed some water and gave ourselves a two minute break on the crossover.

"You're brutal with those drop shots, Toby."

"Ah, it's a tough life. Young and beautiful, but can't read a drop shot until it's too late."

She made a face, as she always did when I tried to sneak in a compliment. She reminded me of myself when I was her age, completely uncomfortable in her own skin. I could tell she was never quite in sync with the other kids at the club, and I'm sure it was the same at school. I could identify. I survived the high school years thanks to my two best friends, but the rest of it was as fun as a canker sore. Who thought up the whole concept of high school anyway? Pedophile Nazis? Who else would make fifty insecure teenagers shower together? Why not save both time and tax dollars by hiring trained child abusers to humiliate us physically, emotionally and intellectually in one intense weekend, and get it out of the way? Then on to college early, but equally humbled.

She got feistier with each set and my win margins in the last two sets were reduced to 6-1, then 6-2. She was ecstatic about winning two games against me for the first time and I had the feeling I should get used to losing more games soon. Ten years ago I'd made a brief fling at the pro circuit and got as high as the 174th ranking in the world. On the one hand, that's damn good. But on the pro tour, it meant I rarely got past qualifying and my prize money was zilch. Neither was it good enough to attract any groupies, so exit pro tennis career. I'd slipped some since then. Still, this girl just took me for two games. Ouch.

"You know, Toby, I should get a bonus for taking two games off you," she said as we headed for my car. "How about you let me play some music this time."

I'm quite the strict driving instructor and usually say no music, but today I decided to make an exception.

"What kind of music were you thinking?"

She laughed. "Like you've got any tapes except the Beach Boys."

"Hey, a classic car deserves classic music."

I'd bought my car with a hard-earned $525 when I was in high school, a '63 convertible Ford Falcon with a two tone, red-over-white paint job. The absolute tops in coolness in my own, admittedly quite unique, opinion. It also had California's last working eight track player. The tapes were so mammoth my glove compartment could only hold three at a time. Lately I'd been in a Beach Boys mood.

Lynn reached under the driver's mat for the key. Luckily my

top was down, since we were the two sweatiest people in SoCal at the moment. The bench seat was intended to only hold two, but we made it three. That put me crammed in the middle and Kemo Sabe by the door. As a gag, my pal Brogan had put the six-foot wooden Indian in my car after I passed the bar, its feet wedged under the dashboard so forcefully I couldn't get it out. I'm sure I could rip out my dash and pull it free, but I'd already lost my best friend Brogan. I was keeping Kemo Sabe.

We left the grounds of the club and turned onto Old Highway 395, *Good Vibrations* filling the air around us. We had it cranked up loud and it sounded like music is supposed to sound in a car: tinny and distorted.

A few cars honked and waved, as usual. They whizzed by so fast I couldn't see the drivers' faces, so didn't know if they knew me, or were just reacting to my stoic wooden friend lodged in the front seat.

"Where to?" she asked.

"How about we drive past your house? I've never seen where you live." I had to go there tomorrow. Might as well learn how to get there.

"You got it. To the castle we go."

Castle?

A few turns later we were rising up one of Fallbrook's endless hillsides, avocado orchards towering on both sides. Some of them had sheep grazing to keep the weeds down.

"So, Toby. Did you like my parents?" She said it almost teasingly.

In all the years Lynn had been playing at Coral Canyon, this was the first time I'd ever met them. Lynn was always whisked to and fro by one of the limos. Neither of her parents had ever come to watch her practice, or compete in a match, even the state regionals.

"What?" Me, stalling.

"Did you like my parents?"

I thought about how to answer for a minute, then got tired of the effort. They didn't deserve it.

"Actually, no."

She turned toward me and gave me a huge grin.

"That's what I love about you, Toby. You're always so honest."

Not any more, I thought glumly.

My only consolation was that maybe I could get the whole mess straightened out, so her parents could tell her the truth. Or I could. For all I knew they were going to assign that job to the limo driver. *Worthington, be a dear and run Lynn over to school. And let her know she's adopted on the way.*

Thankfully, she changed subjects.

"So when's your next date with Rita?"

I couldn't keep down a grin. "Tomorrow."

"So where are you taking her?"

"Oh," I smiled. "Just somewhere."

"A secret location, huh? Well, wherever it is, I bet it's romantic."

When I didn't confirm any planned romance, she pulled over to the side of the road like a mother about to spank her misbehaving toddler. When she even went so far as to shut off the engine I knew I was in big trouble.

"Toby, you are *not* just playing tennis with her again, are you? Or taking her to a bookstore? God!"

"Hey, they serve coffee at that bookstore. And pastries. We had a nice time."

She sighed. "I've seen her with you, Toby. She's ready."

Here was a girl who was half my age and had never been kissed giving me dating advice. The pitiful thing was I could use the help.

Rita MacGilroy and Brogan Barlow had been my two best friends since kindergarten. We'd survived junior high and high school, united in our geekiness. Brogan was the fat kid, Rita the gawky beanpole. Me cursed with a "before" face for a Clearasil ad. I fell in love with Rita even before my adolescent pimples cleared up. But Brogan fell too, and was the first to ask her out. When they got married right after high school, I was Brogan's best man, and still, his best friend. Rita stayed my other best friend, and I had no trouble putting aside my feelings for her, or at least, repressing them so deep even a Freudian couldn't find them. But Brogan died last year and his dying words to me were to take care of Rita, and the two baby daughters I helped them adopt. I knew I had his blessing, and Rita and I were taking tiny steps toward each other.

Mercifully, Lynn got us back on the road. Soon she was pulling up to the gates of Champagne Crest, the mountain-top domain for some of San Diego County's wealthiest families. I'd never been through the gates due to my aversion to the uber-wealthy, and the fact no one entrusted me with the gate code. Half a minute later we stopped before a gated drive. Man, a gated home within a gated community. Talk about snobby.

Lynn waved toward the mammoth structure behind it like she was showing what was available behind curtain number three.

I looked up. "Jeez. Is it a house or a shopping mall?"

I had the feeling I wasn't the first to make that comment.

"You want to come in?" she asked. "We could bowl a few games."

Bowl?

"I don't suppose you have an indoor tennis court in there too, do you?" I asked.

Her eyes twinkled. "No, but I could ask for one for my birthday if you want." She was joking. I think.

"How about we bowl another day. Besides, I think you're just hoping to get out of my side-to-side drill." I always made the last hour of her workout the hardest, making it even more difficult than any match could be, so that real competition was easy by comparison.

She laughed and gave a "caught me" look. She u-turned and we headed back to Coral Canyon.

"I'll take a rain check on the bowling on one condition," she said.

"What?"

"That you promise not to take Rita to a bookstore. And no tennis. Okay?"

Talk about a lack of confidence.

"Okay, deal."

If I weren't a hyper-aware driving instructor, alert for errant vehicles, I probably wouldn't have noticed the black SUV that was parked a few hundred feet outside the Champagne Crest gate, or thought anything about it when it pulled from the curb as we passed, staying a fair distance behind us. A Suburban. Oversized chrome rims. Tinted windows. Whip antenna. One just like it had left Coral Canyon behind us as well. Through a half dozen turns it had still been behind us, although quite far back. I'd forgotten about it when it didn't follow us into the la la land of Champagne Crest, but here it was again. Of course, huge, black SUVs were as plentiful in SoCal as the gallons of gas they consumed, so maybe it wasn't the same one. There was no front license plate, even if I was close enough to read it.

"Why don't you cut through here, Lynn." I pointed up Citrus Lane, which locals knew serpentined up the hill to nowhere, then back to the main road.

"You got it, Teach."

As I should have expected, the black SUV peacefully drove past and didn't follow us.

I didn't bother to look behind us again until we were turning into the club. When I did, there was the black Suburban. *A* black Suburban, anyway. Once again, however, when we turned, it benignly kept going straight.

I hoped benignly.

3

ONLY THREE THINGS stood between me and my date with
Rita. First I had to visit Amanda, one of the birth mothers I was
working with. Then Nevin and Catherine. Finally, shower, shave
and try to handsome myself up enough to be halfway worthy of
Rita.

I was actually looking forward to my first stop. Amanda's
grandmother was known as Granny Grump to the youth of Fallbrook, of which I was once one. I got a lot of client referrals from
doctors, counselors and hospitals, as you'd expect when you
work with women facing unplanned pregnancies. But Amanda
was sent my way by Granny.

My job is pretty simple actually. When a birth mother comes
to see me, I explain how adoption works, then show her couples
I'm working with who are hoping to adopt. Each couple puts together their own profile, with pictures and an introductory letter
describing themselves and what a child's life would be like with

them. I had about twenty families waiting to adopt and Amanda selected Aaron and Charlotte Colburn. They owned my favorite restaurant, a little Italian mom and pop place in town called *Costa Brava*. It didn't matter that neither Aaron nor Charlotte were Italian, or that "Costa Brava" was actually Spanish, the sign inherited from the previous restaurant. The food was great, and it fit tight budgets like mine. It was sandwiched between a dry cleaner and a donut shop, low on style and high on great food.

After just one meeting with Aaron and Charlotte, Amanda was sure they were the perfect parents for her baby. It was a good match. It always amused me when my wild-child birth mothers chose Ozzie and Harriet adoptive parents, wanting a lifestyle for their children that they had rejected for themselves. Or maybe they never had it and secretly yearned for it. Unlike Nevin and Catherine, Aaron and Charlotte were typical adoptive parents, a fantastic couple wanting more than anything to have a family and share their lives with a child.

The adoption also had Amanda's grandmother's blessing, although it may have only been for anticipated extra large portions of Charlotte's cannelloni. Everything was looking good in the adoption until I'd hit a snag with the birth father. I didn't tell Amanda that was the problem when I told her I'd be dropping by.

When I pulled up to Granny's driveway, Bill Clinton and Richard Nixon were guarding the entrance. I'd seen Tricky Dick before, but Clinton was new. Granny was a bit of an eccentric and lined her hundred-yard long driveway with discarded old water heaters, each standing upright, painted in the image of those she admired or despised. She'd started her project about forty years ago to the tune of one creation a month, so that by now many of them were almost shoulder to shoulder. The exaggeration of certain physical attributes was the giveaway to what Granny thought of each person. Nixon had a long, steel protrusion welded to his face, a la Pinocchio. Clinton also had a protrusion, and also from the middle of his body, but it was a few feet lower. At first I thought it was a misplaced arm. Then I realized it was, well, let's say a body part not visible in any presidential portraits. Judging from the size and skyward direction of the appendage, Clinton would be quite proud.

As I crested the top of the drive I could see Granny under an ancient oak, shading her and her tiny house. She was seated in front of a water heater, this one a short, fat solar model. Her paintbrush was flying.

"Good day, Toby," she called out, not stopping her strokes.

If I recalled correctly, Stella Grumpmacher was now ninety-two. It seemed like she'd been old forever but was still going strong. So strong that when her daughter developed a drug problem and took off on the back of somebody's Harley, Amanda was left with Granny. That was when Amanda was in grade school. She'd been a bit of a rebel, like her mother. But then, so was Granny.

"Hi, Granny. Who you working on?"

"Oh don't tell me you can't recognize him?" She was enjoying this.

I checked out the distorted, wide body, with a head no bigger than an apple. Because of her recent feud with our city council, I could take a guess.

"Hmm, I'm guessing Mayor Thompson."

She crowed with delight. "Ding, ding, give the boy a prize. What was the giveaway? The pea-sized brain, or the absence of any balls?"

I hadn't noticed the latter, but now that she mentioned it, there was a definite absence of any bulge. Even less so than on her

Michael Jackson caricature. The Mayor had tried to get an ordi-
nance passed forcing her to remove her water heaters, claiming
they damaged property values in the neighborhood. It was quite
the hot topic in every local barbershop, with those who loved or
hated them as entrenched in their respective positions as old-
school republicans and democrats. But Granny prevailed and the
water heaters, and now the Mayor, were a part of Fallbrook's own
version of Mount Rushmore. I was nice to Granny for two reasons: I genuinely liked her, and I also never wanted to end up a
caricature in her driveway. It was the town's ultimate humiliation.

"I think I'll put the Mayor right by the street where everyone
can see him. Right next to Clinton," she cackled.

She dropped her paintbrush into a rusty tin of water and held
out a hand. "Give me a hand, youngster."

I gently pulled her up. Once on her feet she moved just fine.

"Ya want a beer? Or would you prefer a sody pop?"

Word had it Granny subsisted on almost nothing but beer,
chips and guacamole. From what I'd seen, there was truth to the
rumor.

"Oh, I'll take a Dr Pepper if you've got one."

I followed her into her home, built in the twenties and showing its age, the yellow paint peeling. Granny was a pack rat and
her house was filled with stacks of newspapers, neatly piled almost to the ceiling. It was like being a mouse in a maze. She
compounded the absurdity with rows of empty beer bottles on the
floor pushed flush to the newspapers, like stones lining a garden
walkway. This left pathways so narrow sometimes I had to turn
sideways to pass. Maybe this was why I had to make house calls
to see Amanda. In her enlarged condition she couldn't get out of
the house.

About ten turns later we got to the kitchen and I had a cold Dr

Pepper in my hand. Granny opened a Coors for herself and plopped down at a little Formica table. Sure enough, sitting there was a bowl of guacamole, with diced chunks of tomato, mango, onion and several shades of bell pepper. No wonder she could live on the stuff: she had a half dozen vegetables mixed in there. She took a tortilla chip from the bag, dipped it, and stuffed it into her mouth in one bite.

"Still got my own teeth," she said.

What could you say to that. "Me too," I said.

I wasn't in a big hurry, and the guacamole was damn good, so we ate in a companionable silence for a while.

"You've grown into a handsome man, Toby. Just like your grandpappy. Now there was a man."

She was right about the second part. Everyone in town had loved my grandpa. "I can take you to the eye doctor if you need glasses, Granny."

"Ha. Modest like him too. I can see you blushing under that tan. He could never take a compliment either."

My answer was to fill another chip with guacamole. She could be the Mrs. Fields of guac if she ever decided to market her concoction.

"You here to see Amanda?" she finally asked me.

"Yes. I told her I was coming by. She in her room?"

"Yep. Maybe you can convince her to come out and get some sunshine." She took a pull of the Coors. "Did you know she took out her piercings?"

When I'd first met Amanda a couple of months ago she was in full teenage rebel mode, with about a dozen earrings in each ear, as well as a piercing below her lower lip that was almost long enough to serve as a lance in a jousting competition. If she had any others on her body, I didn't want to know about them.

"So what prompted that?"

"Who knows? I just know she did it on her own. Maybe she's growing up a bit. The hard way."

The hard way was right. Getting pregnant and having a baby at eighteen just to give it to someone else was not the easiest way to get started in life. An act of kindness for which there was no adequate measure.

I finished my drink and stood up. "Okay if I find my way to Amanda's room?"

"You think you can?"

"Sure."

Actually, I wasn't sure, but I figured if I got lost in the maze I could call for help. Granny saluted me with a chip and off I went. With only a couple wrong turns I was soon at Amanda's door. I knocked loudly so she could hear me over her music. She turned it down and said to come in.

She was relaxing in bed reading a *People* magazine with some emaciated model or rock star on the cover. The older I got, the less often I recognized anybody famous. At least famous in the eyes of *People.*

"Hi Toby."

"Hi. Howya feeling?"

"Okay. You come just to ask me that?"

She wasn't being rude, just blunt. Her face was free of piercings as Granny had said, but I didn't comment on it for fear she'd take it as approval and put them back in just to spite me.

"So. . . I called Michael yesterday," I said.

In my first meeting with Amanda she'd identified Michael as her boyfriend, until they broke up shortly after the pregnancy.

"Yeah, so what'd he say? Is he going to sign whatever you need him to?"

"Well, no actually."

"Asshole," she mumbled. I was pretty sure she was referring to Michael. Not me.

"That's not the problem, Amanda. The problem is he says that the last time you two, ah. . . were intimate, was the day before your birthday."

"Damned right it was the last time. For my birthday he gave me a CD, some mix he burned. Like wow, don't spend a whole dollar or anything. Talk about a loser." She looked at me, having evidently missed my point.

"What I'm getting at is that your birthday is July twenty-ninth, right?"

"Yeah."

"Well, you're eight and a half-months pregnant, and your birthday was ten months ago."

"So?" She still didn't get it.

"What I'm saying is that if you and Michael had sex the day before your birthday, that was six weeks before you became pregnant."

Amanda just stared at me and didn't say anything.

"So," I went on, "Unless Michael had the slowest swimming sperm in the universe, he can't be the birth father."

I was trying to lighten the mood a bit, but she didn't even crack a smile. Oh well, at least I amuse myself.

Her eyes ditched mine and found an interesting spot on the wall.

"So what do we do now?" she asked.

"Well, we have to identify the birth father to the court and try to find him. So can you tell me who you had relations with six weeks after Michael? I'm not trying to pry into your personal life, but we have to try to find the right guy."

She finally took her eyes from the wall and looked at me. "Alright," she said. "But I'm not a 'ho like it makes me sound, okay?"

"Amanda, I deal in unplanned pregnancies every day. You're not going to say anything that I haven't heard before, so don't be embarrassed. Just tell me what happened."

Actually, the only one embarrassed by these birth mother stories is me, as sometimes it seemed everyone in the world is getting some hoochey koochey but me.

"Okay," she said. "It was down at the river for the Labor Day weekend. Camping and stuff, you know?"

"Sure."

The river meant the Colorado River, a five-hour drive from San Diego. I'd never been there, but from what I'd heard it featured topless water sports and massive alcohol consumption by day, followed by massive alcohol consumption and sex with new friends by night. Kind of like Easter break at Ft. Lauderdale, California style.

"I had just gotten undressed in my tent, and he just walked right in. 'Thought it was his tent,' he said." She shrugged. "That happens a lot to me down there. Anyway, after that, you know, we just, you know, did it."

Evidently, asking him to leave was not an option, river hospitality and all. I had an image of her getting undressed, a lantern in her tent casting her strip tease image across the wall of her tent like a movie screen. A hundred guys sitting as if at a drive in, drawing straws to see who'd get to use the magic "I thought this was *my* tent" line.

"Did he tell you his name?"

"Hmm. . . Keith maybe. Or Kevin. One of the 'K' names. I didn't get his last name."

Ah, now we were making real progress. A "K" name.

"Oh yeah," she added. "I heard one of his friends call him *Zuley* once, like a nickname maybe."

Great. A "K" name and what sounded like a Spanish nickname. He was practically found already.

"So was he Hispanic?"

"Yeah, but maybe like just half or something. He wasn't very dark."

"Did you ever see him again?" I was hoping she got at least some information we could use to search for him.

"Well, he was still there the next morning, if that's what you mean."

Not exactly what I was looking for.

"Did he tell you where he lived, or worked, or anything about himself we can use to find him?"

"He mentioned some clubs he liked in Riverside."

"Okay, that's a start."

Riverside was city of a half million, located an hour or two inland and best known for its gangs and smog.

"And I know he liked oldies."

"Oldies?"

"You know. The Doors. Beatles."

Yeah. That'll help. At least I could tell the adoptive parents the birth father had good taste in music. A nice hereditary trait. Not to mention those big brass balls to use the *tent* line.

"Can you tell me what he looked like?"

She thought about it and started scrutinizing me.

"He was like you I guess, but a little taller, so maybe six feet. And he was built better. I mean, you know, really primo muscles. And he was younger, of course, like maybe about twenty. Really, really intense blue eyes. And his hair was brown like chocolate, not kind of dirty blond like yours—"

"That's enough of a description," I cut in quickly, wanting to leave with some ego intact. I pulled a *Declaration of Mother* form out of my briefcase, a court form used to identify the birth father. "Just complete this and mail it back to me. If you were only with him the one time, the court will understand why we can't find him, so it's not going to mess up the adoption. You don't need to worry about anything."

"Oh, it wasn't just one time." Amanda perked up with a happy memory. "We did it like four times that night and—"

I interrupted quickly. "That's okay. I don't need to know those kind of details."

"But we did it—"

"No, really. It's private. I don't need to know."

"But—"

"No."

"Okay." She seemed to give up, then snuck it in. "And three more times the next morning."

I looked on the floor to see where my ego had landed. Like I really needed to hear about every other guy in the world being a sexual James Bond. Somehow I'd been cursed with the notion that sex was part of loving someone. This meant I could count on one hand the women I'd slept with. Actually, I could lose a few fingers in a tragic lawnmower accident and *still* count them on one hand.

"So, Toby, is it going to be a problem? If we can't find Karl?"

It took me a second. *Karl?* Oh yeah, a "K" name.

"No. It actually makes things easier. If we don't have a last name or address, there's not much I can do to find him. The court will just terminate his rights as an unfindable father. Don't worry about it."

"Well, okay," she said, stretching like a horny cat remembering her mystery Marathon Man and hoping for an encore. "But if you do find him somehow, you'll let me know, right?"

4

WHEN I PULLED up to Nevin and Catherine's gate I noticed a small brass plaque set into the stone pillar on the left. The word "Guests" was in raised letters, perhaps to assist their sight-impaired visitors, with an intercom button at the top. Below was an arrow pointing further down the street and the words "Servants' Entrance." Which was I? In a burst of confidence I pushed the *Guests* button and was rewarded by an invitation to enter.

I parked the Falcon in the circular driveway next to a fountain likely designed by the Bellagio guy. The only thing missing was the piped-in opera music. Before I got to the door it was opened by a severe-looking Hispanic woman in a maid's uniform. Likely my footsteps on one of the polished stone steps secretly activated a hidden buzzer inside and sent her scurrying to the door.

"Mr. Dillon?" She looked me over and didn't immediately invite me in. Her eyes were focused on my kneecaps as if she'd never seen shorts before. Maybe they were not allowed in the castle. Thank goodness I remembered to dress for the occasion and wore a polo shirt rather than my usual tee.

Hey, it never hurts to overdress.

Out of true curiosity I studied her right back. My parents were disturbingly rich and had a housekeeper come in once a week, but I'd never known anyone with a bona fide servant. Since I'd only seen them in old black and white movies, it took me a minute to adjust to seeing one in living color. She wasn't as friendly as the ones in the old movies, though.

Eventually my knees passed muster and I was invited inside. The entrance lobby rose three stories high, more befitting a hotel than a house. As if on cue Nevin trotted down the eight foot wide stairway. I couldn't help wondering if he'd been lurking at the top of the stairs to make his entrance.

Poser.

"Toby!" Wink. "You find the place okay?"

"No problem." Hard to miss it, considering an African village could live in its shade.

I couldn't bring myself to be so chummy as to call him Nevin. But I wasn't too thrilled with "Mr. Handley" either.

"Catherine's waiting in my study. Follow me."

After more turns than I'd encountered in my recent newspaper maze experience, we arrived, although I didn't think a room of about eight-hundred square feet qualified as a study. His desk alone was half the size of my apartment. Catherine was waiting in a seating area of four tan leather chairs. I sank into mine and almost let loose with an orgasmic sigh. The leather was as smooth as human skin. Maybe not my skin, but the skin of someone who didn't abuse it by smacking tennis balls in the sun five hours a day.

"Hello, Toby." Catherine gave me a smile with more humanity than I'd remembered. Maybe she was more comfortable here. "Would you like some tea or coffee?"

When I paused she said, "We're having some."

"Sure. How about some tea?"

She turned her head and as if by magic the snooty maid entered. What were there, secret summoning buttons? Catherine ordered two teas and "a coffee for Mr. Handley."

Evidently we couldn't begin coffee and tealess, so while we waited Nevin engaged in some small talk.

"I noticed your diploma in your office, Toby. UCLA, not a bad law school. I'm a Trojan myself."

I wanted to ask, "ribbed or regular," but he probably meant USC.

My diploma did proclaim UCLA in large letters, although if you stood closer you'd see the small print beneath it where it said Uncle Charlie's Law Academy. I came from a family of lawyers, but a falling out with my law-for-riches father sent me to his brother, my law-for-people uncle. There I'd become a lawyer under a little known California program called apprenticeship. A person can study under an attorney, just like Abraham Lincoln did in his day, without ever going to law school. Not that I'm comparing myself to Honest Abe, although I did have better taste in hats. Four years later, I sat for the bar and passed, first try. In the snooty world of law though, this wasn't exactly an impressive pedigree. Just one more reason I practice out of a Pro Shop instead of a corporate skyscraper.

There was a tap on the door and Smileyface entered with a tray, then departed without a word. Both tea and coffee must have been brewed and poured, awaiting our selection, as she'd been gone all of thirty seconds.

"Would you like some honey, Toby?" Catherine asked. "It's

from a local hive. Good for your antibodies."

Nevin snorted his ridicule but didn't say anything as he blew on his coffee. I looked at Catherine with new eyes. There was a theory that eating honey from local hives builds your immunities and antibodies. Since the bees got the pollen from local plants, the honey was like little allergy shots. My grandfather had believed in it, and there was no one I respected more. Maybe I'd have to reevaluate this lady. Offering me local honey, and caring about my immunities too.

"Yes, some honey would be great. Thanks." I looked at Nevin when I said it, hoping he'd take it as a tiny dig.

Once we all had our drinks in hand, it was evidently socially acceptable to begin.

"Let's get down to it then," Nevin said. "I didn't want to go into too much detail in your office. We were afraid Lynn would get impatient waiting for you and walk in on us."

"She's at that age," Catherine interjected. "Turning into quite the eavesdropper. We've actually caught her listening at doors."

"Anyway," Nevin said. "When we went to see Anton West he put an investigator on everything. Finding Melanie I mean."

I'd thought part of my job was to find her, so maybe my surprise showed on my face.

"We're just trying to save you some time and make things easier for you," he added quickly.

"Hey," I said. "The more they've done the better,"

I meant it. I was no Magnum P.I. And I don't just mean my lack of Marlboro Man good looks, a Hawaiian estate, muscles and a red Ferrari.

"Good," Nevin said. "They learned that Melanie's father died six years ago, but they were able to find her mother. In fact, she apparently lives in the same house they had when Melanie was growing up, over in San Marcos. Her address and phone number are in here."

He handed me one file and held back a second one. San Marcos was only thirty minutes away, one of the bedroom communities of San Diego, not rural like Fallbrook.

"No one has tried to approach her, though. I thought the P.I.s would scare her so I wanted to leave the contact to you."

I nodded. "Why are you telling me about Melanie's mother? Does that mean they couldn't find Melanie?"

"That's exactly what it means, and they were quite surprised about it. I had the impression they don't fail at this kind of thing very often. They said it's like Melanie just vanished about four years ago. No tax returns. No W-2s. None of her credit cards used. No bank activity. The DMV still has her address as her mother's, but from what they can tell she hasn't been there for years."

"And they checked for a death certificate?"

"Yes, and nothing. They checked every database for any sign of her, alive or dead. Not just local, but international. Nothing."

"Okay," I said, a bit lost. "But I'm not sure I know how you want me to approach this. Do you think I should just go to her mother and let her know her daughter placed a child for adoption, and it's important I find her? Without sharing your names with her, I mean."

Nevin looked to Catherine. "We talked about that. We just have to leave it to your judgment. Whatever you think will lead you to Melanie. One reason we came to you is we assume her mother will know who you are, so she's more likely to trust you. You got a lot of good press a while back."

They were referring to the fact I had more than my fifteen minutes of fame last year. Much more. I'd arranged an adoption for Brogan and Rita. They'd beaten the odds and found success in the movie world. Somebody has to get lucky I guess, you just never think it could happen to someone you know. They rose to what Rita laughingly called the *next* stage. As in, the next Julia Roberts. The next Tom Cruise. When the baby I'd placed for adoption with them was kidnapped, it became one of the biggest stories of the year, staying in the headlines for months. Several people didn't come out of it alive, including Brogan, and here was Nevin using it as strategy. Almost a year later, no one would recognize me walking down the street, but if they heard the words "adoption attorney" while looking at my face, they'd likely remember.

As much as I disliked Nevin more by the second, I had to admit he was right. Celebrity opened doors, even unearned and temporary fame like mine. It might help with Melanie or her mom.

"I hope you don't mind," Catherine said, likely reading my thoughts.

I just shrugged. What could I say? They were users. They'd find and manipulate any angle to benefit themselves. The pain of my past was just a stepping stone to success for them. But since I was doing this for Lynn, and not for them, it didn't bother me. Much.

I thumbed through the file without really absorbing anything. It looked like hours of reading. One page caught my eye. It had Melanie's senior picture in high school, and the DMV photo from her most recent driver's license, dated five years ago. She'd have been thirty then. The school picture bore a remarkable similarity to Lynn. Put them in a room together and most anyone would peg them as mother and daughter. I wondered if Nevin and Catherine allowed themselves to recognize it.

The younger Melanie had a pleasant, open face, eager for the world ahead. I wondered if she was pregnant when the photo was taken and if so, if she knew. A peanut M&M destined to be Lynn. The more recent DMV photo showed a face which had learned some tough lessons. There was a fragile smile, but lacking the innocent abandon. Maybe everyone loses it, except those with a Peter Pan syndrome still living in short pants and playing tennis all day.

"Can you tell me about what Melanie was like when she was working for you?"

Catherine delicately sipped her tea before answering. "She was a very sweet girl, still in her last year of high school when she started, around Thanksgiving. We just needed someone part-time, a pleasant voice on the phone. We didn't really need someone skilled, which was good because we couldn't afford to pay her much back then. Nevin had just started the business and we were scratching for every dime. It wasn't until the VC guys came on board that everything took off."

At the same moment my face showed ignorance over the *VC* reference, Nevin couldn't keep a touch of annoyance from his.

"Venture capitalists," he said. "I was just one more 'computer guy' with big plans and some good software ideas, but no money. A venture capital group saw the potential and ponied up what it took to take us to the next level. Actually a few levels." He gave me what was supposed to be a modest smile.

Now I knew why he looked annoyed. He didn't want to share any of the glory, probably thinking it took some of the gusto from his rags to riches story, at least the one paraded in front of the world in the media puff pieces and when he ran for office.

I knew a little about venture capitalists from my father. They were private investors who bought into promising businesses to grow them, promote them, then sell them, taking a giant share of the profits. Hard for the small businessman to say no when someone wants to hand you a few million dollars to bankroll your dream.

"Was Melanie still around when all that money came in to the business?" I asked Nevin.

"Yes, but why do you ask?"

I was thinking of one local cell phone company, Qualcomm. When they hit the big time, the newspapers were full of stories about the lowliest clerks who were suddenly millionaires thanks to stock options and bonuses. I said, "I've heard about little companies, especially tech companies back in those days, that hit the jackpot and everybody in the company walked away with money. If she left with lots of cash, it'd give her something to use to hide."

"Well, she didn't," he said. "She made minimum wage when she started and she made minimum wage when she left a few months after Lynn was born."

Well, weren't you the generous boss. And it's not like she did anything special for you, like give you a daughter.

"When she quit, did she give you a reason?" I asked. Like being a cheap bastard, maybe?

Catherine took that one. "I think she wanted some distance. After Lynn was born, I think it was emotional to be around us."

I wanted to say that some adoption education and counseling for everyone would have helped with that, but then, that's what you get with a *real* adoption

"Okay," I said. "I'll read over the file and go talk to Melanie's mom—"

"And if you have to give our names, it's okay," Nevin interjected. "Whatever gets you to Melanie."

I wanted to say, *I'd rather not. I'm ashamed to have anyone know I'm working for you.* I changed gears.

"What about the birth father? Did Melanie ever say anything about him?"

"No," Catherine said. "She never talked about a boyfriend, and we never saw her with anyone. I guess it was something we should have asked about, but since she wasn't married, we just didn't think it mattered."

I looked at the copies of Melanie's driver's license and Lynn's birth certificate. Lynn had been born sixteen years ago on September twenty-seventh. That meant she would have conceived in late-December. That would have been in the middle of Melanie's senior year, when she was seventeen. She would have just been starting to show toward the end of the school year. I knew from first hand experience how clever some girls were at hiding their pregnancies with baggy clothes. Just months ago I had a tearful call from a birth mother's mother. She was at the hospital with her fifteen-year old daughter who had just given birth. She'd learned of her daughter's pregnancy just hours before, when her water broke while shopping at WalMart.

It also occurred to me Melanie was a minor at the time of conception, technically making it statutory rape if the birth father was at least eighteen. Could that be part of the reason for the secrecy, and her willingness to participate in a fraudulent adoption? Protecting someone? Maybe an older man she cared about?

Nevin still had one file in his lap. I had to assume it held the blackmail notes. The file he'd given me had a label on the tab with Melanie's name neatly typed. I wondered if he was so anal that he put a label on the one he was holding: "BLACKMAIL NOTES: HANDLEY, NEVIN AND CATHERINE"

Neither he nor Catherine seemed anxious to get to those, but I wanted to get moving. I had a date to get ready for. Tea with these two, local honey or not, wasn't my favorite way to pass the day.

"Are those the blackmail notes?"

He finally opened the file. "Yes. I've got the originals here, and copies for you. Here's the first one we received."

The letter he handed me was encased in a clear plastic sleeve. I felt like I was in an episode of *CSI: Fallbrook.*

"Anton West's investigators went over each letter," he said by way of explanation. "That's how they gave them back to us so we left them that way."

The letter was in the style of an old-fashioned ransom note, words cut from newspaper headlines and glued together on a plain piece of white paper. It was not only old-fashioned, but overly dramatic, like something out of an old Bogart movie. I wondered what it told us about the sender.

The note said:

IF YOU LOVE HER, YOU WILL TELL HER.

Stapled to the back was an envelope, obviously the one it came in. It was postmarked in Fallbrook, meaning it was mailed from within a few miles of their home. I thought of the black SUV which might have been following Lynn—or was it following me, since it happened right after my meeting with Nevin and Catherine? I pushed the thought from my mind. The postmark date was April fifteenth, seven weeks ago.

There was no return address. It was addressed to both Nevin and Catherine, via what looked like a pre-printed oversized business card which had been glued to the envelope.

"What's this?" I asked.

"It's a calling card," Catherine said, with a tone implying I'd just pointed to a chair and asked what it was. I'd seen business cards, but this had both their names, and their home address.

"A calling card?"

"Yes. They're like social greeting cards. You give them out to friends and people who need your address and so on."

Hmm. I'd never heard of such a thing. Maybe you got a catalog with those kinds of goodies when you made your first ten million. Or had an active social life. I had neither.

Nevin walked over to his desk and came back with one of the cards. "Here. This is what they look like before being cut down like on the envelope."

The one he handed me had a phone number and e-mail addresses for both of them under their home address. The one on the envelope had been cropped to eliminate the extra information.

The connection was too obvious for anyone to ignore. "So this had to be sent by someone you know," I said. "Someone you'd have given your card to."

Nevin answered. "We talked about that with Anton's people, but it doesn't help much. We probably gave out twenty thousand last year."

"That seems like a lot." Since I could count my friends on my fingers and toes, I didn't see how someone could give out twenty thousand.

"Not really. It's a political thing. We used to just give them to friends, but then I started to give them out at rallies and speeches during the election, and I could see they went over well. I thought it gave a personal touch and shows I'm accessible. People don't want to vote for someone unapproachable and walled away."

I thought of the two gates I had to pass through to get to their door. "So you really give everyone your home phone number, and e-mail address? Anyone can just call you up?"

"Well, actually, no. The *home* number is a machine which has a personal greeting, like it's ours, but my staff checks it and lets me know what I need to respond to. Weeds out the crazies. Same with the e-mails. We wouldn't give out our actual information."

"But you don't have a problem giving out your home address?"

He shook his head. "Not really. It's public record. Anybody can get it just by calling the Assessor's office. Besides, we've got the gates."

This guy was cold as ice. He reminded me so much of my father I wondered if we were related; or maybe they just knew each other from the same church, worshiping the gods of money and manipulation.

So the calling cards were a dead end. I went back to the note. *If you love her, you will tell her.*

"Did you notice they don't even use Lynn's name?" I said. "Or even say what they're talking about? They never mention adoption."

"That's why we didn't do anything at first," Nevin said. "I just assumed it was some crackpot. Here's the next one that came, a week later."

He handed it to me.

DO YOU LOVE YOUR DAUGHTER?
DO YOU KEEP SECRETS FROM THE PEOPLE
YOU LOVE?

This envelope was postmarked April twenty-second in Fallbrook, and had another cut-down calling card for the address. The letter had the same newspaper cut-out text. The same cheap white paper.

"Lynn is your only daughter, right? They can't be talking about anyone else?"

"No," Nevin said. "Just Lynn. And if you're wondering, the only *secret* we have is the adoption. There's nothing else it could be."

"It's funny they don't use her name though, or use the word *adoption*. Don't you think?"

Catherine leaned forward. "We talked about that. We thought maybe Melanie was worried someone else would see the letter, and even though she wants Lynn to know, didn't want her to learn like that. That fits, don't you think?"

Actually, nothing made sense to me, but her theory was as good as any. I wished Nevin would just hand me the file, instead of doling the letters out individually like Halloween candy.

"Can I see the next one?"

"This is the penultimate one," he said as he gave it to me.

I'd lived thirty-three years on the planet and never once heard *penultimate* used in a sentence. Seen it in books, yes, but never heard it in conversation. I almost ran to his desk to see if he had a *Word a Day* calendar.

It was postmarked on May third, but this one bore an Escondido postmark. My Uncle Charlie's office was in Escondido, although I didn't consider him a likely suspect. Escondido was about twenty miles south of Fallbrook, next to San Marcos, along the freeway on the way to downtown San Diego.

The note said:

BE GOOD, NOT EVIL.
YOU HAVE LIED TO YOUR DAUGHTER.
YOU HAVE LIED TO EVERYONE.
YOU WILL PAY IF YOU DON'T STOP.

I looked again at the envelope and noticed the usual calling card had been modified. Catherine's name had been crossed out, leaving only Nevin's. I looked at him.

"Looks like this one was meant just for you."

Nevin made light of it.

"Like any of this makes any sense? I can't explain it."

You will pay if you don't stop. A threat, but what kind of threat? To his reputation? His life? The notes seemed more concerned with forcing some morality and righting a wrong than with violence.

"Do you have any idea about this reference to lying *to everyone*? Like lying to Lynn is separate." I was thinking it meant family, but it could also refer to employees, constituents. Anybody.

"I haven't lied to *anybody*, Toby. You can't ask me to answer to the charges of some crackpot."

I wanted to say, sure, no lying, except about the adoption. Oh, and the misleading contact cards to people entrusting you with their vote.

"Here's the last one," he said, evidently anxious to leave the topic. "It was waiting for us in the mail when we got home from seeing you yesterday."

JUNE 7TH IS THE DEADLINE.
IT'S NOT TOO LATE TO DO THE RIGHT THING.
IF NOT, GET READY TO READ ABOUT YOUR
SINS IN THE NEWSPAPER. ALL OF THEM.

All of them. Did she mean all the sins? Something in addition to the adoption? Or all the newspapers? I didn't have a degree in

Advanced Ransom Note Analysis, but I didn't need one to see the increase in frustration, and desperation. I could see why Nevin and Catherine thought they came from Melanie. There was a yearning to them, a cry for doing the right thing. For morality. That would fit with a wronged birth mother, denied any contact or emotional validation in making the placement, changing it to a dirty secret. And the crossing out of Catherine's name seemed to indicate Melanie saw Nevin as the principally responsible person. Also, there seemed to be a vagueness which could imply more wrongness than just the adoption. That actually made it look more likely to be Melanie, since she was the only other person privy to both the adoption, and working at his business. She was one of the few, if only, people, who existed in both those worlds, besides Nevin and Catherine themselves.

"I wonder why June seventh." I said.

"It's Nevin's birthday," Catherine said.

Man, did someone have it in for this guy or what? Or was it just a coincidence?

"Doesn't matter what day it is," Nevin said. "What matters is we've got more than a week. Lots of time."

"Lots of time for what?" I asked.

"To find her, of course. To see what this is really about. To put a stop to it."

I shook my head. I couldn't put off asking them any longer.

"Is there a reason you don't just *tell* Lynn. I mean, right now?" I held up the notes. "Wouldn't that end all this? And you left my office so quickly yesterday, I didn't get a chance to tell you, but there's no way to hide from Lynn the fact you're going through an adoption once we officially start it. The social worker and the judge will both want to talk to her. So why delay it?"

I looked to Catherine first, then when she didn't reply, to

Nevin. Finally he nodded.

"We assumed she'd need to know, and yes, we'll tell her, but it's been sixteen years, Toby. Waiting a few weeks isn't going to make any difference, not to Lynn anyway. I'm sure you can understand that."

Actually, I didn't. Not at all. My face must have showed it because he kept going.

"Listen, I'll admit part of this is my own stubbornness. I don't like people telling me what to do. No one's going to tell me what to say to my daughter, or when. But the rest is for Lynn. Don't you think we should know who is out there, making these *orders*, before we act on them? What if Melanie is delusional, or she's become a drug addict? Or maybe this is leading up to a demand for money? I know we'd still need to tell Lynn, but it'd change how we told her. And I'm sure you can see the main problem."

I had no idea.

"Ah, I guess I don't. I'm sorry. What's the main problem?"

Nevin leaned forward and pointed to the notes in my hand.

"They say to tell Lynn. . . Well, how does Melanie know we *didn't?* Even if Lynn knew, that doesn't mean she'd go around sharing it with everyone. And if we did tell her now, how would Melanie *know that we did?*"

Alright, I'll admit it. The thought had never occurred to me. I guess that's why he lived in a twenty-thousand square foot house and made umpteen million dollars, and I spent my days chasing yellow balls. It didn't change the fact that Lynn should be told, but it did change a lot. His question was a good one. What if Nevin and Catherine had told Lynn after the first note was received? How would the note-writer know if they'd done so or not? Did this mean the notes referred to something else entirely? Something the sender *could* verify?

"What about your staff?" I asked. "They'd know what's said in your house." I still wasn't convinced the notes were from Melanie, or if they were, that she was doing this alone.

Nevin shook his head. "They were thoroughly checked out before we hired them, and again when this started. Besides, we wouldn't talk about that kind of thing in front of them."

Catherine seemed anxious to move back to the subject of the adoption itself. That was fine with me. It was probably a mistake for me to put too much thought into the notes. They weren't my job. My job was to talk to Melanie and get the adoption on the right track.

"What about the home study, Toby?" she asked. "Do we need to start something now?"

"Soon, but not yet. We'll do this as a private adoption, not through an agency."

I walked them through the basics. Melanie would need to have several meetings with a specially licensed social worker called an Adoption Services Provider. She'd provide Melanie counseling, then later witness her consent to the adoption. It would then be turned over to San Diego County Health and Human Services, which would do a six month home study. After that, there would be a court hearing to obtain the approval of the judge, and make everything final. Usually the last part was a slam dunk. In their case, even with Nevin's position of power, some judges would not feel too kindly about how their adoption started. We could only take it one step at a time, though.

I heard a buzz coming from Nevin's direction and he pulled out a cell phone as thin as a cracker. I expected him to tell whomever it was he'd call back but he held the phone tighter to his ear and said "yes" a few times. He stood up.

"Cat, I've got to take this. You two go on ahead."

If Catherine was surprised he was relegating our discussion to second place on his priority list, it didn't show. Maybe she was just used to it. We watched him leave, grunting into the phone on his way to the door. What surprised me was his tone of voice on the phone. It was the first time I'd heard tension in his voice. Or was it fear?

I held up the stack of notes. "So Catherine, how do you feel about these?"

"Feel?" she asked.

I nodded. I don't know what I expected to hear. Humanity? Some recognition that they'd robbed both their daughter and her birth mother of everything good adoption had to give? That they were finally going to make things right?

She didn't say anything for a minute and just bowed her head over her cup of tea held in her lap. I wouldn't have noticed the tear if it hadn't splashed into her cup, causing tiny drops of tea to fly onto her pristine white pantsuit. I waited for her to wipe them, but she didn't. They looked so out of place, like mud on a new car, that I almost wanted to dab at them for her. She finally looked up.

"You probably think we're monsters," she said. "I know I do."

I was too stunned to answer, watching the ice lady melt, and wondering what else here wasn't as it seemed. When she went on, it was in a quiet voice I had to lean forward to hear.

"When we first did the adoption, all I wanted was a baby. I didn't think beyond that. And Nevin had his business. That was all he thought about, so Lynn was more. . . for me. It wasn't until Lynn started growing up that I realized we couldn't tell her about being adopted. How could we tell her when we did it the way we did? If someone heard about it, the whole thing could come out.

And once Nevin got successful, then went into politics, forget about it." Her voice took on a slightly mocking tone. "Can't do anything to rock the boat. Perfection is required. Always."

She seemed to realize she had been nervously tapping her foot and stopped. "And sometimes I wonder what Melanie thinks about it now that she's older. Back then she probably went along, not knowing any better, but as she grew up, she must wonder about it. Actually, I'm surprised she didn't contact us sooner. I'd hate us too if I were her."

"But why wouldn't she just contact you and tell you how she feels? Why the notes?"

"You're not a woman, Toby. You wouldn't understand. Can you imagine her on the phone with Nevin? Calling his office or one of his phony home numbers? How intimidated she'd be? She's not like us. She can't go to a high-priced attorney and have him manipulate things for her to get what she wants. For all we know, she's still worried about her part in the whole thing and maybe getting in trouble over it. She's not going to the newspapers. She just wants us to make things right. That's what I think anyway."

We sat in silence, except for her sniffling. Like most males, I'm lost in such situations, where hugs and soft words are needed. I cowardly opted to ask her where the bathroom was and she seemed relieved to have a moment to herself.

"Make a left in the hall, then the first door on your right."

As I opened the door of the study I marveled at the quality of the hardware, as it made absolutely no noise when I turned the knob to open and close the door. Nevin was standing about ten feet away, his back to the door, still on his phone, oblivious to my presence. He was right in front of what appeared to be the bathroom door. I didn't want to interrupt him so I just hung back until he was done.

"No, you listen to me, Julie," he was saying quietly but force-fully. "It's over. We are *done*. Do you understand that? *Done*."

Something made him turn around. His tone was icy when he spoke to me.

"Is there something I can do for you, Toby?"

I feebly pointed to the bathroom just beyond him. He nodded and moved away, as casually as if I'd just found him reading a newspaper. He had to know I heard at least some of his conversa-tion, but if he felt caught in the act, he wasn't about to let on. Of course, he was the man with no secrets, and who never lies.

I didn't need the bathroom. I'd just wanted a break. I stared at myself in the mirror until I become bored, then livened things up with some Robert DeNiro in *Taxi Driver*. After a few minutes I figured it was safe to head back to the study. I'd just sat down when Nevin followed me in.

"Sorry," he said. "What did I miss?"

He sat back down and glanced at Catherine. I didn't need to worry about her, though. She was as composed as when he'd left, the aristocratic face perfectly in place, even her jacket rearranged to hide the small stains.

"Actually, I think we're done," I said. "I'll look at what you gave me and then go visit Melanie's mom and take it from there. Okay?"

"It's all we can do," Nevin said and turned to Catherine. "Hon?"

"Of course, darling," she said sipping her tea, pinky extended.

There didn't seem to be much else to say. I handed the papers back and stood up. "Do you want to keep the originals of these? Maybe have someone analyze the notes? For fingerprints or—"

"Sorry, I should have told you," Nevin said, taking the originals and handing me copies from his file. "We already did that."

Why should I be surprised?

"Anton West's investigator checked them out. The newspaper cutouts are all from the *San Diego Union Tribune,* which practically everyone in the entire county gets."

That was true. I got it and probably so did they, along with another half million people.

"And the paper it's glued to is a generic one every office supply store sells. They said there were partial fingerprints on some of the letters, but we can't compare them to Melanie's. Since she's never been arrested they're not on file anywhere."

I got to my feet and Nevin and Catherine both rose and walked me to the door.

"The investigator's number is in the report," Nevin said. "Give him a call with any questions. Or just bill me if you've got someone you want to run some leads down. We want to save you for Melanie and her mom. Okay, big guy?"

Big guy? Did he just call me big guy? What was I, twelve? Was a pat on the head next? How patronizing could this guy be? The fact he delivered the line with a wink did nothing to lessen its offensiveness.

They stepped outside with me and Nevin's face dropped. "Oh, my God."

At first I thought it was the sight of a '63 Falcon and wooden Indian passenger in his driveway, but he was looking past them both to the street below. A string of cars had pulled up and people were getting out with signs. Someone below saw us and suddenly everyone was waving their homemade signs in our direction: "Handley's a sellout!" "Keep Fallbrook green!" "Save Sandia Creek!"

His face grew red with anger. He shook his fist in frustration and I saw one of the people down below take a picture. Looked like we were going to be in tomorrow's paper. Hopefully, they'd crop me out of the picture. Nevin had taken a beating in the press lately for casting his swing vote on approving more aggressive development in our rural part of the county. I wondered if the irony was lost on him to see the builders bulldoze thousands of trees, then name the developments after the trees no longer there: *Happy Oaks* or *Peppertree Plaza*. The battle of no-growth versus development would never stop, until there were no more trees to fight over.

"How'd they get through the gate?" Nevin growled. He turned to Catherine. "Call security and get them out of here."

Without a word she turned and I took it as my chance to flee. As I drove past the protesters, I recognized a few people and waved, middle-aged soccer moms playing at protesting. I wondered how it would go over with Nevin if I asked if I could hold up one of the signs. I decided it might create a bit of a conflict so drove on past them and headed home.

5

I PULLED UP into my coveted covered parking space, potential space-stealers warned by a custom sign proclaiming "Reserved for Toby Dillon. Violators will be humiliated on the courts." It would have been egotistical if I'd had it made, but it was last year's Christmas gift from Lars.

I hopped out of my car and, although I kept the Falcon and Woody spotless, did a quick visual to be sure everything was ready for Rita. I'd spent longer than I had wanted in tea-talk at Nevin and Catherine's, so had only fifteen minutes to get ready before Rita was set to arrive. Luckily, five minute showers were the norm for me, and a few seconds for my usual finger-comb, so I'd be date-ready in about six minutes. Maybe this is why I had so few dates.

I jumped when a voice came from behind me. "So this guy is walking with his daughter in the park. . ."

I turned and saw Gil the Gardener step from behind the hu-

mongous honeysuckle bush screening the carport from the apart-
ments, his hedge clippers in hand. As usual, he had a joke for me.
The fact I rarely laughed didn't seem to deter him. In fact, it had
become a game. I'd try to keep a straight face no matter how
funny the joke was. Sadly, most of the time it didn't take much of
an effort, but once in a while he got lucky.

". . . And they see these two dogs mating."

"I've heard this one, Gil."

I don't know why I bother. It never stops him.

"So the little girl says 'Daddy! What are they *doing*?' And the
dad says 'Well, darlin' they're trying to make a puppy. . .'"

I started moving toward the stairs to my apartment. Gil followed along.

"Well, that night the little girl walks into her parents' bedroom
and catches them making love, and the girl says 'Daddy! What
are you doing to mommy?' And the dad says, 'Well honey, we're
trying to make you a little brother. . .' So the little girl says, 'Well,
flip her over daddy, 'cause I'd rather have a puppy.'"

"Good one, Gil, but I've heard it before. Guess who told it to
me? You."

"Okay, here's another one. There are these three widows—"

"Stop! Gil, I want to hear it, but I've got a date."

His eyebrows shot up so high every wrinkle was removed
from his face. True, I had a date about every presidential election.
Still, I didn't need everyone reacting with such shock. Before he
could add to Lynn's dating advice, I switched to a subject I knew
would get his mind off my sex life, or lack thereof. Actually,
bumping into him was perfect timing. I'd been planning to com-
mandeer a golf cart tomorrow and hunt him down.

"I've got a side job for you. Have you got the time?"

Gil had been an insurance investigator for State Farm, and a great one, their number one guy handling major fraud cases. When the combination of job stress, an extra hundred pounds and an over-demanding wife gave him a heart attack at age forty-six, he said goodbye to both the job and the wife. He was one of those rare people in life who didn't *talk* about starting a whole new life. He did it.

He let his socially-climbing wife keep everything, and with a small investment bought the landscaping maintenance company that serviced Coral Canyon. The previous owner had employed four guys, all small, hardened men from Mexico and Guatemala, experienced in the demands of laboring in the soil and sun. When Gil became the owner, he became worker number five, out there all day, doing the same work as his men. Gardening and landscaping had always been his secret passion. The pasty, portly man we'd watched sweat his way through the first few months was no more. Within a year he was as brown as his workers and almost as hard. He called working outside all day the Poor Man's Health Club. But he was too good to give up investigating entirely and was my Sherlock when I needed him to be.

"Hey, I started at dawn," he said. "So I can say it's quittin' time. What's up, another birth father search?"

All I normally needed Gil to do was find birth fathers to give them notice of the adoption. Usually this was when all we had was a name, but no address. Even if the birth father was unfindable, the court would want to see a report outlining his search efforts.

"Yeah," I said. "Actually, a couple things. One's a birth father. All we've got is a single name. Zuley. Don't know if it's a first name, last name or nickname. Maybe lives in Riverside. That's about it."

"Description?" he asked.

"About six feet, muscular build, probably early twenties. Likely Hispanic or mixed Caucasian. Only distinguishing characteristic is that he has blue eyes."

Gil didn't write anything down but I knew he'd remember every word.

"Is it Z – U – L – E –Y or Z – O – O – L – E –Y?"

"No idea, the birth mom just heard it spoken, so check both I guess."

"Neither one's going to be very common," he said. "I'm guessing a nickname. You thinking *azul* like Spanish for blue with his blue eyes? That'd be pretty rare for a Mexican guy. So like Bob becomes Bobby, azul becomes Zuley?"

See, the guy's good.

"Sounds like an idea to me. When do you think you can do it? She's due in about a week."

Gil knew I always wanted to find a birth father before the birth if possible, mainly to request a health history to give to the adoptive parents. But also I wanted to make sure he didn't plan to object. Only a couple birth fathers out of every hundred or so wanted to fight the adoption. The biggest fear of most of them was paying child support, so they were thrilled to cooperate. A few, however, wanted to raise the baby. That would be the end of the adoption, unless the birth mother raised concerns about his fitness to parent, then we'd be looking at a court fight, which was the one thing I sought to avoid.

Gil looked skyward at the increasing grayness above. "It's supposed to rain tomorrow, so probably a day off for me. If it's wet, I can have it done by tomorrow afternoon. Fast enough?"

"That'd be great Gil. Bill it to me under Colburn."

"Colburn as in Costa Brava?"

I nodded. A client's identity is protected by the attorney-client privilege, but it extended to the attorney's investigator and staff. Like everyone in Fallbrook, he'd had more than a few plates set in front of him by Aaron and Charlotte. Life in a small town.

"I've got another one too," I said. "Nevin and Catherine Handley are the clients—"

He made a face. "The county supervisor? The tree chopper?"

Our local weekly, *The Village News*, had done a caricature of Nevin with an ax in his hand. I imagined a water heater was in his future.

"Yep."

"Can I pass?" He was serious. He wanted to feel good about what he did, and one thing he liked was trees. He could say no to whatever he wanted.

I knew that if I told him about Lynn, and that he'd be helping her, he'd use every bit of his considerable skill to help, even if Nevin got a side benefit. But even though he'd be bound to keep it confidential, it felt wrong for him to be walking by the courts every day, looking at Lynn, knowing secrets about her even she didn't know. For as long as I could, I wanted to keep it to myself. I wasn't going to tell him about the blackmail issue either. It was just too hot a topic. But I needed his help.

"Of course, you can pass. But can you trust me when I say that I can't stand the guy myself, and I wouldn't be working for him if it wasn't for a good reason? I really need your help."

He didn't even make a show of thinking of it. My asking was enough. That was the benefit of a year of daily chats through the chain link fence which separates the courts from the second fair- way.

"If you need my help, Toby, you got it."

"That doesn't mean I'm going to laugh at your jokes."

He grinned. "It's enough for me to know you're bustin' up inside. Don't worry about it. So what do you need for the tree chopper?"

"It's not really for him, it's more about him. You know he started Human Minds Software about seventeen years ago, right? Down in San Diego?"

He nodded and I went on.

"He had an employee named Melanie Dubravado who worked for him back then. I want to know about every guy who worked there. I don't think there were many back then. They were just starting to expand when she left. And also anyone tied to the business who might have got close to her."

I handed him the pages he'd need from Nevin's folder.

"So, just co-workers?" he asked.

"Yeah, but also business reps, investors. . ." I trailed off and shrugged.

"What do you mean 'investors'? I thought he was a one man show. The rags to riches story."

"I did too. I guess it's part of the image he was selling. But he got funding from an investment capital group. Who they were, and how involved they were, I don't know."

"Jeez, Toby, this is kind of broad. What am I looking for? Anyone who had contact with this Melanie girl? Who her friends were? What?"

It was a good question and it made me focus.

"I guess I'm looking for two things. Someone who could be the father to a child she gave birth to back then. . . that's why I said guys only. But also someone she was close enough to tell secrets too, and who now may want to use those secrets against Nevin Handley. So I guess I shouldn't say guys only. Women too."

"What are we talking? Blackmail?"

"C'mon, Gil. Don't go there, okay?"

He wasn't used to getting half a story from me, but he shrugged and accepted it. He did ask a question though.

"Is there a reason you aren't just asking the girl herself?"

"Yeah. No one can find her. In fact, no one's seen her for about four years."

"And you don't want me to find her?"

"I'd love for you to find her. But when you look in the notes you'll see that some high priced investigators working for another attorney already came up with nada. The one thing they haven't done is talk to her mother. That's what I'm going to do."

Gil gave me a smart ass look. "Oh, 'cause you're so good at that, huh?"

"Shut up."

Gil laughed and pulled out his pruners as we walked through the immense bougainvillea arching over my sidewalk.

"Pray for rain, Toby. I'll have something for you tomorrow."

6

I WAS GETTING dressed in my closet when Rita let herself in and called out from the front door.

"Toby? Are you decent?"

"Yeah."

"Oh well, I'll come in anyway."

Lately there had been a little escalation of the flirtation talk, but talk was all it was. Not that I wasn't enjoying it tremendously.

"I'm in the closet. C'mon back."

My apartment was small. One bedroom with a tiny living room and a kitchenette. It was stylin' though, all the units catering to Coral Canyon's upscale clientele: wood beam ceilings, saltillo paver flooring, and a red cast-iron fireplace which was more for looks but actually worked. When I'd first moved in, a hundred bucks landed me a nicely broken-in leather sofa from a garage sale. Push it against the wall and you couldn't see the previous owner's cat scratches.

With Rita coming over more lately I'd put some effort into the place, painting the walls a shade of what I'd call dark orange, but the can identified it as *Santa Fe Sweet Potato Sunset.* I'd bought a few plants, which I considered next to paint the world's cheapest decorating tool, and bartered a few tennis lessons for an abstract painting from one of Fallbrook's starving artists. I didn't know what the painting was, but it was big and I liked it. Its official title was *Vision number 346.* Sounded like she and the guy who named my orange paint would get along just fine.

For a small place, the walk-in closet was roomy, and when Rita walked in I was sitting on the floor, pulling on some socks. When I saw her I wanted to burst into *You Light Up My Life*, then I remembered that even I wanted to kill Debbie Boone when I heard it. Besides, with the unique reasoning of every male in the universe, I was trying to not make it too obvious I'd die for this girl. Like if she knew, she'd lose interest, so I tried to take the devotion down just a tad. Just call me Mr. Cool. We guys never learn.

She was dressed in some old Levis, torn at the knees. I knew she hadn't bought them that way in a boutique; she actually wore them out working around her property. She'd been raised a Fallbrook farm girl and still liked real work. I wondered what the poor sweatshop laborers of foreign countries thought about the clothes they were manufacturing for American consumers: make perfect new pants, stonewash them to wear them out, then rip them in strategic places. A nation which can't even wear out its own pants. And to think we're the leaders of the free world.

She wore a baggy old tee-shirt and had her hair pulled back in a simple ponytail. Some might think this was her way of going incognito, but she just liked to be as comfortable as possible, especially with the day we had planned.

"Wow, never seen your closet before. That's a lot of tennis shoes."

I went through a pair of shoes a month, easy to do when you spend five hours a day on the courts. The old ones were still too good to toss, so the result was a veritable Imelda Marcos collection, assuming she favored sneakers.

Rita's eyes took in the closet and fell on my blue sport coat and three pairs of slacks hanging in the corner, dwarfed by the dozens of tees and polos filling the hangers.

"Do you have another closet?" she asked.

"Another closet?"

"Yeah. For your suits."

Oh, oh.

The truth was I only had one blue sport coat, plus two pairs of gray slacks and one tan. Since I only wore a suit about twice a month for court, no one saw me enough to realize I only had one suit jacket: a blue blazer. It was surprisingly versatile, kind of like the Swiss Army knife of men's wear.

Until now, I'd been taking a perverse pleasure in having her in my tiny closet with me as I was getting dressed, even if it was only putting on my socks. There was a level of casual intimacy I didn't want to let go of. As if I could somehow keep it going into infinity, we'd morph into husband and wife and share a million such everyday moments.

I could understand her question. I was a lawyer after all, and a person would expect a closet full of suits. Other than hiding my feelings for her for most of my life, I'd never lied to her and didn't want to start now.

"That's all I've got," I admitted.

"But there's only one."

She wasn't being critical, just honestly confused. Can't say that I blamed her. I explained about the pants rotation, ending weakly with, "So really, it looks like I have three outfits."

Outfits sounded like a girl's term, but I didn't know what else to call them.

"I do have four ties," I added hopefully. "So it really looks like four outfits, don't you think?"

The truth was I didn't care much about clothes, or how I looked in them, especially monkey-suits. Shopping for a big TV? Fun. Shopping for a computer? Fun. A car? Fun. Clothes? No thanks. Besides, who'd want another suit when they could spend the same money and get a new, perfectly weighted, graphite racquet with a slightly oversized head? I only had seven racquets, and a guy can never have too many.

Any other woman would have cut loose with a remark or two about my wardrobe failings, and they would have been well-deserved, but Rita just smiled.

"Are you ready to go?"

How I loved this girl.

And go we did.

7

THE DRIVE TO my grandfather's place took only fifteen minutes. He'd bought sixty acres when the land was plentiful and cheap, and like everyone in Fallbrook back then, had planted an avocado grove. Three decades later, the trees soared forty feet, and their broad, green leaves provided a comforting canopy of shade. His land was in an area not yet touched by much subdivision and most of the property around him belonged to the big avocado collectives. From the high point of his property the view was nothing but a sea of lush green. San Diego was sixty miles to the south and Disneyland ninety to the north, but here we could have been in the middle of Costa Rica. A secret paradise.

Before Rita and I got started on what we'd come for, we took a walk in the grove. The trees were mature enough that we didn't even have to duck. The crop was coming in nicely, about three hundred avos a tree. We'd played in the grove as kids. Hide and Seek and Capture the Flag. It was filled with memories, but all I noticed today was that when I took her hand in mine, she stroked a finger against my palm. She'd never done that before.

"I sure miss your grandfather, Toby."

There was nothing I could say to that. My grandfather had been my hero. My role model. Back in the early days he'd been Fallbrook's only lawyer and he volunteered as many hours for others as he did for pay. The grove and his boat had been his passions, sharing them with me every weekend as I grew up. Our project had been his boat.

"This is going to be fun," Rita said. She gave my hand another little squeeze.

What I hadn't told Lynn was that my date with Rita was going to be spent varnishing the teak walls in the salon of my grandfather's boat. I guess it was actually my boat since grandpa willed it to me, but I always thought of it as his. When I'd asked Rita how she wanted to spend the day, she asked if she could help me on the boat. No one had ever worked on it but grandpa and me, and since he'd died, just me alone.

My grandfather had bought it for scrap value. A 1942 Stephens fifty-two foot motor yacht. The diesels had blown and no one wanted an old wooden boat. He'd had it craned in and set into a cement cradle in the ground, so now green grass surrounded its hull rather than water. A lot of people had thought my grandpa was a bit nuts when he did it, but for less than the price of an old trailer he had a classy wooden home, built by craftsmen that cared. We'd built a few steps against the hull to access the aft deck, and from there you entered the salon. The built-in sofas and bookshelves left ample room in the center, with a compact galley forward. Up front, split stairs rose to the pilothouse, and descended below decks to the cabins.

It was intended to be a simple place to sleep for when my

grandpa stayed until dark working on the grove. Sometimes though, I wondered if the real purpose of the boat was for us to spend time together. He knew I didn't fit in at my rush-to-achievement-and-money home. Some of my best memories were of my grandpa and me working side-by-side, always with old-fashioned hand tools, not electric, allowing us to talk as we worked. If every boy in the world had worked at his side, there would be no gangs, drug abuse or violence. He was the master and I was his apprentice, although I later realized what he was teaching me had nothing to do with carpentry.

It was one of those oddities of life that his own son, my father, rejected everything my grandfather had stood for, and now headed one of the biggest and most ruthless law firms in San Diego. My dad's humiliation over a son cleaning tennis courts, and running what he termed a "worthless do-gooder" law practice out of a storage room, only increased his enmity. I got on fine with my brothers, Curtis the oldest, Brent next, then me. Each of us were two years apart in age, but light years in lifestyle. They'd adopted my father's and worked for his firm. Contact with me would incur the wrath of papa, which was usually enough of a potential threat for them to ignore me. So my family may have been lost to me, but the boat embraced me like I was still a small boy in my grandpa's arms.

I'd spent the last month sanding down the flooring and walls, then staining them in warm tones. The walls were solid teak, and the floors were two inch planks of dark teak with light ribbons of holly in between. Today was relatively easy, putting on a nice satin varnish to give the wood a nice glow, and some protection from moisture. I taught Rita how to apply the varnish so it wouldn't puddle in the bevels.

After about an hour and a half I said, "How about a break?"

I didn't need one, but I wanted the day to be fun for Rita.
She smiled. "Great."

We went out to the deck. I'd had a new awning made with
wide blue and white stripes and we sat under its shade in some
Adirondack chairs. We turned them to face the valley view
spreading below us, the sun warming our backs. I'd brought a
cooler and filled it with things I knew Rita would like: some
wine, cheese and crackers, and a Dr Pepper for me. Nothing too
original in that, but sometimes basic is best.

Rita had grabbed the week's collection of mail from the rusty
mailbox on the way up, and now she thumbed through it.

"Hmm. . . what's this?" She held up a magazine. "Since when
do you subscribe to *Cosmopolitan*?"

I'd gotten them before. "Look at the label. I bet it's for Bea
Nolan down the road."

She did, and it was, but that didn't stop her from looking at it.

"Check this out, Toby: '*How well does your man know you?*'"

Suddenly my mouth went dry. *Your man?* She said it lightly, a
game we were about to play. Still, was that how she thought of
me?

"Ready?" she asked.

"Ready."

Was it my imagination, or did my voice just register an octave
higher?

"Okay," she said, mimicking a gossipy teenager's voice.
"Question number one. What color are your true love's eyes?"

What a dumb question. What guy didn't know the color of his
dream girl's eyes?

"No peeking," Rita said, turning her back to me with a laugh.
"I'm waiting."

I took a deep breath. "Green. . ."

"Good. Question number two—"

". . . except around the outside edge where there is a thin ring of blue. . . and when you're outside in the sun, it makes your eyes look almost aquamarine. . ."

"Oh." She said it weakly, like it fell from her lips.

". . . And near the center, your irises are surrounded by these tiny flecks of brown. A few more in your left eye than your right."

She turned to look at me, her face taking on an odd expression. I knew I should stop, that I was giving it all away. So much for Mr. Cool. But I couldn't stop. I could only look into those eyes I was describing.

"When we were kids, the little flecks were darker, like milk chocolate. . . I always thought it looked like those little freckles that arched on top of your nose jumped into your eyes."

I finally shut up. Rita got out of her chair in what seemed like slow motion. My first thought was that I'd risked too much and she was leaving. But she walked over to me. Without a word she sat down on my lap, sitting sideways so she could face me. She put her face to mine. Her lips to mine.

Her tongue slipped into my mouth the same time her arms wrapped around me. There was no mouth so warm, so smooth, so sweet. I'd kissed her once in our youth. My first kiss, shared with the girl I'd believed was the only girl I could ever love. Almost twenty years later and I still believed it.

I felt like every fiber in my being was in my tongue at that moment, exploring a perfect universe. I don't recall giving my hands permission to roam her body, but suddenly they were, and by some miracle, she wasn't objecting. If we'd been in a movie, we'd be getting naked by now, headed for the bedroom. The instant intimacy of our generation. But she and I weren't like that.

Never had been. I knew our courtship was going to be slow. Just the kissing alone I'd stretch into forever if I could. I was in no rush. I wanted this girl for life.

Just as I thought this, my body betrayed me. Well, not exactly betrayed me, but gave me away. Rita, in other words, was no longer sitting on a flat surface. I was embarrassed, as if I were sixteen and on a first date. But she didn't pull away. In fact, she actually seemed to be unconsciously pushing herself down into me, moving rhythmically.

A few more little circle moves with her hips and I decided to say to hell with the slow courtship and the forever kiss. All I wanted was to get her in the bunk downstairs and get naked with her. Not in two months or two weeks or two hours. This very second. I put one arm under her legs and one around her back to lift her up and bring her there. She didn't protest.

Then my cell phone rang.

Why the hell did I bring my cell phone? I ignored it, but Rita didn't, breaking from our kiss.

"You better get that."

"No," I said, pulling her back to me. "It'll stop in a second."

But she gently resisted my efforts.

"No. You really should get it."

I knew she didn't really care about the phone call. The look on her face told me she realized we were going too fast. That may sound ridiculous in light of the fact we'd been friends for most of our lives, and kinda sorta dating without calling it that for several months, but I understood. Still, I knew we'd crossed into new territory. I'd waited forever; I could wait a bit longer.

Rita extricated herself and stood up. This left my excitement painfully obvious. She looked down and giggled. Toby Dillon, tentmaker. I couldn't help it and laughed too. The phone had stopped ringing but now started again. I was laughing when I said "Hello."

It was Lynn and she only spoke for a few seconds. The tent collapsed and the laughter died in my throat. I told her I'd be right there. I looked up at Rita who'd stopped laughing too when she saw my face.

"I'm sorry, I've got to go. That was Lynn. Her father's been murdered."

8

THERE WASN'T MUCH conversation on the way back to my place. Rita had met Lynn a few times but didn't know about her parents hiring me. She assumed I was going there as a friend. Actually, that's why Lynn had called me. Nothing more. But my mind was already racing, thinking about the notes and the threats we'd taken as idle.

I dropped off Rita at her car, pausing only long enough to kiss her. Our goodbye kiss had the restraint of a prom kiss on the doorstep with parents watching through the curtains, but it held the promise of the passion from just moments before.

The good feeling ebbed away as I got closer to Lynn's house, and my thoughts went to her. A teenager losing her father. Not just to death, but to murder.

There was a patrolman at the Champagne Crest gate, and through its iron bars I could see a phalanx of emergency vehicles. He radioed my presence and someone gave the okay to send me through. Just as I drove in, a news van pulled up, but was kept outside. This was going to be big news. Nevin Handley wasn't just a major politician in the county, he was San Diego's version of a mini Bill Gates.

A second policeman was at the gate to Lynn's house. He told me I'd been cleared to go up but I'd have to leave my car on the street.

"What's with the Indian?" he asked, looking genuinely perplexed.

As I walked up the driveway I could see banks of floodlights set up around a small building barely visible through some trees in a distant corner of the property. The crime scene people were already there in force and there was a lot of activity around the structure. Comparatively, the house was quiet. As I approached the front door Lynn came running out. She launched herself into me with enough force to almost knock me down.

She was crying when she'd called me and she wasn't close to being out of tears now. They flowed the minute she held me, her body racking with sobs. Finally they stopped and she let me go.

"Marcel found him. In the weight room."

Talking about it made her face contort with anguish all over again and a few more tears trickled out, but this time without the sobs. I only knew Marcel by name as Lynn had mentioned him a few times over the years. She never used the word *butler*, but that'd likely be the closest description to what he did.

"Toby, I heard them. The police. They were standing right outside. I heard them say my dad was *murdered. . .* Why would someone murder my dad?"

Nevin Handley may have been a jerk in many ways, but he was still her father. Taught her to walk and to talk. To me he was a client, and a father to my friend. I owed him something.

"Tell me what happened, Lynn. From the beginning."

As soon as I asked her, I wished I hadn't. I was asking a girl to relive learning of the death of her father. But I couldn't take the question back. Actually, she seemed relieved to verbalize the thoughts racing through her head, maybe hoping they would replay differently in the telling so he was alive at the end.

"In the afternoon my dad went down to work out, in the gym. We called him to dinner on the intercom but he didn't come, so mom sent Marcel down." Her eyes lost their focus. "Mom and I made a pie together for dessert. . . she's been spending more time with me lately. . ."

She turned toward the lights set up below, what must be their gym. I turned her toward the house. "Let's go inside, Lynn."

But she didn't budge. Her eyes came back to me.

"And Marcel called us from there on the intercom. Mom got it but I could hear him screaming. Screaming to call an ambulance. So mom called 911 and we ran down. . . And we found him."

I was still cursing myself for asking the question and tried once again to get her in the house—to do anything but relive finding her dad's body. Not that she was going to be thinking of anything else. I got her moving toward the front door and out of sight of the gym. But she kept talking as we walked, my arm around her.

"He was on the weight bench, his arms just hanging down. Marcel was doing CPR. . . but dad never came back."

So far, it didn't sound like murder. More like a heart attack. I wasn't going to ask her about it though. When we got inside I let her lead us to where she wanted to go, and we ended up in a comfortable room that was one of the few areas I'd seen in the house that didn't look like a museum. There was a sofa, some armchairs and a TV. We sat down and she put her head on my shoulder. Her breathing grew so deep that after awhile I thought maybe she was so exhausted she'd fallen asleep, but when the click of heels sounded outside, Lynn's head raised in time to see her mother enter the room. She didn't look surprised to see me. Lynn or the police must have told her I was coming.

Lynn got up and walked into her mother's arms. Catherine gave me a little nod toward the door and I assumed she was giving me the hint to go and leave them alone. But when I got into the hallway I realized she'd been telling me someone was waiting for me. A policeman.

"Mr. Dillon?"

I nodded.

"Can you follow me please?" It wasn't really a question. "Detective Hawkes would like a word with you."

Winston Hawkes. I'd got to know him last year when Brogan and Rita's adoption turned bad—a missing baby with a critical medical problem facing us like a ticking time bomb. He'd proven himself a good, smart cop who cared more about results than the politics of police work. We'd approached the threshold of friendship when the case ended, and had since crossed over it, sharing more than a few beers, or in my case, Dr Peppers, over Charger and Padres games on TV.

We got to the little gym and the cop stopped me outside.

"Wait here, please, sir."

That was fine with me. I had no desire to see a dead body. The only problem was that the cop had left me by a window and I didn't have the willpower not to look inside.

Nevin's body was on the floor, next to a padded bench press. It had stirrups on posts at one end to hold a barbell, although there were no weights there now. His neck was red with a strip of abrasions across it.

"Hi, Toby."

I was so preoccupied by the sight of the body I didn't even hear Hawkes approach. He had about twenty years on me. In a movie he'd be played by Morgan Freeman, assuming he'd accept a supporting role. His ebony face was glistening from the heat of the lights. Or maybe it was the pressure sure to follow this case. He gave me a smile but one without any humor.

"Hi, yourself," I said. "Is it true? Was he murdered?"

"Where'd you hear that?"

"His daughter, Lynn. Overheard two of your men talking up by the house."

He made a face.

"So it's not true?" I persisted.

He thought about his answer for a second then said, "Yeah, looks like it is. I already talked to the wife, but that's not the way I'd like a kid to hear about it. Was it two of the uniforms?"

I didn't know and shrugged to tell him so. He had weightier things on his mind than chewing out two cops for talking out of turn. At least for now.

"Mrs. Handley was down here with me when the uniform at the gate said you were here. She tells me you're her daughter's tennis coach."

I nodded.

"Seems like a funny person to call when your father dies," he said, his eyes sharp. "Your tennis pro."

"We're good friends. Have been for a long time. Fifteen hours a week on the court together and you can't help it."

That's what I said, but what I was thinking about was the questions which might come next. Questions I wasn't prepared to answer just yet, and it wasn't going to sit well with Hawkes when

I didn't. I could only hope he wouldn't lead the conversation that way, and instead assume I was nothing more than Lynn's friend.

"Why were the cops saying he was murdered?" I asked.

He didn't rush to answer, but finally did.

"The press is already out there. As soon as we refuse to label it an accident they're going to start hinting foul play, so that's tonight's number one news story, whether I like it or not. But that doesn't mean you need to share any details."

I nodded. Besides, talking to the media was one of my least favorite things to do. Hawkes filled me in.

"The servant came down to get him for dinner. Found him on his back, on the bench. A barbell was on his neck—one end anyway. The other end was on the floor. The paramedics pulled him off the bench when they tried to bring him back. Already dead, though."

My eyes went to the window as Hawkes spoke. Near the body I saw the barbell, maybe five feet long with a few steel disks at each end. Maybe seventy or eighty pounds total, not much weight when it comes to doing bench presses.

I tried to imagine Nevin doing some presses, just toning with a low weight. If he'd had a heart attack the weight could have fallen to his neck, and one side slid off when he died. There had to be more to make it murder.

"How do you know he didn't just have a heart attack or something?" I asked.

Before he could answer, the technician who'd been dusting the barbell for prints came outside to speak to Hawkes, pausing to look at me first.

"It's okay," Hawkes said. "What've you got?"

"Well, the deceased's prints are all over the barbell, *except* where you'd usually put your hands." He put his closed hands about two feet apart in front of him. "There's nothing there. Some of the butler guy, but they're at one end only. Looks like he just flipped the end of the bar on the vic's neck off, like he said, trying to help him."

"Thanks," Hawkes said. "Let me know when you've got more."

I could see the murder theory making sense if there were no prints where Nevin's hands should have been, but they could have been innocently wiped away by the butler or the ambulance people who must have been the first on the scene. Besides, if Lynn overhead the cops correctly, the police had thought murder even before they realized there were no prints where they should have been on the barbell.

I asked my question again. "So why do you think it was murder, and not a heart attack?"

Hawkes nodded to the departing tech.

"Weren't you listening?"

"Yeah, but you were talking murder before you heard that."

He sighed, like he wished he hadn't started the conversation with me.

"Whoever did this probably thought it'd look like a heart attack, but the coroner knew right away. He could feel the crepitus in the neck. . . all those soft bones in there. . . completely pulverized. 'Crunchy, like Rice Crispies,' he said. Even if he had a heart attack, he'd be able to lower the weight. He wouldn't just shut off like a switch. And the blue all around the mouth, which shows suffocation. You're not going to see that with a natural death."

That meant someone stood above Nevin and pushed the barbell into his throat, suffocating him, pushing so hard they'd crushed the bones in his neck. I tried to imagine someone he trusted standing over him, spotting for him on his last few reps, then when his arms were exhausted and he couldn't lift the bar even once more, pushing it down until he was dead. Or someone had come in without Nevin seeing him, focused on his workout. The lack of Nevin's fingerprints where they should have been on the bar only made it clearer. That's where the killer had gripped the bar while he pushed it down, either wearing gloves, or wiping off his prints afterward.

"So, Toby," Hawkes gave me a look, seeing my mind racing. "You have any idea who might want him dead?"

Ahh, there it was. The question I'd hoped not to hear. My problem was that I couldn't reveal anything Nevin and Catherine told me without their permission. The notes. A threat. Melanie. All of it.

Nevin was dead, and normally that would end my obligation to keep the attorney-client privilege, but Catherine was my client too. If she'd told Hawkes about the notes and the threat, he'd be asking me about them. But he didn't, which meant she hadn't told him. Had she just been in shock and didn't think of it? I had to assume she'd want the police to know. A threat to Nevin's life, even a vague one, seemed about as big a clue as could be. I was silent too long. Hawkes knew I was holding something back.

"Damn it, Toby! Talk to me."

Hawkes moved closer, invading my space. The last time we'd worked together he'd learned I'd kept things from him during his investigation. Since I was on the side of the good guys, he overlooked it. More than overlooked, I think he secretly rooted for someone trying to take down bad guys, by whatever means. But he wasn't going to fall for my innocent act again.

"I'm sorry," I said. "I can't answer that yet."

You'd never guess we were normally friends by the look on his face at that moment.

"Listen, I let you skate with withholding evidence once. I'm not going to do it again. If you know something, anything, relevant to this you've got to tell me. Now."

I just stared at him. The sad thing was that part of the attorney-client privilege included even telling someone the *identity* of your client, unless they gave permission. I could have taken the heat off myself by telling Hawkes that I had an attorney-client privilege with Nevin's wife, and that barred me from giving any information. Cops never liked the rule, but Hawkes would have to accept it. But it would put suspicion on Catherine if she refused to let me speak, which was why a client's identity was part of the privilege.

"Tell you what," I finally said. "I think I can get permission to talk to you by tomorrow. Okay?"

I owed Hawkes that much, and I couldn't imagine Catherine wanting me to sit on the information about the notes. He wasn't mollified, though, and let me know it.

"Sergeant Crowley," he bellowed over my shoulder.

I turned to see the policeman who'd escorted me down walking toward us. Hawkes nodded toward me.

"Escort this gentleman off the property, please."

Ouch.

"Wait," I said. "I'd like to say goodbye to the family first. I've got the right to do that." I could get pissy too.

"Whatever," he grumbled. "And just so you know, Toby, we've already established Mrs. Handley and the daughter were together in the kitchen at the time he was killed. The butler confirms it too. They were working in there for hours. They're not suspects."

His eyes bore into me. He was a smart guy. He was telling me he knew the issue was attorney-client privilege, and that my client was most likely Catherine or Lynn. He wanted to make sure I passed along their *innocent* status to get their cooperation. I probably shouldn't have said I needed to stop by the house, as that likely put the thought in his head.

"Got it," I said.

He nodded me on my way and the sergeant escorted me back up to the house.

"I'm going to wait here for you, Mr. Dillon. When you're ready to leave I'll escort you to the gate. We can't have anyone walking around the property while we're investigating the scene."

I promised him I wouldn't run out the back door, then pushed the bell. Smileyface answered, the first time I'd seen her tonight. I asked for Catherine and she let me inside, but kept me standing by the door. When she spoke her tone was disapproving.

"Mrs. Handley is putting Lynn to bed. Are you sure you need to speak to her?"

The last thing I wanted to do was disturb them, but I also had to talk to Catherine.

"Actually, I do. But I don't want you to interrupt them. How about I just wait until she comes out, then you tell her I'm here?"

She didn't seem to like the idea but she walked me to a living room, the kind where it looks like no one actually ever sits down. The sitting area was in the middle, with several yards of empty floor space all around. The walls were covered with paintings, all lighted like we were in Versailles. I wondered who thought to turn them on at a time like this.

So much time passed that when Catherine came in I was half lying on the sofa, almost falling asleep. I stood up.

"I'm so sorry about Nevin, Catherine."

Such a lame thing to say when someone dies, but what else can you say?

"Thanks for coming to see Lynn. I'm glad she called you. She. . . she doesn't have a lot of friends, I'm afraid."

She sat down and I did the same.

"I was surprised the police wanted to speak to you," she said. "Can I ask why?"

"The lead detective, Winston Hawkes, you met him?"

She nodded and I went on.

"You know about the kidnapping case when I did Brogan Barlow and Rita MacGilroy's adoption last year. He was the detective on it." After a pause I added, "He's good."

"Did he tell you what he told me? That it looks like Nevin was killed? Not an accident?"

"Yes. In fact, he asked me if I had any idea who could want to harm him. Technically, I can't answer that question without your permission. I had the impression you didn't tell him about the blackmail notes, and that one had an implied threat to his life."

She looked at me steadily. "No, I didn't."

She didn't add anything, just let her statement sit there.

"Well. . . can I tell him?" I asked.

Without a word she got up and closed the double doors leading into the room. When she walked back she was more focused. Intense actually. She spoke softly but firmly, like she didn't want anyone to overhear, but also to be sure I did not misunderstand her feelings.

"No, you do *not* have permission to tell him about those notes."

"But Catherine, we have to tell—"

"No, we don't have to tell him anything about them. Listen to me, Toby. Do you really think a little woman like Melanie overpowered Nevin and killed him?" She stared me down. "She wrote those notes because we left her no choice. Nevin treated her. . .

we treated her terribly. We turned something which should have been all about Lynn, something that we could all rejoice in—Melanie and us—and turned it into something dirty. People don't keep *good* things secret, just things they're ashamed of. And the more time that went by, the more impossible it became to even think about making it right. Thank God she's finally doing something about it, because if she left it to Nevin and me, it'd never happen."

What she said made sense, but it was still too much of a coincidence that the notes came at this time, particularly the one less than two weeks ago. *You will pay.*

"Let's say you're right," I said, "and the notes have nothing to do with what's happened. What does it matter? What's the harm? For all we know there's more to those notes than we know, and the police can find out."

But she just shook her head.

"I can't believe you say there's no harm, Toby. Can you imagine what will happen if instead of *you* finding Melanie and talking to her, a policeman does it. . . asking about blackmail notes. . . and murder? Do you think she'd want to cooperate with us?" Her voice faltered a minute as she corrected herself, realizing there was no more *us.* "With me."

"Okay," I said reluctantly. "I can't tell him anything without your permission, so he won't hear anything about it. But I want you to know I think it's a mistake."

"I'm sorry you don't agree with me," she said. "I wish I could make you understand. More than anything I've got to watch out for Lynn. Suddenly, I have no husband, and technically I don't have a daughter. I just know if the police know about all that it'll end up in the news within a day or two. You know it too. It's just what happens. I truly don't care about myself, but Lynn would be humiliated. And poor Melanie, who did nothing but give us a daughter, will be made out to look like a suspect." She leaned forward with intensity. "And *that's* why we aren't going to say anything."

"So what do you want me to tell Hawkes? He can tell I know something, and that if I'm not talking to him it's because you're a client. He made it clear you're not a suspect, but claiming the attorney-client privilege is going to make him think I'm holding back something which reflects negatively on you."

"So much for the attorney-client privilege," she said pointedly.

Without warning, the tough façade crumbled and she brought her hands up to her face, covering it as if to find the composure she was losing. Just as quickly she stood up, her signal our conversation was over.

"I'm sorry. I just can't talk about this any more. I'm fading away by the second, and I want to go check on Lynn."

She walked me to the front door and I turned to her with one last question.

"Is there anything I can be doing for you or Lynn? Anything at all?"

Her eyes locked on mine. "Just find that girl, Toby. Find Melanie. Please. I don't want to worry about losing my daughter too."

9

BY THE TIME I got home it was getting close to midnight. My first thought as I went to bed was a selfish one: I was going to be sleepy tomorrow and I had to get up at dawn to blow off the courts. Unless Gil's promised rain came, that is. My second thought was how sad my bed looked. It had never struck me as odd before, but suddenly the single pillow on one side of the double bed hit me as a veritable icon of loneliness. It was a country song waiting to be written: one pillow on a bed made for two.

My last thoughts as I drifted to sleep were not of Lynn or Catherine or Nevin or murder. They were only of Rita.

The morning brought rain, and for the first time in a long time, I was glad to be free of my tennis obligations. I'd been set to take over the nine a.m. morning clinic for Lars, but now I could concentrate on finding Melanie. Or trying to. I wasn't sure how Nevin's murder affected anything. If Catherine was right and Melanie had nothing to do with his death, nothing had changed. If she was wrong, who knew what awaited me? I tended to think Catherine was right, though.

The best thing about the rain was that Gil could go to work for me. When the phone rang midway through my second bowl of Raisin Bran, it was him. He'd been able to start on things yesterday and said he'd have more by two. He proposed meeting at Costa Brava. He didn't have a cell phone, part of his "less is more" philosophy, so he'd be unavailable to me until then.

I'd been through the file Nevin had given me. Melanie's mother's name was Cindy Dubravado. Thanks to the investigator's report I had her address and phone number. I thought I'd have a better chance of success if I just dropped by to see her. The report said she was retired, so the odds seemed good she'd be home in the morning.

It was only a thirty minute drive to San Marcos. On the way I worked through the different approaches I could take with her. If I told her of the adoption she'd understand the importance of reaching Melanie, but what if she didn't even know of the pregnancy and the adoption which followed it? Melanie could end up being furious with me for having told her. Not only did I not want to violate her privacy, I also didn't want to do something that would make her so angry she wouldn't cooperate in completing the adoption.

By the time I pulled up to the house I had a loose plan in mind. I felt like a football coach. I had a plan, but I also had a backup plan. And if the backup plan didn't work, I had a backup backup plan, although that one basically just involved groveling and begging.

The small stucco house was in an older but well-maintained neighborhood. I smelled the cookies baking through the screen door even before I knocked. I'd lay ten-to-one odds we were talking homemade chocolate chip. If things went just right, I'd leave with Melanie's address in my hand, and some cookies in my stomach.

The woman who came to the door was pleasant looking and in her early sixties, complete with apron bearing "World's Best Mom." She was still wearing oven mitts that could have come from the Aunt Bea Mayberry collection.

"Good morning," she said. "What can I do for you?"

Suddenly I felt guilty for my planned approach, but protecting Melanie's secrets, not to mention Catherine's, gave me little choice.

"Hi," I said. "Is Melanie home?"

Man, am I an original thinker or what?

"I'm sorry, Melanie hasn't lived here for quite awhile. Are you a friend of hers?"

"Yes, but it's been a long time, back in high school. We kept in touch for a while, but she stopped calling a few years ago. Is she okay?"

"I'm sorry." She smiled kindly. "I'm not sure if I caught your name."

"Toby. Toby Dillon."

The name shouldn't mean anything to her, but I had to give her one and couldn't very well lie about my name.

"I thought I knew all of Melanie's friends from St. Francis. I don't recall ever hearing yours."

"Oh, I went to a different school, but we worked together at Human Minds back then."

She considered me for a second then pushed the screen door open.

"Why don't you come in."

The door opened into a small living room with the patented

grandma-era floral print sofa and chairs. I was hoping she'd detour through the kitchen and come back with a plate of cookies, but all she did was peel off the oven mitts.

"You have a nice home," I said. "Are you retired?"

Toby Dillon, master at small talk.

She gave me a bitter smile.

"Not willingly. I was with Langdon Pharmaceuticals for a long time. I was just short of my pension when we got shut down a few years ago." She grimaced. "Lawyers."

Oops. That had been one of my dad's class actions. Langdon made heart stents. When some of the recipients died of heart attacks, he'd brought a class action that had bankrupted the company. I recalled the company's defense had been a good one: the people who got the stents were more prone to subsequent heart attacks due to their existing cardiac problems, so of course some died. But as always, my dad won. So a few people got rich—relatives of the deceased, and of course, my father and his firm. And nine hundred people lost their jobs. Welcome to litigation in America.

As I was thinking this, a light went on in her eyes. Not a nice light either.

"Wait a minute. . . Toby Dillon. . . You're part of that family of lawyers, aren't you? You're the one who does the adoptions."

She said it like an accusation, and in her case it was justified, at least about my father. I held his law practice, as I did most of the legal profession, in pretty low regard. Lawyers should exist to solve problems, not get rich creating them. But she wouldn't believe me if I told her that. She gave me a piercing look.

"You never worked with Melanie did you? She would have mentioned that."

So now she realized I was not only a liar, but the son of the lawyer who put her company out of business. Things were not looking good for me. Worse, any shot I had at some cookies just went out the window. I was just thinking I'd better switch to Plan Two when she took the matter out of my hands. She sat back and fixed me with a challenging stare.

"I'm guessing you're here about Melanie's daughter."

10

TALK ABOUT KNOCKING a guy's feet out from under him. Not only did she know about the adoption, she knew why I was there. This lady's mind worked like mercury.

"Listen," I said. "I'm sorry for not being truthful with you before. You're right, I'm an adoption attorney. . . and I really believe in what I do. And part of that is respecting the privacy of everyone involved if they want it that way. That's why I couldn't say why I was here. What if you didn't know Melanie even had a baby? I didn't have the right to tell you about it. Only Melanie does."

She considered what I said and seemed to accept it. Maybe even appreciate it. "So why are you asking about this now? You weren't an attorney back then. Lynn was born sixteen years ago."

For the second time inside a minute she had me almost speechless. One, she knew Lynn's name. I guess there was no reason she shouldn't. Melanie likely knew from Nevin and Cath-

erine, and if her mother knew about the adoption, there was no
reason for her to have also not mentioned the name they chose.
Still, it sounded strange coming from her mouth, like she thought
about Lynn every day. The other thing was that she knew Lynn's
age without a moment's thought. That'd be expected if Melanie
had raised Lynn and she was a traditional granddaughter, but not
with a child placed for adoption. I was getting a weird vibe, like
Scully and Mulder were going to walk into the room and make
me a part of an *X Files* episode. Luckily, they'd been off the air
for ages, so I knew I was safe.

"You're right," I said. "Obviously I wasn't an attorney back
then, but I've been asked to help now."

"Don't you think your family's done enough already?"

Give it up lady, I thought. A son can only pay for so many of
his father's sins.

"So," she went on. "What is it you need to *help* with? Melanie
certainly didn't ask for it."

"Well, since you seem to know all about the adoption, you
probably also know that all the papers weren't done which should
have been. That's what they want to get done now."

"*All* the papers? Are you kidding? As I recall there weren't
any papers. Melanie didn't know any better back then. She was
just a kid. But she told me about it all later, when she was old
enough to realize the Handleys should have known better. And
then to let her go like she was just another employee. . ."

Every bit of her anger was justified, and I shared it. But she
threw me with the last comment.

"What do you mean, let her go? I thought she quit."

"Oh no. Nevin Handley cut her loose. Not that he did it himself. Too big a coward for that. Had one of his new employees tell
her they had to cut back. Then it's in the papers just a week later

he'd signed some big deal and suddenly Handley's a millionaire. The man is a piece of work."

Is?

She seemed to know everything going on so I was surprised she hadn't commented on Nevin's death. But I hadn't noticed a TV in the living room, and I'd stepped over the newspaper in the driveway. Could she have missed the news about Nevin's death? The media was already hinting of possible foul play, but didn't have any of the details yet. The *Union Trib's* story had included my name; the vultures had spotted me going through the Champagne Crest gate. At least I was identified as a "mourning friend of the family" and not as their attorney. Still, it was attention I didn't want. I wasn't sure if telling her of his death would make her more or less likely to cooperate in getting me together with Melanie. All I knew was that I was not only a bad liar, I was tired of doing it.

"Mrs. Dubravado, maybe you haven't heard, but Nevin Handley died last night."

I couldn't quite get myself to say "murdered," and since the media hadn't discovered that fact yet, it wasn't information I should share anyway. Besides, there was only so much I could throw at the poor lady at once. The look on her face told me it was shock enough. She may have despised him for the way he'd acted toward her daughter, but he was still the father to her biological granddaughter.

"How. . . how did he die?"

"Ah, I don't have all the details. I know he was exercising alone—lifting weights—and they found him dead. A heart attack maybe. They aren't sure."

She seemed to have a hard time processing the fact I was here about the adoption at Nevin and Catherine's behest, yet Nevin had just died. I tried to fill in the gaps.

"They came to see me about it just a couple of days ago. Nevin dying doesn't change the fact we need to set things straight. It's important for Lynn's security and. . ."

It was time to play my trump card.

". . . So Catherine can finally tell Lynn she's adopted. They never felt they could with the way they did the adoption."

I wasn't being manipulative—I never would be about adoption. It was the field I was dedicated to. But I also knew she'd want to do what she could to make Lynn aware of her history. And maybe the next step would be for Lynn to ask about her birth parents. And grandparents. Maybe even meet them. Every person, adopted or otherwise, can never have too many people loving them.

"So that's why I need to talk to Melanie as soon as possible. With Nevin dying, if anything it's even more important now."

She sat back. Her anger was gone. But I could tell she wasn't ready to send me to Melanie's door, so I prodded a bit.

"Can you tell me why she disappeared?"

From the look on her face, it might have been the wrong question to ask, but after a moment she spoke up.

"I remember Melanie when she was just becoming an adult. Just starting her life. All that hope and promise. . ."

I thought of the face on the girl in the high school yearbook and knew exactly what she was visualizing.

"Sometimes," she said, "it just disappears. . . Or is taken away."

"Taken away?"

She looked away. "It happens. People take and take. And at some point you give up. For Melanie it started with getting pregnant, then being rejected by the father, then the Handleys."

"Wait. Did you say rejected by the *birth* father? *Lynn's* bio-logical father?" Maybe she could not only point me to Melanie, but to him as well.

But she just glared at me. "You're going to tell me you don't *know?*"

Her anger threw me.

"No," I said. "How would I know? The Handleys don't know and—"

"Oh, like hell they don't know. They're protecting him, just like before. You all make me sick."

"You're saying the Handleys know who he is?"

She looked at me again, really scrutinizing me.

"You really don't know, do you?"

I just shook my head. "Will you tell me? Why is it such a se-cret?"

"Why? Because like always, money wins. Power wins. And no, I won't tell you. Let your own clients do that. That's the least the cowards can do."

This lady had been one step ahead of me since I walked into the door. She knew more than I did it seems, and she wasn't tell-ing.

"Okay, I'll ask them. Ask Catherine, I mean. But I still need to talk to Melanie."

She just stared at me, evidently as uncertain about me as she was before.

"Please, Mrs. Dubravado. Tell me how to find her. I think I can make things better. For all of them."

If my sincerity mattered, she'd tell me. She stared at me for awhile, then reached for a pen.

"She doesn't have a phone. At least, I don't have a phone number if she does. She just drops by every few months or so.

Doesn't call first or anything, just comes."

She looked at the open door.

"It's why I never leave. I don't want to miss her if she comes."

She wrote an address on a magazine cover and tore it off.

"This is the only address I have. It's where I write to her, and where I forward any mail. Not that she gets any anymore."

She handed me the scrap of paper.

"My daughter is very. . . alone. You really think you can help?"

"Yes. I do." I meant it.

She was still for a long moment before she spoke.

"Okay then."

And with that she got up and left me there. I'd wanted to ask about the address she'd given me. If she had Melanie's address, why couldn't she visit her? But it was clear she considered our conversation over, and it didn't seem right to follow her into the kitchen and ask more questions. Besides, I had the address now. I could see for myself.

As I walked alone to the door I felt haunted by a sense of wrongness I couldn't shake. I'd spend part of the morning with Lynn's birth grandmother. A person Lynn didn't even know existed. Part of a family wronged and hurt by distant events, and by secrets I'd yet to learn.

11

THE ADDRESS SHE'D given me was 45067 Rice Canyon Road #325, San Diego. I knew Rice Canyon. It was a winding road that started at Interstate 15, halfway between Fallbrook and downtown San Diego. I'd stopped at the exit maybe once in my life for gas, but couldn't recall an apartment complex or office building there.

It was still only eleven o'clock and even if the drive there took me forty minutes, I'd have time to make my meeting with Gil for lunch at two. The drizzle turned into a light rain so it ended up taking me closer to an hour. The street number I was looking for was only one block from the freeway. It was a strip mall, and 45067 was a *Mailboxes and More* store.

It figured. A mail drop. One of those private mailbox rental companies. I'd always thought only fledgling at-home businesses used them to give the appearance of an actual office address, but I guess regular people used them too. The window of the store also told me I could buy shipping supplies, make copies, send FedExes and get my passport photo taken.

I knew they'd refuse to give up a box holder's phone number or true address, so I had to go into duplicitous mode again. This time I had no compulsion about using trickery. I doubted another tale of love and loss was awaiting me, hopefully just a grumpy clerk sneaking cigarettes behind the counter between customers.

"Hi, I'd like to ask about renting a box."

The clerk wasn't grumpy, nor did he smell like cigarettes. He looked right out of high school, and badly in need of a Kleenex. He slurped his reoccurring snot up his nostrils with enough force to power a wind turbine.

"What size you want, and for how long?" He didn't wait for an answer and gestured to a price sheet taped to the counter. "Here's the prices. Tell me when you're ready."

I needed a box for about one day, but that wasn't on the rental options, so I asked about the monthly rates.

"Can you show me the small boxes you have available?"

He rolled his eyes as if to say "They're all the same." But he reached for a key ring with one hand, and a binder with another.

"Sure," he said, getting up.

When I'd entered the store I looked for box number 325. It was a small one, about four inches square, at waist height. There was an entire wall of them, most equally small, but some up to a foot square. They were in the front half of the store, with a second door leading to the retail side.

"What have you got in the three hundred range?" I asked.

He seemed used to people requesting specific numbers. He opened his binder and thumbed pages until he found the one he wanted.

"Well, I've got 328, 347 and 392. They're the only vacant

ones now, in the three hundreds anyway."

Without being too obvious I glanced at the page he was reading from. I was hoping each customer's contact information
would be there. Instead, though, just the expiration date on each
box rental was listed. I turned my attention to the three boxes he
had available. Box number 328 was in the same row as Melanie's,
just three over to the right. I indicated that one.

"Can I see in the box?"

"You want to kick its tires, too?" he asked.

Wise guy. But he opened the little steel door and stood back.
It was as I'd expected, steel walls extending straight back about
eighteen inches to an open back. Through it I could see a back
room where someone could stand sorting all the mail into the correct boxes. There was a small Post It note hanging from the back
of the box.

"What's that?"

He squatted a bit and looked inside.

"Oh, that's just the old customer's instruction notes. Like if
you want us to call you when your box is full, or you got a package too big for the box. We'll hold oversized for you but you pay
extra past the first day."

I told him I'd take the box and we walked back to the counter.
I had to fill out a contract and show a driver's license and a credit
card.

"What happens if someone doesn't have a credit card?" I
asked. I was thinking of the investigators finding no current credit
information for Melanie. Maybe someone rented the box for her.

"What do you care, man?" he said. "You got a card."

He snorted up some snot again.

"I bet your mom or dad own this store."

He looked surprised.

"Yeah, how'd you know?"

"I don't know. Just a hunch."

He bent back over the forms. I had to sign one saying I wasn't using the box for any fraudulent purposes. I was given a copy of a privacy statement saying that my identity and other personal information would only be divulged by court order or by order of the Postal Inspector General.

"So if I want to leave you special instructions on when to call me, that's no problem?"

"No problemo, man. Part of the service."

"I'm not sure what options I have. Can you tell me what most of the other box holders do?"

"Well, some come everyday and just check their boxes. If there's an oversize we leave a note and if it's nine to five, just come to the counter and we get it out of the back. The guys who need us to call are usually the ones who only come in when their box is full, or they get something like a registered letter or a FedEx. You know, like that."

"Yeah, a friend of mine has a box here, I think. Melanie Dubravado?"

When he just gave me a blank look I continued.

"I think she has you do something like that 'cause she doesn't come in every day."

In a perfect world, Runny Nose would have said, "But she does come in everyday, right at three o'clock." Or maybe, "Yeah, she has us call whenever she gets a big package and then she comes right away." But he didn't say either of those things.

"Hey, man, we've got like five hundred boxes here, ya know. We just look at the number and toss it in. Most of the people just get their mail and leave. No one comes in to buy stuff or anything."

I'd noticed they charged $1.99 for a color copy. No wonder business was lousy.

He handed me two keys and explained one was for my box and one was for the front door. I could get my mail twenty-four hours a day. When they closed they locked both the front door accessing the boxes, and the second door to the store. My key would open the front door.

I had a plan in mind, but I'd have to come back when they were closed. Besides, Gil was going to be waiting for me, as was a plate of Aaron and Charlotte's chicken parmesan, angel hair pasta and a Caesar salad on the side.

12

I WAS TEN minutes late, but still ended up arriving a few minutes before Gil. The lunch crowd was just finishing up and I was able to snag my favorite corner table. They'd painted a Tuscan villa scene on one wall and I wanted to be near the painted fireplace since it was a rainy day.

Gil arrived with a serious look on his face.

"I just got a call from my mother. Her two best friends had strokes yesterday. They live in Miami Beach, see, and they're all retired widows. . ."

As he often does, Gil likes to start his jokes as if they're true stories, although he's too bad an actor to pull it off. At least I hadn't heard this one about three widows in Miami Beach.

". . . So she tells me, they're sitting down at the beach and this guy comes right up to them and exposes himself! Right there on the beach! Well, before you know it, eighty-six year old Mrs. Rabinowitz has a stroke, right there on the beach. Then, a second

later, ninety-five year old Mrs. O'Houlihan has a stroke right after her. . ."

I played along and said, "What about your mom?"

"Oh. . . she refused to touch it."

He sat back, content, ignoring my groan. Now that his joke
was out of the way, he got down to business.

"So I read in the paper this morning you've got a murdered
client, Toby."

"Who said anything about *murder*? That's not confirmed."

He snorted. "Give me a break. I worked with the cops on
cases for twenty years. I know when they're looking at a murder.
The cops who made the 'no comment' statements are on the
homicide detail for God's sake. It's obvious."

He was making me feel like an amateur, which actually I was
when it came to things like murder.

"So, Gil. What've you got?"

He pulled a sheaf of papers out of his briefcase.

"Got a list of the employees at Human Minds when Melanie
Dubravado was there. There were only two other ones besides her
and the Handleys back then, both men. I'm still working on any
criminal histories or something which may make one of them
stand out. I should have that tomorrow. But here's the interesting
thing. You also wanted to know about other people there she
might have had contact with, besides employees. So I went online
to get the names of the people who invested in the business—"

"You can just get that online?"

"If they're a California corporation, yeah. They've got to be
listed with the Secretary of State. Easy to find if you know your
way around. Anyway. . . this is good, Toby."

"I'm waiting."

"Get this. I can't trace it."

He seemed thrilled by the news.

"I don't get it," I said. "That's good news? Why?"

Mister Insurance Fraud Expert was in his element and his face was glowing.

"Toby, listen. When you buy a business, or acquire an ownership stake, like with venture capitalists, you have to register it with some branch of the government. If it's a California corporation, it's with the Secretary of State in Sacramento. Non-corps are just with the county government. They want to keep track of who owes taxes, who gets served papers if there's legal action. Like that."

"I got it."

Actually I didn't, at least not what that had to do with what I wanted.

"Okay. Well, sometimes, companies don't want you to find out who the real owners are, so they use what they call 'dummy' corporations. You've heard of those, right?"

I had, vaguely. I nodded.

"They create a blind you can't get past. The thing is, to set up an effective blind, you can't make it obvious you're setting up dummy corps. Okay?"

Asking for a more complete explanation seemed like a waste of time. He'd get to the point eventually. That's all I cared about. Just like I didn't need to know how Aaron and Charlotte prepared the chicken parmesan I was waiting to order. I just wanted it put in front of me.

"So I go through six dummy corporations. *Six!* All technically legit. Here's the kicker, though. The last trace I can make on it ends with a corporation registered in, get this, the Cayman Islands."

He sat back like the proverbial Cheshire cat.

"And that means, what?" I asked. "His investors have good tans?"

"Ha, ha. There's only one reason companies register in the Caymans. Same with their banks. They are completely confidential. They refuse to divulge ownership records to *anybody*. Even foreign governments. You can't trace it."

Gil was right. It was intriguing, but I wasn't sure how it helped me. I wasn't interested in the sanctity of Nevin's tax liabilities. Still, I was curious.

"Sounds illegal. Why wouldn't that have come up when he ran for supervisor?"

"Hey, you can look into this stuff, or you can *look* into this stuff. I know how to *look*. But remember, this all happened a long time ago. Sixteen years. And none of this is technically illegal. But probably the biggest reason is that most everyone would have stopped at finding the initial venture capital group. No reason anyone would look to see who owned *them*. And then looked to see who owned *them*. And so on. You only do something like that when you're a cop looking for dirt, or the world's greatest retired fraud investigator."

"Okay, so we can't trace who's the real owner of Human Minds. You're saying that means we can't find out who may have been there checking out the business and maybe getting to know Melanie?"

He sighed.

"Yes, that's right, but you're missing the point. The point is, *dirty money* bought into Handley's business. You don't go to all that trouble to hide where the money's coming from for no reason."

At the sight of my blank face, Gil leaned forward and spoke even more quietly.

"Toby, you're still not getting it. What I'm saying is. . . this is *mob* money. Handley's business is owned by the mafia."

13

THE MAFIA? I was out of my league here. I was just trying to find a birth mother and right a wronged adoption.

"Are you sure about this, Gil? You're not looking for dirt 'cause he's chopping down trees?"

"Very funny. Believe me, Toby. It's dirty money. Usually that means it's organized crime. Maybe not the mafia, but some other criminal enterprise. Drug cartels, big prostitution operations, bookmakers. It's all some type of organized crime."

So much for just dotting the i's and crossing the t's. I felt myself sinking deeper and deeper.

"I guess the police will want to know this," I said.

"Damned straight. Especially if the guy's been murdered. These guys play rough sometimes."

A worried look crossed Gil's face.

"What?" I asked. What could be worse than all this?

He didn't answer right away, and when he did, I wished he

hadn't.

"The thing is, Toby, when I was getting this information, some I could get on the spot off the computer data bases, but some I had to order, stuff that's on microfiche. This was before I came across the Cayman Islands connection. Anyway, I gave them your name and address to send the records to."

I could guess what this meant, but I wanted to hear Gil say it.

"And that worries you, why?"

"Well, I don't think it's exactly a great idea to have your name down as looking into records that organized crime doesn't want looked into. You know? These kind of guys tend to have people. . . reporting to them when someone start digging."

Great. Still, I couldn't imagine them caring much about what some small town adoption lawyer was doing. It's not like I was the Attorney General or something. All the same, I was going to stay away from any weight rooms for awhile.

Charlotte interrupted visions of my untimely demise and handed us menus, not that we needed them. She also gave me a shoulder hug. I'd been their favorite customer since I told them Amanda had chosen them. Now they were days away from being parents for the first time.

"Where've you been, Toby?" she asked. "How are we going to pay for our adoption if you're such a stranger?"

"What do you mean? I'm here twice a week." Any more and I'd have to buy all new, bigger tennis shorts, and I wanted to stay in my 32s.

Aaron and Charlotte and I had agreed on a barter. Rather than charge them for the adoption, which would usually be a couple thousand in legal fees, we agreed to two hundred free meals, fig-uring the meals times ten bucks made us square. My concern was that they were so grateful, they weren't keeping an accurate total and were going to stretch it into free meals forever.

"I think today's number twenty-nine, right?" I said. "And you can put Gil's on my tab today too, so now we'll be at thirty."

"Oh no." She smiled. "I think you're only at about ten. But I'll check."

See. It was like that. Nice people.

Charlotte left with our orders and Gil leaned forward with more.

"I've got something on Zuley too."

"Man, you're fast."

"Not really. It's just knowing where to look. Anyway, on Zuley I came up dry on a property records search under both spellings as a last name, but came up with something when I talked to a cop friend in Riverside."

That was one of the advantages of having an experienced investigator, rather than try to do some of this stuff myself. Not only did he know how to find information fast, he knew people like cops who could get what we needed. He reached into his briefcase and pulled out a few loose sheets. A man's photograph was on the top page and he turned it around to face me.

"Zuley?" I asked.

"I don't know if it's your Zuley, but he's *a* Zuley."

The photo was clearly a booking photo. I could tell it had been sent to Gil by fax so the quality wasn't great. It was in black and white, so I couldn't see if the eyes were blue. He looked like he could fit the description Amanda gave me though—young, handsome and somewhat Hispanic looking in a young Ricardo Montalban kind of way.

"So what's the word on him?" I asked.

"You can read the basics on him here on the booking sheet. That picture is from three years ago, by the way, the only time he was arrested. He's twenty-four now. Six-one, one ninety. Full name is Christiano Warren De Lara."

Not exactly a "K" name, but a hard "C."

"Warren?" I asked.

"Anglo mother, Hispanic father. Guess they each got to choose a name."

"How's this make him a Zuley?"

"He's actually quite well-known, in Riverside law enforcement circles, anyway. When I asked about knowing a Zuley, he knew right away who I was referring to. I guess it's a nickname. Like I guessed, the blue eyes, that's azul in Spanish. Americanize it into slang and it's Zuley."

"So is he in jail now?"

"Far from it. They picked him up on a nickel and dime drug sale a few years ago, not enough to do any time for. Evidently the guy's smart. They think he's moved up, running a meth lab with a whole slew of dealers. Can't prove it though. They say he's a savvy guy."

I looked at his picture again. He looked more like a college athlete than a drug dealer.

"He doesn't look like a druggie," I said.

"Probably he's not. Most of the ones that survive sell it, not use it."

Maybe my hope that this guy wasn't the birth father was coloring my judgment, but I couldn't see him hanging out at the Colorado River for a weekend. That was more college kid stuff. I said as much to Gil.

"Toby, you are so naïve. He was obviously down there with his guys selling dope. It's party-time down there, man. Get real."

Okay, then. I guess I had to face the reality this was probably the guy. I'd sort of hoped we would just be dealing with an unfindable birth father. Although the drawback to that was no chance to get a paternal health history, the advantage was we didn't have to find him, give notice, or worry about an objection. Now I was stuck with a mini drug kingpin.

I also worried about how Aaron and Charlotte would handle the news. Last time I spoke to them, we all thought Amanda's old boyfriend was the birth father. Of course, I'd have to run the photo over to Amanda to confirm it, but I was already resigned to the fact this was Amanda's Zuley. She'd be my next stop after lunch. Might as well get it over with.

By the time Charlotte brought our food, the lunch crowd had left and Aaron hung up a "closed" sign. They brought some plates for themselves and joined us, as they always did when I ate there, customers permitting.

"You said you might have some news on the adoption?" Charlotte said as they sat down.

I showed them the picture of Zuley, and filled them in about the news that Michael was not the birth father. I also told them about Zuley's background and that my next stop was going to be to show his picture to Amanda. I think we all knew that he was our guy, though. I watched as Aaron and Charlotte exchanged a look after hearing everything. Suddenly the birth father had gone from a white college boy to a Mexican drug lord.

I've had adoptive parents pass on an adoption for several reasons. Usually it had to do with the birth mother, concerning issues like prenatal drug abuse which could affect the baby, or wanting an ethnicity matching their own. I'd also had some pass on placements where conception was by rape, not wanting to adopt a child conceived by violence. Personally, I always thought a child came into the world pure, regardless of how the conception occurred, but not everyone agreed with me. But here the concern was the birth father, and the knowledge that he was selling poison to people. To kids. And with drugs and selling it comes violence. What if he didn't like what he might see as *his* baby being placed for adoption? Would he use his resources to find them? Hurt them? If these thoughts didn't occur to Aaron and Charlotte, it was my job to discuss them, and I did.

So we sat and talked about these very things. They weren't thrilled with the turn of events, but neither were they backing away. Finally, Aaron turned to me.

"Toby, we've been committed to Amanda and the baby since the day she picked us. We've thought of him as our baby since that moment. So if it turns out Amanda used drugs while she was pregnant, that won't change anything for us."

Charlotte spoke up. "And if the baby is white or black or brown, that doesn't change anything for us, either. I mean, we hope for ten fingers and ten toes and all that, but this will be our baby no matter what. But. . ."

"But what?" I asked, when she trailed off.

Aaron continued for her. "The one thing we don't want is to have to fight someone for a baby. We just couldn't face bringing home and loving a baby, then a long time later giving him back because someone is fighting us in court. Do you understand?"

I did, perfectly. On the one hand, I couldn't see a drug dealer wanting to go to court to fight an adoption—not exactly an impressive work history to a judge. But I also had to admit that in the few cases I'd had where the birth father objects, it was usually a guy who the world knew should not be a parent. It was obvious to everyone but him.

I told Aaron and Charlotte I'd drive over to see Amanda right away and confirm our Zuley was her Zuley and let them know. And I also promised if Zuley was the guy, I'd try to reach him as soon as possible to see if he'd cooperate with the adoption.

When Gil and I left, we stood outside for a minute.

"I hope you don't mind," he said, "but I'm going to pass on serving this Zuley guy any Notice of Paternity papers, okay? These drug people are scary, Toby. You should have the cops serve him. That's what they're for."

Usually I had Gil serve legal documents since he did it in a more personal and less intimidating way than the police would. After all, I wanted these guys' cooperation, not make them feel threatened. But I understood where he was coming from, and he was right. He said he'd keep working on the Human Minds employees' criminal histories and I settled into my car and called Amanda to say I was on my way.

I'd been keeping an eye on my rear view mirror lately, watching for the black Suburban. I'd assumed at the time it was following Lynn, but there was a chance it had been following me. If it was following anybody, that is. Now with Gil's mafia talk, I had something else to worry about.

14

THE DRIZZLE HAD stopped although the sky stayed gray and cloudy. That was enough of an excuse to put my folding top down and welcome the sky. If I had to put the top up more than five times it was a bad year for SoCal weather.

There was a law somewhere that said Beach Boy music could only be played on sunny days, so this morning I'd filled my glove compartment with the Grass Roots and the Doors. I was playing *Midnight Confessions* the third time in a row by the time I got to Amanda's.

It was a five minute stop, just long enough to have her confirm that my picture of Zuley was the tent-invader of her sexual dreams, and to see that Mayor Murphy's visage now occupied the spot of honor at the entrance to Granny's driveway.

I stopped by my office just long enough to prepare a Notice of Paternity form, the document each birth father had to be served, and a Waiver of Notice, which he could sign to show his agreement to the adoption. I also grabbed my Thomas Brothers map book and hit the road.

Gil had already told me serving Zuley was a job for the cops, and he was right, but I had a couple hours of daylight left, and wet courts meant no tennis this afternoon. Amanda's baby was due any day and both she and Aaron and Charlotte deserved to know if Zuley was going to be a problem. Plus, it was important to get a health history before the birth if we could. Sometimes some quick decisions had to be made if there was a birth complication, and knowing if Zuley was allergic to certain medicines would help us all protect the baby.

The booking sheet Gil had given me had an address but no phone number. I'd considered checking the yellow pages under CRYSTAL METH, DEALERS and CRYSTAL METH, MANUFACTURING, but I only had San Diego County books, not the ones for Riverside.

According to Gil, the cops said Zuley didn't live at the address listed, making it nothing more than a drop box, like Melanie's. Evidently, it was a house he'd bought for his parents. Hmm, a drug dealer who cared? It made me think of the televised trials of serial killers. They'd argue "sure he slaughtered forty-seven people and their pets, dismembered them and put them in his freezer, but he was good to his mother. So cut him some slack."

Thanks to light traffic I made the drive to Riverside in just over an hour, and followed the map to the address for Zuley. I was expecting a run-down house in one of the gang-dominated neighborhoods, but was surprised to find a small but beautiful older home in one of the more established areas of town.

The girl who answered the door was in her late teens and had the same half-Hispanic look of Zuley. I guessed I was speaking to a sister, although Gil hadn't thought to give me any information on Zuley's family. I tried to look non-threatening, which for me wasn't too hard.

"Hi, I'm looking for Zuley. Is he around?"

She looked me over, spotting me for the stranger that I was. "Who are you?"

Fair question. I realized at that moment that unlike my under-cover trip to the mailbox store, I had no plan. Perhaps the original thought and deception I'd used there exhausted my limited reser-voir in the bag-of-tricks department. When in doubt, go with the truth.

"My name is Toby Dillon and I'm an attorney. Is Zuley your brother?"

She nodded but didn't volunteer any information. At this point my first goal was for her not to see me as someone bringing legal woes to her brother.

"I'm not here to make any trouble for him," I said with my most sincere face. "I just need to talk to him about someone he knows who needs his help."

That was honest enough without letting her know about the pregnancy and adoption. I only gave that information to the birth father directly for a few reasons. One was just to respect his pri-vacy, but the other one was more practical. Sometimes the birth father will be relieved adoption is being planned, and he's off the hook for child support and parenting duties, especially when the pregnancy resulted from a casual encounter and he could barely remember who he slept with. But that same birth father could become a headache if his parents learn of a baby on the way, and want their grandchild, or to force their son to "be responsible." Of course, in my mind, placing a child for adoption *was* being re-sponsible—putting a child above their young male egos. But to each their own.

She looked at me doubtfully. A lawyer on your doorstep, for some reason, is rarely seen as a cause to celebrate. We fall even lower than Jehovah's Witnesses. Maybe that was because they come bearing gifts, even it is only a free copy of *Lighthouse* magazine.

"He's not here. Do you want me to see if I can find him?"

If he wasn't there, I didn't know what that meant. Maybe she was going to call him and let him know the joy of an attorney making house calls awaited him.

"Sure. Thanks."

She was gone so long I was about ready to take a seat on the front steps, but she finally came back.

"He's over at *Miguel's.* He said you go can meet him there if you want. It's a bar over on Magnolia by the bowling alley. Do you know where it is?"

I didn't, but I knew the general vicinity and she told me enough to know I could find it. When I walked to my car I took a subtle look at an old low-rider Chevy that had pulled to the curb a few houses down while I'd been waiting. No one had gotten out and I could see two heads outlined in the front seats. As I pulled out I saw them do the same, on my tail. I wasn't overjoyed at the escort, but I didn't take it as a threat. I assumed that they were sent to watch over the sister, and to make sure I was alone. At least I imagined that was the kind of precautions drug dealers took.

When I approached the freeway entrance, I seriously thought about just getting on it and heading home to the sanctuary of the comfy apartment, the storage room office and the tennis courts that made up my contented little life. But I didn't. Amanda, Aaron and Charlotte, and the baby that was due any day deserved the

best I could do. So when I got back on the freeway, I turned
west, toward *Miguel's,* my escorts behind me.

15

EVERY BUSINESS WITHIN five blocks of *Miguel's* had bars on its doors and windows. The only exception was the bar I was about to enter. From the looks of the place, the clientele was too rough for anyone to even consider breaking in. The criminals were already in there, drinking.

The sun had disappeared on my drive over, and with the new darkness came a few ladies who were plying their trade on the corner. The Mexican rap music blaring from inside drowned out my Jim Morrison, turning him from a tough rebel into a pansy by comparison. I found a parking spot in one of the few slots open under a burned out street light. When I looked up, I realized it had been shot out and never replaced. The graffiti on every visible surface of the bar and the surrounding buildings told me I was in gangland central. If that wasn't a big enough clue, the guys hanging out at the door of the bar, with their skull caps and tattooed arms and pierced faces, told the tale. I had the feeling I was the first white man ever to enter *Miguel's*. I hoped to be the first white guy walking out too.

I looked around for the low-rider Chevy, but my escorts had disappeared. I assumed they were telling Zuley I'd arrived, and was alone. Before I could take a single step toward the bar I was surrounded by the ladies from the corner. Maybe they assumed the only reason an Anglo would venture there was for the pleasure of their company. Or maybe they saw Kemo Sabe and one of them said, "check out the guy with the woody in the car."

They made a few offers, some only speaking Spanish and describing their services in very effective sign language. I politely said "no" as I moved to the door, leaving behind a few mutterings of what sounded suspiciously like "homo" in Spanish.

The crowd inside was young, rough and punked out. Thankfully there was no theatrical moment of silence as the skinny gringo breaks the color barrier, but I could tell my arrival had been noted. I made a quick loop through the place with no sign of Zuley. I went to the bar where the bartender was eyeing me as if I were trouble. Like trouble as in wiping my blood off his floor.

"I'm looking for Zuley," I said, trying to not make myself sound like a gunslinger in a Western movie. "Have you seen him?"

"*Que?*"

"Zuley?"

"*Una Corona?*" He held up a bottle.

"No, gracias. I'm looking for Zuley."

"*No cervesa?*"

I had the feeling he wanted me out of there, and if Zuley wasn't there, out was where I wanted to be. I wondered why I'd been sent here if he wasn't even here and started to get a bad feeling. When I got back to my car I could see the shape of a man leaning against it. It was too dark to see if it was Zuley. As I got closer he looked up and the light from the beer signs in the window was enough to tell me that he wasn't. It also told me this guy was trouble.

"You the lawyer?" He said *lawyer* like he'd say *cockroach.* It didn't seem the time to show off that cockroach was one of the few words I knew in Spanish, *la cucaracha.* He gnawed on a fingernail as he said it and then spit whatever he'd bitten off in the direction of my feet.

"Yeah, that's me. Did Zuley send you?"

He laughed and held up his right hand, which he curled into a fist.

"He sent the both of us."

It didn't take a genius to know the fist was meant for me. I hadn't been in a fight since I was in third grade, and I didn't win that one. At least the girl who'd punched me lost her recess. I don't think this guy was worried about getting a time out.

What's a guy to do? I was in Mexican gangland in a dark parking lot. The few people near the door were more likely to place bets on how many punches it would take to put me down than call 911. I considered asking the fistmaker if I had time to run over and place a bet on my going down in one punch. At least I'd come out of it with some money. Maybe enough to pay for the dental work.

He started swinging his arm around in a windmill like he was Muhammad Ali, toying with me. Like an idiot I was hypnotized by the moving fist, the *sucker* in sucker punch. When he finally sent it arcing toward me I threw up an arm to block it, just in time to realize the real blow was coming from the other fist. His hand crushed into my stomach, deep enough to feel what I had for lunch. My body folded over, like a jackknife, struggling to find some oxygen in the air.

I was so focused on trying to breathe that I didn't even see the knee which came up to my face, only the blackness that followed.

16

I WOKE UP sitting on a floor, in a corner. I wouldn't actually call it sitting, more like a rag doll sprawl. All that was missing was the chalk outline around my body. I did a slow inventory to see what worked and what didn't. One major body part slow to reach full operating speed was my brain. But slowly things came back to me. I thought "erase, erase, erase," but nothing changed. I would have tried the Dorothy in Oz trick of tapping my heels together, but I couldn't feel my legs.

I realized things were finally starting to click cranium-wise when I became aware they'd changed my shirt. I'd come in wearing a white one, and this one was brown. Then I realized it was dried blood, covering the entire front and already crusty. I must have been out for hours. I felt around to find the origination point of the blood. The winning body part turned out to be my nose. The clue was when I touched it I cried out in pain. This announcement that I was awake earned me a halfhearted kick in the side. I knew Mexico was known for its soccer players, but I could do without a personal demonstration of their fancy footwork.

I heard, "Tell Zuley he's awake." Then, "Get on your feet, lawyerman."

I turned my head to see Fistmaker and another guy standing above me. From my vantage point on the floor they looked about ten feet tall. I wondered if it was a good time to tell Fistmaker's pal that he should ask for nose hair trimmers this Christmas.

Unless I was watching the San Diego Charger cheerleaders perform, the floor probably wasn't the best place to be, so I struggled to move myself into a sitting position. From there, with the help of the wall, I was able to get to my feet. If only the wall would cooperate and stop moving.

I was in a small windowless room. There was no furniture but an old metal desk and behind it, a chair. On the desk there were three cellular phones and an old-fashioned, boxy desk phone. There were two doors and I could hear machinery behind one. I had the feeling I was in Zuley's meth lab. Command Central. At least I'd found Zuley.

Or he'd found me.

While I stood in place I feebly moved my arms and legs in very small doses. If it were a video it'd be *Get Fit! The Abe Vigoda Way!"*

Fistmaker came up next to me and gave me a shot to the kidneys with a finger. He nodded toward one of the doors. The one without the sound of machinery behind it.

"Go. In there."

I moved forward, finding after a couple steps I was actually able to walk without shuffling. When I got to the desk I put both hands on it to steady myself. At that moment the phone rang. One of them anyway. Without even thinking about what I was doing, I picked up the receiver of the old clunky one with my right hand, instinctively keeping my arm straight, with the receiver down low at my waist. Then with a quick turn of my shoulders and twist of my hips, my arm slingshoted out in a perfect backhand arc, reaching top speed as the receiver reached the outer nadir of my swing. The end clipped Fistmaker neatly under the jaw then continued high above my right shoulder, which I held in a perfect follow-through, like John McEnroe used to do, or a golfer admiring a three hundred yard drive.

The Man Formerly Known as Fistmaker went down like he was made of jello, except he didn't bounce when he hit the floor. In fact, he didn't do anything. Just laid there.

I had no master plan of escape. I didn't have a second move ready to go, such as twirling the phone receiver by its cord over my head like some nunchakus, taking out Fistmaker's pal, and fighting my way through whoever and whatever was behind the doors. Jackie Chan I wasn't. What I was, was just one angry guy. Some primal defense instinct buried deep in my medusa oblongata had spoken before I could tell it to shut up. Fistmaker's second-in-command took in his friend on the floor without much interest and pulled out a gun as casually as I would my wallet.

A voice came from the door I'd been told to walk through.

"Enough, Pedro."

I turned. Filling the doorway was a too-good-looking guy in his twenties taking in the scene with a slight smile.

Zuley.

17

"I'LL SEE YOU now," he said, stepping aside.

What did this guy think he was? A dentist?

As ominous as the two guys were that I'd just had the pleasure of meeting, Zuley was calm, and if not friendly, at least not waving a gun or a fist in my face.

He went behind a desk that matched the utilitarian tone of the one in the other room and sat down.

"Sit," he said, indicating the single chair facing the desk.

I sat. Spread out on his desk were the contents of my wallet, neatly lined up. Also my cell phone, keys and the legal forms I'd brought for him. The latter had been folded in my pocket. Now they were lying open.

"Maybe I should hide my phone so I'm safe." He grinned. "Nice move by the way. Tae Kwon Do?"

"No. Classic one-handed backhand. A mixture of John McEnroe and Rod Laver. Except they were both lefties."

He laughed as casually as if we were having lunch. His voice had no hint of a Spanish accent, and if it wasn't for the goons outside the door, and the gallons of meth likely boiling in the next room, I could have been talking to a young CPA.

He picked up the Notice of Paternity and looked at it, although I had the feeling it'd been on his desk for hours and he'd already read it. It basically said he was alleged to be the father of Amanda's baby and that he had the right to object, in which case a trial date would be set. If he didn't do so within thirty days his rights could be terminated by court order. Because it was a legal document, however, it took four pages to say it. He waved it at me.

"You want to tell me about this? Looks like you're telling me I'm going to be a father."

I still wasn't at my best, and I had the feeling I needed to be to talk to this guy. He already seemed smarter than half the lawyers I dealt with. Not that that's saying much.

"Do you remember Amanda?" I asked.

His look told me he didn't.

I said, "About nine months ago she was at the Colorado River over the Labor Day weekend. You and she spent some time together in her tent."

Recognition sparked in his face.

"Ah, earring girl. Yeah, I remember her. Pregnant, huh?"

"Yes."

He seemed to be the kind of guy who liked to run things, so I let him take the lead. I was going to follow every grandma's advice, "Speak when spoken to," but in my mind I modified it to add "And live."

"Yeah," he said, shaking his head. "I remember running out of hats with her. She was somethin'."

I'd heard the term *hats* for condoms before. Toby Dillon, expert in all things prophylactic.

"And she's sure it's me, huh?" he asked.

"She said there was no one else for a couple months before or after. So yes, she says she's sure."

He considered that then glanced at the document he was holding.

"So what's this about adoption? She doesn't want a baby, huh?"

This was where I had to be careful. Although this guy seemed intelligent and reasonable—if you discount his murderous hoods and drug empire—some of the birth fathers I'd encountered considered their spawn the second coming of Christ, to be cherished by any woman lucky enough to give birth to the Chosen One. Of course, usually these same birth fathers would never even want to see the baby, or support the mother. The baby was *her* problem. After all, he did enough work contributing the sperm.

"The thing is. . ." I stumbled as I decided whether to call him Zuley, Mr. Zuley, or He Who Holds My Life In His Hands. I ended up just skipping the personal salutation entirely. "Amanda is only eighteen. She's like a lot of young girls. She wants to maybe go to college. One day get married, have a family. If she raises a baby now, when the pregnancy wasn't planned, it's not fair to the baby, or to herself."

I paused to see how I was doing so far. He was listening, so I plowed ahead.

"But there's tons of people, fantastic people who will make great parents, who can't have kids, usually for some medical reason. So Amanda can not only create a family for people who will be wonderful parents, but provide the baby with a loving home, where that child will be the center of their lives."

I was afraid it came out clumsy, like a speech. But hopefully he felt the sincerity behind the words.

"What about blood tests and stuff like that?" he asked.

I hated that question. Usually guys asking about blood tests followed it with the statement: "I want one."

"If you want a blood test, we can do one. The court doesn't require one though. The only time they do is if you want to object to the adoption. Then you'd have to first prove you were actually the birth father. . ."

I didn't really want to go into the rest of it. I wasn't his lawyer, but I still had the duty to be honest with everyone I dealt with, even if it was someone on the other side of what we wanted to accomplish. So I plowed ahead.

". . . and if you are, then you have the right to go before a judge and argue the child would be better off with you than the adoptive parents. Basically, whoever the judge thinks will be the best parents for the baby. . . wins."

It was more complicated than that, but it was accurate enough for drug dealers, even smart ones.

He didn't seem to like what I'd said though.

"If it's my kid, why do I have to prove anything? Why should I have to prove I'm better than someone who isn't even blood?"

It was a fair question, and one asked by every birth father with a desire to object. I hoped that wasn't where this one was heading.

"The difference. . . do I call you Zuley?"

He nodded.

"The difference, Zuley, is that you and Amanda aren't married. If you were, you'd have the same rights that she does and we'd need your consent. But non-marital fathers have less rights. I just have to show the court that you got that notice. . ."

I nodded to the Notice of Paternity in his hand.

". . . And if you don't object in court, your rights will be terminated."

He grunted and said nothing. I couldn't read his thoughts, but just in case they were running along the lines of *How many pieces should we chop Toby Dillon's body into, and where should we dispose of them,* I thought I'd put on an affirmative defense.

"Just so you know, right before I came in here, I called someone I know at the Riverside PD and told them I was meeting with you."

I hoped the meaning was clear. Chop me up and when I don't appear, he'd be answering questions he'd rather not be facing.

He didn't even look at me when he spoke, sounding amused.

"No you didn't. I've already gone through your cell phone and redialed the last few numbers."

Then he did look at me.

"Don't worry. I'm not going to kill you."

Then he added, "Yet."

After staring me down he laughed.

"Just kidding, lawyerman. No one's going to kill you, and I'm sorry about the beating. Sometimes the guys like to have a little fun. Looks like you got some payback, though."

He put down the Notice form and picked up the Waiver. It was the form which said he waived his rights.

"So why are you here, Toby?"

He hadn't used my name before and I took it as a good sign. What was next, a guided tour of the meth lab? *We're not like the other meth labs. We don't cut our product with baby powder, and we boil it until it is just right, so you get the very best high, with almost no chance of a bad trip.*

"You could have just sent these papers," he said, waving his hand in the direction of my bloodied nose and shirt. "No offense, but you kind of invited all this. Showing up unannounced at my parents' door. You know?"

I nodded, and did the only thing I could think of. I told him the truth. That I needed his health history. That I wanted his cooperation. That I was hoping to walk out the door with a signed Waiver of Notice, so Amanda and Aaron and Charlotte could start the baby's life without worrying about a problem later.

He nodded as if to say he liked what he heard. He leaned forward.

"So tell me about these adoptive parents."

With those words, I knew I had him. So tell him about them I did. Even asked about his family's health history and got answers. When I finished he sat back. I'd hoped we were done, but evidently we weren't.

"Here's my problem, Toby. I run a pretty good operation here. Two, three more years, and I'm out of the life. Never have to work again if I don't want to, if I make it through."

He looked at me to see if I understood.

"What I'm saying is for me to survive, it's not enough that I'm smarter than everyone else doing what I'm doing. They've got to be scared shitless that if they cross me. . . if they dishonor me. . . they're dead. You know?"

It wasn't exactly how I ran my business, but I understood.

"All these guys who work for me," he went on. "They've all got a bunch of kids, but none of them are *fathers*. Do you know what I mean? They just don't want someone taking something that *belongs* to them, even if they don't want it."

He was even smarter than I thought.

"So here's my problem, you come in here with your papers, which my guys *see*, and now they think I've got a kid coming. So

I *have* to fight for it, or at least kill the messenger. You see my problem?"

I didn't like the part about the messenger but thought silence was my best option for the moment.

"So this is what we'll do," he said. "I'm going to sign your form here giving up my rights. . ."

And to my shock that's just what he did, then handed it to me.

". . . and you're going to fold it up and put it in your pocket where no one can see it."

I did.

"And now I'm going to send you home. But before I do, my guys are going to hear you beg for your life and apologize for having the wrong guy. Got it? And I'll probably have to punch you. Just go with the flow. Can you handle that?"

I thought he was joking about the punch but there was no humor in his eyes, just business. I nodded. He wrote down something on a piece of paper and handed it to me.

"Here's a phone number where you can reach me. You or the kid needs something. You get word to me."

He waited until I had it safely in my pocket, then bellowed through from his desk toward the door.

"Pedro!"

Pedro stuck his head in, and through the open door I was overjoyed to see Fistmaker still on the floor, not moving. Now fighting at one hundred sixty-one pounds, Toby "The Telephone Terror" Dillon. Put me in HBO's Ultimate Fighting Championship, as long as I got my phone.

"Yeah?" he said from the door.

Zuley nodded to me with disgust.

"Get this asshole out of my sight."

Pedro dragged me out of my seat before I realized I had a part to play. I hadn't had a significant theatrical role since second grade when I'd received glowing reviews for my portrayal of a sheep in a school play. Then my job was to baa incessantly. This wasn't going to be that much different, and it wasn't hard to sputter with fear as I turned back to Zuley.

"I'm so sorry. This girl is just really screwed up. You, you aren't even the right guy!"

Zuley shook his head with disgust. I hoped it was part of his act and not a reflection of his opinion of my acting skills. He slowly walked around the desk until he stood in front of me. He grabbed the front of my shirt and dragged me skyward until I was on my toes.

"Yeah, well here's a little goodbye from me."

Nothing hurts so much as a blow you're waiting for. Better it be unannounced. While Zuley's left hand held me up, his right hooked to my stomach. It hurt, but I could feel him pull my shoulders down at the same time with his other hand, making it look like the blow doubled me over. The whipping of my head got my nose bleeding freely again, which added to the theatrics of the moment.

A spattering of my blood appeared on Zuley's shirt. When he noticed it, he turned back to me.

"Asshole," he said under his breath.

And with that he delivered a backhand slap that whipped my head to the side.

Man, this guy's some actor! At least, I hoped he was acting.

"Take him back to his car," Zuley said. "I'm done with him. And don't forget the hood."

Hood?

He turned his back on me as if I wasn't worth any more of his attention. My new captor brought me back to the room where we'd started and grabbed a dark pillow case from one of the desk drawers. He tossed it to me.

"Put this on."

I can describe nothing as terrifying as having a hood on your head. Completely vulnerable and helpless. But I told myself the reason for it was to not see where I was, so I couldn't lead someone back here. That meant I was getting out of here alive so I did as I was told.

I heard the tearing sound of duct tape being torn from a roll, and felt the pillowcase being taped around my neck, like a noose, making it impossible for me to raise it over my head. With one hand roughly grabbing me by the back of my shirt he marched me through a few turns before I felt the cool air outside. I could hear a car door open but when I was pushed inside, I realized it was the trunk that had opened. I was unceremoniously dumped in and the lid slammed shut. I had to fight the urge to pull the tape off and remove the hood, but to do so would have likely resulted in more pain, or death, when the trunk was opened. So fighting claustrophobia and fears of asphyxiation, I tried to make my mind go elsewhere. I was back in Rita's embrace, on the deck of my grandfather's boat. For twenty minutes she held me.

When the car finally stopped, I was dragged from the trunk without a word and dumped on the ground. I heard the car drive away. It took me several minutes to unwind the duct tape and get the hood off. I didn't know where I was, just that it was an alley and I was alone. My cell, keys and wallet had been dropped next to me. When my unsteady legs got me to the end of the alley, I could see that I'd been left behind the bar where I'd started. A glance at my phone told me it was just after three in the morning. The bar was closed and the parking lot was empty. Even the hookers were done for the night, or maybe they were just occupied indoors. Unbelievably, both the Falcon and Woody were unmarked, as pristine as when I'd left them. Evidently asking for Zuley gave your possessions protection.

I got in my car, turned the heat on full to combat the shakes which suddenly settled on me, and headed home.

18

MY MIND WAS empty as I drove. I was on autopilot. At one point I wondered if I was lost. I wasn't recognizing any of the freeway signs, like I was in a foreign country. Was I in shock? Did I have a concussion? Or was my brain still dwelling on my stupidity for letting this happen to me?

At some point though, I knew where I was and my senses returned. I was just happy to be alive, and to have accomplished what I set out for. More than once I patted my pocket to confirm the existence of Zuley's signed Waiver. It was going to be a nice call to Aaron and Charlotte, as well as to Amanda, to let them know the good news. The rest of the story they didn't need to hear.

When I got home I headed straight to the shower. No five minute shower this time. I gradually turned the water hotter and hotter, eventually sitting on the floor and letting the steaming water fall over me. The adrenaline rush of my survival had ebbed and I likely couldn't stand up even if I wanted to at the moment. My head, my stomach, all of me, ached. It forced my thoughts back to my post-college Peace Corps days. I'd seen such poverty there, poverty so severe it was often synonymous with death, human values abandoned by some in the quest for survival, yet inexplicably heightened by others. Extremes of good and evil. Choices made.

Tonight was like that. Men with no discernable recognition of the value of life. And the dichotomy of Zuley: smart, at times even charming and thoughtful, but also pumping poison into the bodies of the young and weak for money and power.

When I finally found the strength to rise to my feet, my thoughts had changed without any conscious intent. From darkness to light. From Zuley to Rita. From beatings to a baby about to be born. From kidnapping to a new family being formed.

Before I finally climbed into bed I turned off my alarm and unplugged my phone. Although I was supposed to be up early enough to blow off the courts, any early-risers would have to deal with any stray leaves or caterpillars themselves.

I woke up at just after noon. I don't recall ever sleeping that late, but I needed it. Thankfully, despite recent life experiences to make a good nightmare, I had a dreamless sleep.

Usually, every morning I do a set of stretches, then go down to the courts to stretch again before I play. There'd be no tennis for me today, but I did the stretches anyway. It was a chance to check out how my body was doing. Actually, below my neck I was in decent shape. The only real blow I'd taken was to the stomach, and although there was a big bluish-purple bruise, it hurt less than it looked like it should. The problem was above my neck. I'd never had a broken nose, but I feared I did now. When I inspected it in the mirror, it wasn't crooked, but it hurt like hell.

For that matter, so did my whole head.

I'm not a big medicine taker. In fact, my medicine cabinet has a toothbrush, toothpaste, dental floss, Tylenol and ear swabs, not even enough to fill even half a shelf. I'd taken three Tylenol last night, brazenly exceeding the manufacturer's instructions of taking a maximum of two, and did the same this morning. I knew the pain wasn't going to go away, but hopefully the pills would keep it from getting worse.

I called Fallbrook's oldest living doctor, Dr. Hagerty, still practicing in his eighties, who said he'd see me right away, squeezing me in during his lunch. His niece had remarried last year and I did a step-parent adoption for her and her new husband. I didn't do adoptions to get favors in return, but it seemed I got them. I was just doing my job, but for some reason people were grateful for it. More so than for a root canal anyway. At the moment I wasn't complaining about the special treatment.

I wasn't sure what the reporting duties of a doctor were regarding a patient who was a victim of a crime, so I just told him I'd been in a fight with a person I couldn't identify. He gave me a pretty thorough going over before finally pulling on a rubber glove.

"Okay, Toby, drop the pants and bend over."

"Wait a minute! What's that got to do with getting hit in the nose?"

He cackled and pulled off the glove.

"Nothing, actually, it's my poor man's concussion test. If you bent over without a word, I'd be thinking concussion."

Old codger medicine, got to love it.

"About your nose, though, Toby. It's not broken, but you broke the blood vessels in there. I'd recommend you avoid tennis for a couple of days, okay? Run too much and the blood's gonna flow. Should be fine after that."

I didn't have any health insurance so talked him into two tennis lessons in exchange. He said he'd give them to one of his grandkids and they'd give me a call.

From the car I called Amanda, then Aaron and Charlotte, and gave them the good news about Zuley. I also passed along the health information he'd given me, which was basically that he was disgustingly healthy. I could have gone to the police and filed assault and kidnapping charges against him, but it seemed futile. Besides, in an odd way I felt we'd made a deal. Not that I wouldn't turn him over in a heartbeat if I could. There's nothing romantically roguish in being a drug dealer, no matter how charming he might be.

I headed back to Coral Canyon. The day had broken clear so Gil was somewhere on the course. I helped myself to a golf cart and found him on the twelfth hole, attending to some azaleas adorning the tee box. I filled him in, leaving nothing out. He shook his head.

"You're lucky to be alive, Toby. What's your next trick? You going to stick bacon in your pants and run through the lion's den at the zoo?"

"No, worse. I've got to go tell Catherine what you learned about Nevin's business. I didn't think to ask you yesterday. Do you think he *knew* it was dirty money buying into his business?"

Gil looked off for a second.

"That's hard to say. The way you can usually tell is if the business is consistently losing money. Then you know the main purpose of the company is really to launder. And you'd have to get into the books for that."

I left Gil to his azaleas and got his promise that once he got off duty he'd get back to work on the criminal background check on the Human Minds employees. That was harder information for him to come by because what he was after was in law enforcement data bases, technically off-limits to him.

I was two holes away when I realized that for the first time I'd escaped without hearing a joke. Maybe things were looking up. I headed back to my office and checked for messages, but there was nothing that couldn't wait. I wrote a letter to Melanie, telling her about Nevin and Catherine's desire to finalize the adoption and asking for her cooperation. I thought of it as Mailbox Strategic Plan 1. On my way out I'd pop it in the courtesy mail slot for customers in the Pro Shop, and remind the counter girl, Hilary, not to forget to swing by the post office or drop it in a mailbox on her way home.

I also had Strategic Plan 2, which I thought might get me to Melanie quicker. I put a copy of my letter to Melanie in a shoebox, adding some of my favorite books about open adoption. I thought the books might put Melanie in the right frame of mind to cooperate, but also because I needed a plausible reason for sending her a box when a small envelope would do for just a letter. I wrapped the box in bright red paper. A big red box would make it easy to spot someone carrying it out, especially if someone other than Melanie came for it. If I were a high tech private detective I'd implant a tracking device, but I wasn't, so I went with the low-tech option: easy-to-spot leftover Christmas wrapping paper. Later today I'd drop the box off at Melanie's mail drop.

Yes, there was even a Strategic Plan 3, although it bordered on the illegal. No, I take that back; it was completely illegal. But like most illegal plans, it was likely to work faster than the other options. To put it into effect, however, I had to wait for the cover of darkness.

The last thing I did before I left my office was to call Catherine and ask her if I could come over. On my way out I grabbed some adoption books from a collection I kept at the office, some of them the same ones I'd packaged for Melanie.

There was still one policeman at the Champagne Crest gate, likely to keep the media from sneaking in. I still hadn't been entrusted with the entry code so I called from the gate phone and was buzzed in. It was mid-afternoon so I assumed Lynn would be home from school. I needed to be careful since she still didn't know her parents had hired me. As far as she knew, I'd never spoken to them except about her tennis when they came to my office a few days ago. All these damn secrets.

When I walked up the driveway I looked down to the weight room. No cops. Smileyface escorted me straight to the study. I was expecting Catherine to be in the casual arrangement of chairs where we sat before, but she was looking comfortable behind Nevin's desk. She didn't come around the desk to shake my hand, so I just went to one of the two chairs in front of the desk and sat down.

"Hi, Toby. Thanks for—"

Her eyes widened a bit.

"Are you okay? What happened to your nose?"

Dr. Hagerty had said the nose was fine, but I'd be stuck with the rainbow shading for awhile.

"I'm fine. Just a little household accident. But I have some news on Melanie."

I knew mention of that would get us past any questions about my nose. She leaned forward eagerly.

"You found her?"

"No, but I met with her mother. She's a nice lady. I think you'd like her. It turns out Melanie told her everything. The pregnancy, the adoption, you and Nevin as adoptive parents. Even the fact the adoption was never finalized legally."

Catherine's face showed her surprise.

"How does she feel about. . . What did she say about it?"

"I think there's some anger there, a lot actually, on her own behalf, and for her daughter."

I had to go lightly here.

"Catherine, can I ask you something?"

"Of course."

"You want me to help get the adoption finalized legally. And you want to do that to protect Lynn as being unquestionably part of your family, and so you can finally tell her she's adopted. Something you feel she deserves to know. Is that right?"

"Yes. You agree, don't you, that she should know?"

"Oh, without a doubt. I just thought that. . . well, have you thought about after you tell her, how she's going to feel? About being lied to for all those years? Not with mean intentions, but not the truth just the same? And that there's going to be her curiosity about her birth family. Maybe wanting to meet the birth mother who gave birth to her?"

This woman just lost her husband and it wasn't the time to push too much on her, but if she was pressing me to find Melanie now, these were issues which could come up any day, depending upon how Melanie reacted. I owed it to her to at least start getting her mind thinking in that direction. Even more, I owed it to Lynn, since it was she who would be the one really facing these issues.

Catherine looked lost.

"To be honest. . . I have, but I just. . . all I can think about is getting the legal part fixed, then figuring out the rest. I don't know what else to do."

"I understand. I brought you some books that I think may help.

Help you help Lynn, actually. I know you're busy now, but. . .'"

I put the books on the desk and she reached out for them.

"Toby, that is very nice of you. Thank you."

"You're welcome. There's a couple other things I need to talk to you about."

My hesitation told her it wasn't something she was going to want to hear. She didn't say anything and waited for me to tell her.

"You know we have to try to find Lynn's birth father too, right?"

"Of course. You explained that."

"Well, Melanie's mother wouldn't tell me who the birth father is. But she said to ask you. That you know."

"Why would she say that?"

"I don't know. The real question is if it's true. *Do* you know who the birth father is?"

"Absolutely not."

It hurt to see the lie so clearly on her face.

"She said you were covering for whoever it was," I persisted.

"Why would we do that? Back then, or now?"

That was the question. I had no answer.

"Okay then, I guess I'll just have to ask Melanie when I find her."

"Yes, I guess you will."

It came out of her mouth oddly, like *and that's when we want you to know.*

"Fine. Just one last thing." This one was going to be even harder. "I've been checking into people tied to the business back when it started, when Melanie was there, someone who—"

"I told you, Toby, those notes have nothing to do with Nevin's death. I don't see why you persist in that."

"I'm not talking about the notes. I'm talking about the birth father. He almost certainly had to be someone she knew at school or work—"

"Why don't you just wait until you talk to Melanie and ask her?"

"Because so far I can't find Melanie, and maybe she won't even tell me when I do."

I wasn't feeling too sorry for Catherine at the moment. If she'd be honest about who the birth father was, I wouldn't have to look in this direction.

"Alright then," she said. "What about those people?"

"Well, we looked into the venture capital people too."

"And?"

"And we stumbled into something we didn't want to find."

"Who's this *we* you keep talking about?"

"You told me to hire who I needed to look into things. So I brought in someone who knows a lot more than me about that kind of stuff. Anyway, what he told me was that the venture capital people were actually controlled by a corporation, which was controlled by another corporation, which was controlled by another one . . ."

She was the wife of a successful businessman and pretty savvy in her own right. She knew this wasn't heading anywhere good.

". . . And the trail ends with a Cayman Islands corporation," I finished. "A blank wall."

"Cayman Islands," she repeated softly.

She knew what that meant even without being married to a successful businessman. Anyone who'd watched Tom Cruise battle his corrupt law firm in *The Firm* did. She looked around the room and muttered, "Asset seizure and forfeiture."

The term had been in the media a lot lately, with more and more corruption by big business and politicians being uncovered. Enron was the start of a new age of corporate accountability. The public was calling for more than slaps on wrists. Now, the government's most powerful tool was seizure of every item that flowed from the illegal transaction. The fact that some of the money came from legitimate sources was little defense. Perhaps as Catherine looked around the room her thoughts were that if this was true, she could lose everything.

"Why are you telling me this, Toby? You think this has something to do with Nevin being killed?"

She knew the answer and I didn't need to respond, or ask the obvious question that was to follow.

"Yes," she said. "You can tell the police about it. You have to. For Nevin."

"You can tell me not to," I told her. "If no one's ever found it before, they may not this time either. I discovered it working for you. It's protected information, attorney-client."

"Tell them."

"You're sure?"

"Tell them."

"You know that if it means what I think it means, you could lose everything."

"Tell them."

"And the notes? Can I tell them about those now?"

"*No!* The notes are for you. No one else. Don't ask me again."

Talk about strange. She was willing to lose everything to help get to the bottom of her husband's death, and know the true nature of his company, but the notes were off limits.

"Okay." I stood up. "Can I say hi to Lynn?"

She just nodded. I don't know if she even noticed when I left the room. When I went through the door Smileyface was there waiting for me. I didn't know the protocol to see Lynn. Did I just walk up and knock on her bedroom door, or have Smileyface tell her I was here? I went with the latter.

She excused herself and came back quickly. There must have been intercoms connecting every room.

"Miss Lynn will see you now. Will you follow me please?"

I'd never been in Lynn's room before. For some reason I was surprised to see the kind of things I should have expected in a teenage girl's room: posters of girlish-looking boys who were probably rock stars, and teenage girls with short tops showcasing belly button rings. After the obligatory "what happened to your nose?" questions, for which I'd devised a tale of my clumsy encounter with a door, we sat on the floor and talked for awhile. She didn't bring up tennis until I got up to leave.

"Do you think we can hit some balls tomorrow, Toby? I just wanna hit something. Ya know?"

I did, and despite Dr. Hagerty's cautions I said I would. We both had some frustrations to work out. Lynn's blows would be striking at those who killed her father. Mine would be at my captors yesterday. I'd never been the victim of a crime, and what I didn't expect was the feeling of emasculation. The intelligent half of my brain told me I was powerless to fight multiple guys, not to mention guns. And duct tape. Still, part of me still raged against it. I had the feeling Lynn and I were going to have quite the war tomorrow. And we'd both be the better for it after, some of our demons exorcised.

19

I WASN'T EVEN out their driveway when my cell rang. It was Hawkes and he got right to the point.

"You didn't call me yesterday, Toby."

"Sorry. Was I supposed to?"

"I thought we had an agreement. What happened to the 'I should have something for you tomorrow'? I know you know something, and I don't want any of that attorney-client crap."

Catherine didn't give me permission to talk about the notes, which was what I'd been referring to at the time. But since then Gil had stumbled onto the illicit money in Nevin's business, and that I could talk about. Hawkes would never know that wasn't what I was going to tell him the first time.

So I told Hawkes all of it, from the dummy corporations to the Cayman Islands blank wall. I didn't need to spell it out for him. He lapped up the information, said he'd talk to his department's white collar crime unit and let me know what came of it.

He sounded like a kid seeing a shiny red bike under the Christmas tree, new murder suspects just around the corner.

Next on my to-do list was to drive out to Melanie's P.O. box. If I mailed the box to her it would take even more time to get there, so my plan was to deliver it in person. When I got there it was just before closing time, five o'clock. There was a girl behind the counter and I gave her the bright red box.

"Hi, I was going to mail this but thought it'd be faster just to drop it off. Is that okay?"

"Sure," she said, exploring one of her nostrils with a finger. I watched as it disappeared up to the last knuckle. Yesterday's clerk had been a boogie slurper, now this.

"Is the guy who was working here yesterday your brother?"

"Yeah, how'd you know?"

"Just a guess."

I turned to leave then turned back as if I'd just thought of something.

"Hey, is that package too big for her box? I don't want it to get returned to me or something and it's important she gets it right away."

"Oh no, it's no problem. We just call 'em when they're over-size."

I was just about to find a subtle way to ask her when she planned to call when she gave me what I wanted.

"I gotta close up in a couple minutes, but someone will call them tomorrow. I'm sure they'll pick it up soon."

I thanked her and walked outside. I'd noticed she said she'd call *them*, and *they* will pick it up. Was that because the box was taken by a business, or maybe a couple? Or just because it was a simple term to refer to anyone, and she had no memory who that specific box belonged to?

The box was my nine-to-five option, and hopefully word of a package waiting would spur the box number 325 owner to come and get it pronto. But I also had to be ready for someone coming after hours, just coming for the regular mail in the box.

Unless I parked right in front of the store's plate glass window, which wouldn't be too discreet, I was going to need some binoculars to see when the mailbox was opened. Thinking of binoculars made me wonder if there was a clear sight line between my balcony and the "French" swimming pool. I'd hate to buy them and only use them once.

Only Strategic Plan 3 was not yet operational. My stomach was growling and S.P. 3 required a few purchases, so I hit the road. Three exits down the freeway I found a large shopping center that had everything I needed: salad tongs from *Target* and a mechanic's mirror from *Kragen Auto Supply*. For my stomach there was a *Jack in the Box*.

Usually, I'm a pretty healthy eater, but since I recently cheated death, I felt I could let it slide with some of the worst junk food in America. Worst as in artery-blocking, not taste. I ordered a combo meal of two jumbo tacos, substituted onion rings for the usual French fries, well worth the thirty-nine cent premium, and a large Dr Pepper. I spent an extra thirty-five cents for a *Union Tribune* to read in the car while I ate. Woody was comforting company, but he didn't add much to a conversation.

When I made it back to *Mailboxes and More,* it was closed as I'd expected. All the other businesses in the shopping center were small and shut down for the night, with the exception of a nail and hair salon, which seemed to be doing a good early evening business. They were several stores down, though, so there shouldn't be any passersby to mess up my plan.

I used my key to open the outer door leading to the mailboxes and heard it lock automatically behind me. I opened my box. No mail as expected. From my bag of new purchases I took the mechanic's mirror. It had an extendable handle with an adjustable, small rectangular mirror at the end. I'd seen them used by car repair places to see in hard-to-get-to spots. Kind of like a jumbo version of what a dentist uses, but with less saliva.

I pushed it through my box and turned it toward the back of Melanie's box. I had to pull it out and adjust it a few times to get the mirror angled just right, but eventually I was able to see the back of her box. And as hoped, there was a Post It note dangling from the top. Written on it was:

OS, FX 619-555-2845

I didn't care what the letters meant. I assumed they were codes regarding when to call her as the box owner. What I was after was the phone number.

That might have been enough, but I was going for more. I looked behind me to be sure the sidewalk was still empty. At this point I was probably crossing into some federal crime territory. I took out the salad tongs, and stuffed my arm all the way through the hollow box up to my shoulder.

Toby Dillon, postal proctologist.

I pointed the tongs back toward me and brailled my way over three boxes, dragging the ends to count the dividing metal of each box. When I reached the third, I pushed them inside and tried to will the letters into the tongs. It was like one of those claw machines where you try to grab an elusive stuffed animal for fifty cents. My game was free, however, and I didn't come away empty-handed.

I looked at the letters I'd fished out. I wasn't planning to open them; I'd only sneak so low. But I wanted to see who they were addressed to. If not to Melanie, maybe to someone who would be easier to find. Find them, and find Melanie.

There were three letters. They bore postmarks over the last seven days, telling me the box didn't get much mail, and they didn't come often for it. But none of the letters bore Melanie's name. Each was what looked like personal correspondence. They were to Darrin Farlow, Deanna Grayson and Jenna Mahr respectively. The names meant nothing to me, but I wrote them down, along with the return addresses. Two of the three return address names bore the same last name as the person the letter was addressed to, so apparently family members. Putting the letters back was harder than getting them out, but I managed.

Now that I had Melanie's phone number, or at least the phone number of someone who knew her, the question was how to best use it. The decision would have to wait until tomorrow, though. It was only early evening, but yesterday was still taking its toll and I was fading fast. As I drove home I called Gil. I didn't tell him about the tong-mirror adventure—no need to describe criminal activity when you don't have to. But I did tell him about dropping off a bright red, shoebox-sized package at Melanie's mailbox, and there was a chance someone could pick it up, or the letters. If so, I wanted that person followed.

Gil wasn't the action style of investigator, and he had a day job anyway, but I wanted to pick his brain. I couldn't spend my days and nights in front of *Mailboxes and More* in the chance someone would come. Still, I wanted all the bases covered and he might have a good idea.

"How about Ignacio?" he said.

Ignacio was one of his Guatemalan landscape workers.

"Ignacio? He doesn't even speak English. And doesn't he

have a broken foot?"

They'd been trimming a giant Eucalyptus tree and one of the large branches had fallen on his foot last week. He was out of commission for awhile.

"He has to speak English to watch through a window? Besides, he could use some extra money. How about you give him ten an hour and pay for his gas?"

This was a top flight investigative team all right.

"Okay, deal," I said. "Can he get there early tomorrow? And give him some binoculars. He'll need them to see who opens the mailbox or walks out with the box. And make sure he follows whoever it is, even if it's not Melanie."

"Got it. He'll be there."

By the time I got home I knew there was one last call I had to make. I never thought I'd dread calling Rita, but I was. For the last month or two we spoke on the phone every day, at least for a few minutes, if nothing else planning what we would do for our twice weekly get-togethers. Maybe now I could legitimately call them dates.

Should I tell her what happened to me last night? I didn't want to worry her, but I also wanted to share my life with her, the good and the bad. Plus, she'd soon see my nose in its blue and purple glory.

I reached for the key to my apartment in its usual spot above the door, hidden in a niche in the molding. As I touched it, I felt my knees go weak. I always slip the key in with the teeth pointing up and to the left. It wasn't a security measure, it was just one of my compulsive tendencies. My eyes confirmed what my fingers had already told me. Someone had taken it out and replaced it, backwards.

My thoughts flashed back to Zuley inspecting everything in

my wallet. That included my driver's license and home address. Fistmaker, and his possible desire for some payback also came to mind. And there was an unknown person who had killed Nevin, with Gil leaving a trail straight to me as he looked into the company. For a person who prided himself on having no enemies, I was suddenly feeling very threatened. Did the replacing of the key mean they'd come and left? Or did they replace the key to not alert me, and they were waiting for me inside? I could also be making something out of nothing. All my friends knew where I kept my key and it wasn't unheard of for one of them to let themselves in wait for me, or drop off a racquet to be restrung.

I opened the door and took a quick look from the entry. Nothing seemed different. The place was so small there was nowhere for anyone to hide, except in the closet or under the bed. I turned on the lights and slowly walked through the rooms, picking up one of my racquets on the way as the ultimate weapon.

No one.

Still, I could feel someone had been here. I walked through the place a few times before it registered what was different.

I found it in the bedroom. Specifically, on the bed. My breath caught in my chest and I realized Rita had come while I was gone, driving all the way from Los Angeles just to make the delivery.

Or was it a statement.

Where there had been one lonely pillow, now there were two.

20

I DID CALL Rita that night, but she didn't mention the pillow and neither did I. Its presence was all that needed to be said. Suddenly discussing our next date took on all the importance of a presidential election, the Super Bowl and the Wimbledon finals all in one. Actually, more. It wouldn't be a date; it would be *the* date. I also didn't mention my adventures from yesterday. That was an issue I'd deal with later. I didn't want to let any sadness cloud the moment.

We agreed she'd drive down Friday. Usually, we alternated trips and it was my turn to drive up there, but I think she favored Fallbrook over L.A. In fact, I kept hoping she'd move back. It's not like she was a struggling actress who had to live in town for last minute auditions and day-player roles. She called her own shots. And now she wasn't even working, focusing on full-time mommyhood.

She said she'd bring the kids, which didn't quite fit in with the night of passion I had playing out in my mind, or the implied promise of the pillow left on my bed, but I'd trust Rita to work it out however she was comfortable. Women did these things much better than my gender.

I woke up feeling great and at my usual dawn time. My face even looked better. I blew off the courts, washed away a few spots of bird poop, and when Lars asked me to take over the morning clinic for him at nine, I ignored Dr. Hagerty's advice and said yes.

The morning clinics went from nine to ten-thirty. They were free for club members and fifteen bucks for non-members. Lars let me keep half of the nons' money, so with only a few of the fourteen people present today being club members, that meant I'd pocket about eighty bucks.

I liked to change Lars' usual routine just to shake things up a bit. I started everyone out with a three ball serve and volley drill. Half the players took one side of the courts and grabbed three balls, serving the first one then following it in and volleying the rest of the balls at the net. On the other side of the net the player's job was just to be a backboard and return everything. After the last ball you'd backpedal to the baseline and do it all over again. After twenty minutes we switched sides, then took a break. Everyone grabbed some water and some shade and broke up into little groups to talk about new racquets, kids or whatever.

Gil came up to the fence and spoke through it.

"Hey, Toby. You hear about the lady that hit a sixty-seven out here yesterday?"

"Five under par? You've got to be kidding. Who?"

"Well, I don't know her name. The way I hear it three guys were looking for a fourth to join them the next morning at seven, and this lady asked if she could join them—"

"C'mon Gil. I don't have time for one of your jokes right now. I'm in the middle of a clinic."

". . . So she said she'd get there at six-thirty, or six-forty-five. Next morning, there she is at six-thirty, and she goes out and shoots six under par! The guys can't believe it so ask her to join them again the next day, and she says, I'll be here at six-thirty or six-forty-five. . ."

"Gil, if this joke is one of your sex jokes, at least lower your voice. I got ladies here." Ladies who probably told dirtier jokes than the guys.

". . . So she shows up the next day at six-thirty, but this time she plays *left handed*. The times before, she played *right-handed*. And what's she do? She goes out and shoots seven under par! So these guys are totally amazed. And one asks her, 'How do you decide if you are going to play right or left-handed?' And she says, 'It's up to my husband. He sleeps in the nude. Each morning I pull the sheet down. If he's pointing to the right, I play right-handed. If he's pointing to the left, I play left-handed—'"

"Gil, since I'm not going to laugh, why not just stop now?"

He went on like I hadn't spoken.

". . . So he asks her, 'What if he's pointing straight up. . . ?' And she said, 'Then I'll be here at six-forty-five.'"

I gave him a heavy sigh. At least he'd lowered his voice for the punch line.

"Thanks so much Gil, for sharing that winner. I can't wait to share it with, ah, nobody."

But he just gave me a big grin.

"Got something for you," he said. "On Handley. Something big."

"Yeah? What?"

He leaned close. "*I figured it out. I know* who's behind Handley's business. The source of the dirty money."

He had my full attention.

"Can I first point out that I'm a genius?" he said. "Because you are going to be so happy, in your excitement you may forget to worship the person who made it all possible."

I gave a little bow.

"Gil, let me take the opportunity to remark on your genius, not only in your remarkable investigative skills, but your finely honed sense of humor and joke-telling abilities. Oh, and the Mel Gibson profile. Was that enough for you?"

"I noted some sarcasm at the tail end there, but I'll ignore it. Okay, get this. . . there's no way to pierce the corporate shield with the Cayman Islands registration, but even there you have to list the lawyer who registered the corporation. It's some guy named Tomaso Destrada, there in the Caymans.

"How does that help us?"

"Patience, Grasshopper. Listen and learn. By itself it doesn't. But this is what I did. I indexed his name to see if he registered any *other* corporations. Brilliant, huh? And what do I find out? That he's listed for just one other corporation, and it's based right here in San Diego. Not exactly a coincidence, ya think?"

"And you're going to tell me who? Or drag this out until I think of more movie stars you might resemble?"

He ignored me.

"The Trash King." He smiled. "Julian Toscano."

Toscano was a somewhat infamous figure in San Diego. Nicknamed the Trash King by the media, he owned the county's largest refuse service, and despite the obvious conflict of interest, the county's main dump as well. He also had a string of strip clubs and had married one of the headliners. In her day she was professionally known as Miss Bodacious Pumpkins. I'd never

seen her perform, but the Toscanos' photo graced many a newspaper and I had to admit her pumpkins were bodacious, and I'm
not even a big pumpkin kind of guy.

"Julian Toscano, huh."

"Yeah, just the kind of guy who'd love to have a county supervisor in his pocket. And guess who owns the six hundred acres
being developed in Sandia Creek? The one getting all the pro-
tests?"

"Toscano?" I asked.

"Yup."

There'd been talk over the years of Toscano being "connected," a charge which seemed to go hand-in-hand with the
refuse business, evidently for good reason. But he managed to
keep a likeable roguish aura about himself, and he occupied a
spot at the top of the county's movers and shaker's dog pile.

Gil's information wasn't conclusive proof, but common sense
said we'd found the true owner of Human Minds. But why would
he kill the golden goose, the county supervisor giving the
"thumbs up" to every development he wanted to build, and
probably every requested rake hike in trash fees? I said as much
to Gil.

"I don't know," he said. "I'd just stay out of Big Julie's way if
I were you."

"What?"

"I said, stay out of his way."

"No, what's that about *Big Julie*?"

"Don't you ever read the society pages? Everyone calls him
Julie. Big Julie. He probably started when he saw *American Gigolo*, back when Richard Gere was cool. Not that he'd admit it."

"Gil, what *the hell* are you talking about?"

"Don't you remember that movie? All those great songs from

Blondie? Gere was a gigolo and all these women would do anything for him. His name was Julian, but they called him Julie."

I didn't care about *American Gigolo,* Richard Gere or Blondie.
I'd stopped listening after *Julie.* That was all that mattered. If
there'd been any doubt about a connection between Nevin and
Toscano, there it was.

The day of Nevin's murder I'd thought I'd overheard Nevin
breaking up with a woman. Julie. Forcefully telling her *"It's over.
It's done."* But it wasn't a she. It was Toscano. Maybe Nevin had
taken too big a beating in the press for his bulldozer votes, or
maybe he just wanted out. Whichever, I doubted Toscano was
someone you walked away from. And Nevin hadn't walked away.

One more bombshell for Hawkes; one more headache for me.
I didn't want to tangle with The Trash King. I thanked Gil for the
information, thinking sometimes you learn more than you want
to.

I went back to my tennis players, all of whom had rested long
enough and wanted to get back on the courts. I went with some
cross-court drills and then some quick volleys and before I knew
it, it was ten-thirty. Best of all, my nose hadn't spurted any blood.

I had time for a shower and a homemade sandwich, then
headed to my office. Lynn was set to come at three, so that left
me with some free time. I hadn't done anything yet with the
phone number I'd copied from Melanie's P.O. box. My brilliant
plan was to call and ask to speak to Melanie Dubravado. Yes, I
thought of it all by myself. Unfortunately, this remarkable plan
was stymied by the fact that when I dialed it, there was just a
beep to indicate I was being recorded. Not even a message. Nothing. Just in case I dialed wrong, I tried again. The same thing
happened.

I hung up, unsure what to do. On the one hand, I hesitated to leave a message to call me, not knowing who might be hearing it. On the other hand, my letter to her, discussing the adoption in full, was probably going to the same place where the phone line went. So what was the difference? I called one more time and heard the same beep.

"Hi, my name is Toby Dillon, and I'd like to leave a message for Melanie Dubravado. Melanie, I'm an attorney in Fallbrook and I'm working with the Handleys. It's very important that I speak to you right away. Can you please call me?" I gave my phone number and left it at that. Nice and vague if someone else heard it, but enough for her to know what it was about. Later I'd give Gil her number and see if he could trace it to an address. Or maybe Ignacio, the incapacitated Guatemalan gardener, whom I preferred to think of as my *international operative*, would come back with word he followed someone to Melanie's location.

Staring at me from my desk were my notes about the three letters from Melanie's mailbox. I pulled out the phone book. If either the senders or the receivers could be located, I could perhaps get to Melanie through them. A reasonable assumption if they all got their mail at the same place.

Before I could look up the first name, I was interrupted by a knock. Since I didn't have a secretary, Hilary gave the wall a tap from behind her counter to tell me someone was there to see me. Since I only did a couple of adoptions a month, that meant only about a knock a week to tell me birth mothers or adoptive parents had arrived. She was more than happy with my buying her lunch once a month to say thanks.

I wasn't expecting anyone, so shouldn't have been surprised when I opened the door and my first sight was of Hawkes, testing a putter on the Pro Shop's tiny astroturfed putting green. He looked up and saw me.

"Hey, Toby. Check this out."

He looked down on a three foot putt, tapped it, and sent it two feet past the hole.

"Just where I was aiming." He grinned.

"They give my clients a ten percent discount on equipment," I said. "I guess they could stretch that to include you."

He raised the putter to look at the price tag.

"Two hundred forty! No thanks. I'll stick with the one I got at Sports Chalet for twenty bucks."

He put down the putter and walked over.

"Thought we could talk about Nevin Handley some. Got time for a beer?"

"Sure," I said.

We walked over to the club's restaurant, a good place to go if you liked average food at high prices. But at least there was a nice view of the course. We looked out from behind the tee box of the tenth hole, a perfect spot to feel good about your golf game watching everyone slice their tee shots into the woods. He got a Michelob on tap and I went with, big surprise, a Dr Pepper.

"Thought I'd give you an update on things," Hawkes said. "Since you know the family, maybe you'll have some thoughts."

"Sounds good. Thanks." I knew he wasn't sharing information just to be nice. Part of it was payback for the information I'd given him, and ungrateful cop that he was, he was probably hoping for more. Little did he know I had a juicy nugget for him. But not yet.

"The coroner confirmed what we already knew," he said. "It was definitely murder. Murder by dumbbell. That's gotta be a first. Anyway, no prints to help us. So the killer wore gloves, or wiped down what he touched."

"I thought I saw a security camera by their front door," I said.

"Did you guys check that?"

"Yeah. It's a basic set up, though. Just takes stills when it's motion activated. And it only covers the front of the house. Would have been nice if the killer walked up the driveway, but you know those bad guys. Never cooperating."

"So, how'd the guy get in there?"

"Typical rich people security. They've got the big pillars and the gate, with a security camera and all that showy stuff in the front, but around the rest of the property, it's just a five foot fence. Anybody could have climbed it."

"What about the first gate to get into their neighborhood? Any problem getting past that? Or maybe a camera down there?"

"Toby, those gates are just designed to keep out salesmen, not killers. All you've got to do is wait for someone to drive through, then follow them in when the gate's still open, or walk around them. And no, there's no camera down there. We checked out the whole area. Most of those homes don't even have fences, or if they do they're just horse fences, so there's really no security. We canvassed all the neighbors. No one saw anybody. No surprise really considering all the trees and vegetation between the houses. You could walk an army through there and no one would see them."

"How about with the Cayman Islands thing? Any luck there?"

Hawkes paused to take a long pull at his beer.

"Man, what a headache. Give me good ol' blood and alibis any day. I gave it to our financial crimes guys and they said pretty much what you did. A blank wall, Caribbean style. We got one thing though."

His eyes sparkled like I'd seen them do before when he was excited about something.

"Handley *was* dirty. I mean, he knew the money propping up

the business was. It's one thing for those tech companies to lose money for a few years, but his was *always* in the red. Definitely laundering. The question is for who."

I thought of Catherine. *Asset seizure and forfeiture.*

"Does it look like there's a motive for murder in there?" I asked.

Hawkes shrugged. "Who knows? It'd help if we could ID the people behind the business, of course. But yeah, they could have had a falling out about anything. . . Handley wants a bigger cut. Or he wants out. Who knows?"

We both nursed our drinks, the sugar in mine picking me up, the alcohol in Hawkes sombering him. Time for my little bombshell.

"You know the Trash King?"

"Julian Toscano?" His eyes narrowed. "What about him?"

I told him about the shared attorney who registered the corporations, and my overheard conversation with *Julie.*

Hawkes lost interest in his Michelob.

"I can subpoena Handley's cell phone records and check the origination of the call," he said. "That'll connect 'em. Won't prove murder though."

He paused to scrutinize me.

"Toby, where are you getting this stuff? No offense, I don't doubt you're good at adoptions and tennis, but I've always had the impression the corporate world wasn't exactly your thing. Now, suddenly you're Mister Insider? Even our top financial crimes people aren't coming up with the stuff you are."

I spread my hands. "What can I say? I'm a man of hidden talents."

I wasn't trying to take Gil's glory, but if I gave his name to Hawkes, he'd soon figure out I didn't know about the dirty money angle when I'd inadvertently hinted I knew something the night of the murder. That would bring the blackmail notes back into play. With a solid lead on Nevin's killer, maybe it didn't matter anymore and Catherine was right. If she was, I shared her desire to protect Melanie from any questions.

Hawkes looked at me doubtfully, but what could he do? He'd just got the golden ticket courtesy of moi, although he was looking like it was a ticket he didn't want. I gave him the Cayman lawyer's name and he promised to let me know what he turned up.

"I'll tell you something, Toby," he said. "I'm going to be walking on eggshells here. Toscano is as powerful as they come. He's put something in every pocket in this town. And if he's behind this, you can bet he never personally got his hands dirty. Everything would be insulated."

I gave him a "what can I say" shrug and got up.

"The drinks are on you," I said, leaving him to mull over the bureaucratic infighting that would go into looking into Toscano. All I knew was it wasn't my problem.

I had a few minutes to get to the courts by three, and I could make it if I jogged. I ended up getting there just as Lynn did, although I didn't recognize her car at first. Instead of a limo, she got out of the driver's side of an older Toyota Corolla. Climbing out of the passenger side was Catherine.

Lynn caught my look. "The housekeeper's car," she said. "I asked mom if I could drive over and she said yes."

The second biggest shock was that Catherine was following Lynn onto the court. In the eight years Lynn had been playing at the club, no one had ever seen her parents in attendance, never watching like all the other moms and dads. Catherine walked up to me a little hesitantly.

"Toby, am I allowed to stay. . . and watch?"

I tried to act like it was a sensible question any parent would ask. "I guess that would be okay. Why don't you grab a chair?"

I wondered if her pampered bottom had ever sat in a six dollar resin chair before. I glanced over and saw she seemed to be handling it okay. As Lynn and I worked through the lesson, then moved into a game, I stole a few more glances at Catherine. She was completely enthralled by her daughter, lost in wonderment at her skills. I know the pride I felt in my students. I can only imagine how much more powerful the feelings are for a parent.

During a break she walked over and kept her voice low.

"Toby. . . she's *fantastic*."

"Yeah, in more ways than one."

Catherine stayed the entire time. As she was leaving she mentioned the coroner had completed the autopsy and they could finally schedule the service. It'd be on Saturday, three days from now. She said they hoped I would come and I said I'd be there.

I had no idea what prompted her visit, and the first ever mother-daughter driving lesson. I wanted to think it was a good thing, but part of me wondered if she didn't want Lynn and me talking alone. Suddenly I was suspicious of everyone. But what could Lynn know, or have seen, that Catherine would worry about her telling me?

21

IT WAS A day of surprises on the court. First, Catherine showing up. The second was an hour away. It was Wednesday, which meant tonight was doubles play. Unlike the morning clinics, Wednesday night doubles was by invitation only. In other words, be an A or double B ranked player, or don't come. I never liked playing under lights and usually skipped night play, but I looked forward to Wednesday nights. It was the only time Lars and I actually got to play each other, and we had something close to sibling rivalry going on the court.

I ran home for a quick dinner and to change into a fresh shirt, and was back on the court just before seven, ready to greet the first players. The one I didn't expect to see was my brother.

"Brent?"

He grinned. "Hey, little brother. Got time to knock some balls with me?"

No words were coming out of my mouth.

Brent held his arms out. "So, what do you think?"

I was impressed. "Hey, lost some weight! You look good."

I tried not to think about it, but it hurt to realize almost a year had gone by. At least he'd put the time to good use and had dropped about twenty pounds.

"I started playing again. Lots, actually. Over at Ivy Ridge."

Ivy Ridge was a big tennis club in downtown San Diego. I tried not to show any feelings. It was bad enough for my family to ignore me, but to do so even on a tennis court was too much. As if he could read my thoughts he added, "You're an hour away. No way I could come here all the time."

"So. . . you came by to play?"

"Yeah. I called and found out about doubles night. I was hoping I could get you to myself though." He grinned. "You better watch out, I got my strokes back."

Brent and I had played daily as we grew up. He was one of those kids who excelled at everything. He was varsity football and baseball, and showed such promise my dad had him transfer in his junior year to a Catholic school powerhouse a few cities away with eyes on a big college scholarship. Like most promising athletes, though, he peaked in college and just ended up happy with a degree. He'd have to make his millions in law and not on a field. Despite being a great athlete, he gave up tennis when he was twelve. That's because by the time I turned ten, I was beating him. The difference between us was it was the only thing I was good at. He had cheerleaders eating out of his hand, and could do no wrong in school or at home. So, rather than continue to lose to me, he just quit.

The people who came for doubles were starting to arrive. Usually about eight or ten showed up, and we'd switch partners and rotate so everyone could play, taking up a couple courts. One of my favorite lady players was there, Janice. She was now confident enough in her game that she was starting to come out for hardcore doubles, giving it right back to the guys who went in for smash mouth play. I told everybody I was going to sit out a few games, and walked with Brent to the furthest court, giving us some distance from the others.

"Really, you want to play?" I asked him again.

He pulled off his warm-up jacket. I noticed it was a designer brand and his shorts, shirt and jacket all bore a matching blue stripe. The day I wore matching tennis gear was the day I'd ask Lars to shoot me. For women, that's fine. For guys. . . give me a break.

"Let's go," he said. "Prepare to lose."

Yeah. My ass.

We hit some easy balls from the baseline. He was better than I thought he'd be after all the off years, even with a year of fresh lessons under his belt. And he still moved like an athlete. As we warmed up I started cutting loose with some power and lots of topspin, sending him so far back he was in danger of crashing into the fence. He was a gamer, though, I'll give him that, and went for every ball. That's a Dillon for you. Never give up.

After awhile I signaled it was time for a break and we grabbed some water.

"So, what's with the weight loss? And the tennis? You're too young for a mid-life crisis."

I meant it as a joke, but his face darkened a bit.

"Oh, just time to get back in shape is all. . . and Suzanna left me."

Both my brothers had married into the plastics industry: their wives. Not unpleasant women, but as artificial as they come. Still, it's no fun to see a marriage end.

"I'm sorry to hear that. When did this happen?"

"Almost a year ago."

Jeez. Some family. No one tells me anything.

"So," I said. "How are mom and dad? Still alive?"

He got my meaning.

"I'm sorry, Toby. It's just. . . you know how dad is. You jerked him around pretty good."

As I recalled it, I had just refused to be controlled, but I wasn't going to try to convert my brother. Still, refusing to work for my father's firm and become his moral clone shouldn't mean family disownership.

"Guess what," he said. "I've got an adoption case."

"What?"

"An adoption case. You think you're the only one who handles them?"

"No, but that's hardly what you guys do."

My father's firm, Dillon, Dillon and Gillings, had forty-six attorneys and was one of the most successful in San Diego. My dad was the controlling partner as everyone senior to him had retired or died. He usually didn't allow his firm to take pedestrian cases like adoptions or divorces. He wanted clients with deep pockets, usually corporations.

I couldn't risk some sarcasm. "So. . . what? You coming to me to learn how to do them right?"

"Actually no, I'm here because you represent the adoptive parents."

"What?"

"You represent Nevin and Catherine Handley. Well, Catherine Handley."

There was no way he could have that information. "How do

you know that?"

"Because I've been retained by Melanie Dubravado."

22

"YOU REPRESENT MELANIE Dubravado?" Maybe if I said it out loud it would make sense to me. Who was this woman? I'd envisioned her as penniless and manipulated. To hire any big money law firm to talk to me was a shock. To choose the one run by my family was an even greater one. Did she choose Brent *because* he's my brother? Maybe as a way to manipulate me?

"She got your message," Brent said. "But she's not ready to talk to you yet."

Boy, that was fast. And it sure wasn't the way I imagined things going down, but it was a start.

"Okay," I said. "So do I talk to you, and you talk to her? Sounds kind of circular to me, but if that's how you want to do it. Fine."

What I was really thinking was about how my father's firm operated. They were specialists in the art of billing. The only other individuals who got away with similar business practices were third-world dictators, living in a golden palace while their countrymen died of starvation and dysentery. In any other profession, the practitioners of this would be incarcerated, or at least, tarred and feathered. But in American jurisprudence, it was the status quo, which is why I'd chosen to work for myself, out of a storage room.

I could imagine my brother dragging the case out, making complications where none were needed, just to keep the billable hours flowing. Plus he'd bill for all the time spent on anything in any way related to her case. Her bill at my brother's three hundred hourly rate would likely include: shopping for a new racquet, travel time for the one hundred mile round trip to Coral Canyon; an emergency preparatory tennis lesson; the time spent in the match; purchase of a new tennis outfit and racquet; and a post-match masseuse. Of course, he could have accomplished the same thing in a five minute phone call to me, but why bill for a tenth of an hour when he could stretch it into six hours? After I took him apart on the court, I wouldn't be surprised if he also billed her for the psychotherapy sessions he'd be needing to rebuild his confidence.

I didn't know where Brent thought he was going to get the money for representing Melanie, unless she had some secret wealth. Then it hit me. The law required adoptive parents to pay for a birth mother's legal representation if she desired private counsel. Usually, it'd be in the range of five hundred dollars or so, but Brent had found a deep pocket. He'd be sending his bill to Catherine Handley. For the first time that night I laughed. I wasn't glad to see Catherine possibly lose everything she had in the near future, but I'd enjoy seeing Brent's face when he learned his anticipated bill payer was due to be on the receiving end of a governmental asset seizure action. I couldn't wait to pass along the advice to Catherine to hold off on paying his bill.

"What's so funny?" he asked me.

"Oh, nothing. What did you want to talk about?"

"Well, I understand your client wants Melanie to sign a consent. She has no problem with that. In fact, she wishes they'd done it sooner. I'm curious, though. Is the fact that Nevin Handley died going to create any problems?"

It was a fair question, although his asking it showed he didn't understand anything about adoption, and hadn't taken the time to learn.

"That's no problem. This is what needs to happen. Melanie needs to meet with an Adoption Services Provider. That's a special kind of counselor. The one I usually use is named Sherry Rosman. They need to have two meetings. The first can be as soon as Melanie's ready. In that meeting Sherry will make sure Melanie understands how the process works. Then they meet ten days later, so Melanie has time to think about everything. In that second meeting she can sign her consent to adoption. After that she's got thirty days to revoke the consent. If she doesn't, and very few women do, then the consent is permanent on the thirty-first day."

Brent gave me his best lawyer face.

"I think she prefers to sign her consent in front of a judge and make it permanent right away."

The poor guy. He must have seen the TV movie a few nights ago. That was how they did it there. Top-notch legal research, Brent. I decided to be kind.

"I think you might be thinking about adoption laws in some other state. Each state is different. Some let you sign in front of a judge and it's permanent right away, but California gives a birth mother thirty days in a private adoption. It can be faster through an agency, but it's more bureaucratic, so we're doing this one as a private."

He nodded like he'd known that all along.

"Fine then. I think we can agree on that. What about the father?"

"Nevin?" I asked

"No, the real father."

I hadn't liked Nevin, but I had to defend him, or at least the group he was a part of.

"Adoptive parents *are* the real parents, Brent. The real parents are the ones who teach a baby to walk and talk, and take care of that child every day. That's what *makes* a mother and a father. Are you talking about the *birth* father?"

I almost felt bad. Brent looked so embarrassed. Well, I *almost* felt bad, but didn't.

"Yes, the birth father," he said.

"Okay. Melanie has to fill out a form called a Declaration of Mother. It's signed under penalty of perjury and names the identity of the biological father. We file that with the court—"

"Which judge?" he asked.

"Bornman, over at the north county courthouse. It's filed where the adoptive parents live."

I looked to see if he was still following my Adoption 101 lecture. He was and I kept going.

"Then we need to give notice to the father. He can sign a consent, or waive his rights. Or he can fight."

"What if she can't name the father? Or won't?"

"Well, there is no *won't*. She can't refuse, or lie to the court. But if she *can't*, like if it was a one-night stand or something, we can terminate his rights as a John Doe."

I wasn't sure if he knew, and if he did know, if he'd answer me. But I needed to try.

"So which is it, Brent? Does she know who the father is? Separate from all this legal stuff, it would be really helpful to get his health information. Soon Lynn will be old enough to be getting married and have kids. For herself and her children that stuff's important."

He nodded but didn't answer the question.

"I'll ask her about it," he said. He paused for a minute then added, "I guess the last thing she's worried about is that she and the Handleys never did the adoption the right way, lying at the hospital about who the mother really was and everything. What's going to happen there?"

"I don't think you need to worry. Melanie was a kid back then. It's the Handleys who'll be seen as manipulating things. And it sounds like they've got that all worked out already."

He knew what I meant by "worked out." That's how people in their financial and legal stratosphere did things. It was my dad's daily trade, therefore Brent's as well.

"Who are they using?" Brent asked.

"Anton West."

He nodded. The name was enough to know that end was taken care of.

"Now, I've got a question," I said. "No offense, but why does Melanie feel she needs an attorney for this? We all want the same thing here. No one's fighting."

What I was really thinking was that I didn't want to work through my brother on this. I wanted to talk to Melanie directly. I wanted to tell her how fantastic Lynn was. I wanted to see what her feelings were about the future, maybe meeting Lynn and Catherine. Helping to heal some wounds there'd been no bandages to fix. I couldn't do these things through my brother.

But Brent just gave me the party line.

"Toby, everyone's entitled to an attorney. You know that. And especially here. This is being done sixteen years later than it should have been, through no fault of Melanie."

He had a point there. Still, I wanted Melanie sitting next to me, not my brother.

"So what do you say?" he asked. "Play a set?"

It was nice to see business was done and he still wanted to be a brother and hang out some. Or maybe he was planning to extend his billing time by talking business during the match. Either way, I was going to crush him.

"Sure," I said.

We hit a few to get warmed up again after so much time sitting. My goal was to win all six games and not give up a point. That would be almost impossible against even an average player. Even a pro makes unforced errors, and I wasn't a pro. And to Brent's credit, he was a much better than average player, although he wasn't nearly as good as his tennis coach had convinced him he was. Little brother was about to give him a lesson in humility.

Actually, I was downright cruel. I moved him back and forth, hitting each corner near the baseline over and over again. I'd mix in different degrees of topspin, and the occasional slice. He lost any smidgeon of confidence before we even finished the first game, and left as a shattered shell of a tennis player, held together only by his designer outfit and matching visor.

23

THE FIRST THING I did in the morning was call Gil to see if he had a report from Ignacio. He had and the news was good. A man had picked up the mail and package at four-forty-five yesterday. Ignacio copied his license plate number and followed him until he stopped at a padlocked, heavy wooden gate before driving through.

What's with all the gates? Everybody in this case seemed to have a gate to hide behind, and it seemed all of them would be better off without them. So far, the bars hadn't protected them from any of life's cruelties.

Gil gave me the address. He said it was about fifteen minutes from the P.O. box into Rice Canyon, in a mountainous area with few visible houses.

"We can index the address with the County Assessor and see who owns the property, right?" I asked.

"Already did it," Gil said.

Why should I be surprised?

"And?" I prompted.

"It's registered to Andrew Wellington. Remember him? *The Well Place?*"

Actually, I did. There had been a lot of press coverage on the guy over the years. He'd go off on a rant every so often about something: chlorine in the water, growth hormones in the food, TV violence leading to copycat crimes. Actually, half the time I agreed with the guy. He had a commune called *The Well Place,* centered around natural living.

"Yeah, I do remember. So Melanie is living in his commune?"

"Looks that way," he said. "You want me to dig into the guy's background?"

"No!"

I realized I'd shouted and took it down a notch. I'd almost died following up on his Zuley lead. I didn't know if I could survive more.

"I mean, no thanks. I don't think that will be necessary. Let's just assume he is what he appears, okay?"

I hung up and thought about what he'd told me. It was nice to know we'd tracked Melanie down, but it really didn't matter anymore. Brent was involved now, and that meant I was barred from contacting her directly. Once someone is represented by an attorney, the opposing lawyer can't communicate with them without the permission of the other attorney. I didn't consider myself as *opposing*, but technically I was. At least now I could stop the sherlocking with the names from the three envelopes.

I called Catherine to tell her about Melanie responding to my letter, and her living at *The Well Place.* She'd heard of it and said she'd never heard anything bad. It occurred to me that Catherine might even fit into their naturalist themes, local honey bee proponent that she was. I also told her the contact from Melanie was through an attorney, my brother. That brought an odd silence. Maybe an expected silence, as who wouldn't be surprised by that turn of events? Finally she spoke.

"Did you ask him about the notes?"

Talk about stupid. I'd completely forgotten to ask him if Melanie had mentioned writing the notes, and if she did, to make sure she knew that there were no hard feelings from Catherine.

"I'm sorry, Catherine. To be honest, I didn't even think about it. I'll call him and ask about it."

I didn't waste any time and did exactly that. I got Brent's secretary, Elizabeth, on the phone. She'd been his assistant since he passed the bar a dozen years ago. I'd met her a few times and we exchanged some small talk. I told her I was calling about Melanie Dubravado. She had me spell it and said she'd have Brent call me when he got back from court.

I called Amanda, but no signs of labor yet. Any minute though. I imagined Aaron and Charlotte were staring at their cell phones, waiting for the word to rush to the hospital. I had some other cases going and I spent a few hours knocking some paperwork out. By noon I was done. That was it. The rest of my day was for Rita. And the night, if things went as planned.

So much had happened in the two short days since The Pillow, I hadn't even had time to be nervous. Normally, I would have fretted over what I could honestly describe as the most anticipated event of my life. So maybe I should have been grateful for the criminal anarchy surrounding me.

I realized about an hour before she was set to arrive that we hadn't even talked about what we were going to do. Well, I knew exactly what *I* wanted to do, and what she hinted we would do, but that was more the *end* of the date. I briefly wondered if I should take the pillow she left and put it on the sofa, so she could see it as soon as she came in as a subtle reminder. Okay, not so subtle.

The phone rang and it was Rita, calling from the freeway. She'd just realized we hadn't talked about our plans either. Jeez, we went from flirtation right to boring old married couple, with none of the fun stuff in between. Actually, I couldn't imagine a better way to spend my life than watching her grow old.

She asked if we could meet at the boat. There would be some daylight left for the kids to gently chase the Monarch butterflies that seemed to magically fill the small meadow by the boat this time of year. I could remember the same meadow as a child. Standing like a scarecrow for what seemed like forever, waiting for one of the giant butterflies to land on me. My grandfather, who somehow knew all the truly important things in life, one day gave me a bright red tee-shirt just before resuming my scarecrow butterfly quest. "They'll think you're a giant flower," he'd told me, and sure enough, it worked.

I arrived at my grandfather's a half-hour early, as if it would get Rita there sooner. I'm a list maker, and to fill the time I walked through the boat noting work needing to be done over the rest of the month. I even included some things I'd already done, just for the feeling of accomplishment I got as I immediately crossed them off. Likely a deep psychosis there. Pseudolistosis.

Except for one wall left to varnish, the salon and galley were finished. The built-in sofas proudly held new cushions, and the bookcases my favorite books. One item I ticked off my list was depositing a trap in a small hidden compartment built into a hollow under the stairs where they rose up to the bridge. My grandfather had built it and the joinery was so perfect it was invisible to the eye. In cleaning it up I'd discovered some animal droppings inside, so had bought a monster-sized rat trap. It looked lethal enough to break my fingers if I triggered it, so I barely breathed as set it down inside. The woods surrounding the boat were filled with varmints always looking for shelter and it appeared one had somehow breached the hull and discovered a hideaway.

Below, the two cabins were finally pristine after months of work. The master cabin had a queen-sized bed with about eighteen inches to spare on each side, with the same teak walls and two-tone teak and holly flooring of the salon. The crew cabin—not that a landlocked boat deserved the term—was more utilitarian. It had two lower berths angled into the bow, and the walls painted a gleaming white. When Rita had brought the kids before we'd put their traveling playpen between the bunks on the floor and it fit like it was designed for the spot. With the door open we could hear them from anywhere in the boat.

At the moment though, the master cabin was getting all my attention. I'd brought clean sheets and made the bed look as inviting as any hotel. It was just missing the mints on the pillows, but if things went as planned, she wouldn't notice.

The only room still untouched was the engine room. The twin diesels had been pulled decades ago so it had served as my grandfather's storage room. A lot of his old belongings still filled it and I liked the fact I could still smell him there, the scent of the once-a-day cigar he smoked clinging to the boxes and clothes. Going through them would be to admit he was gone, and I wasn't ready for that.

I heard the slight tap of Rita's horn and bent down to walk outside through the little ground-level aft door we'd cut out to pull the engines. I walked down just as Rita was lifting Remy and Emma out of their safety seats, then taking each by the hand as they wobbled toward me. Rita gave me a chaste kiss. Damn, I knew I should have brought The Pillow, and stood in the driveway, waving it like a matador.

I handed Rita a flat gift box.

"For Remy and Emma," I said.

She opened it. Inside were two tiny red tee-shirts.

She looked at me curiously. I just said, "You'll see."

The hour we spent in the meadow could not have been more perfect. Every dad dreams of reliving his own magical childhood moments in his children's eyes, and even thought Remy and Emma weren't my kids, in moments like that they could have been. We felt like a family, and it felt damn good. At one point I looked up into the heavens and thought I saw Brogan's face in the clouds, nodding his approval of my taking care of his family.

We'd planned to go out to dinner, but the kids had exhausted themselves so much in their excitement over the butterflies that we each ended up carrying a sleeping child up the hill. A quick change of weather quickened our steps back to the boat, as the descending sun seemed to pull ominous dark clouds out of nowhere to take its place.

The kids didn't wake up when we lowered them into their playpen, its padded floor making a perfect crib. Nor did their eyes open or the blissful smiles alter as Rita changed them into clean diapers and jammies.

We were in the salon and settled on the sofa before she asked about my nose. The bruising had turned yellow, which while not exactly attractive, blended in with my face better than purple. I told her the Zuley story, but left out the more terrifying elements. She didn't need to hear about a gun in my face or a pillowcase duct-taped over my head. A plain and simple punch to the nose was enough to describe the incident, even if that meant she was cheated by not hearing about the theatrics of my telephone back-hand.

Mid-story, my arm went around her like it had been created to reside there. Her head fell to my shoulder and my head to hers. Very comfortable. I'd preloaded one of her favorite movies in the DVD player and reached for the remote. She'd mentioned recently that she hadn't seen Cary Grant's *To Catch a Thief* in ages and had been aching to see it, so I'd made a trip to Blockbuster.

She turned to me and gave me a shy kiss. "You remembered! You're sweet."

I had the feeling we were both a bit tense now that we were back here, conscious of what was on each other's mind. We were right at the point where Cary Grant and Grace Kelly were watching fireworks explode over the French Riviera when we became aware of the rain. Not just any rain, but a thundering downpour. It felt wonderful to be in the comfy confines of the boat, warm and snuggly, with a tempest outside. Suddenly, Rita sat upright.

"My car! I left the windows open!"

She reached for her keys and headed outside, me a few feet behind her. It was only a hundred feet to the car, but we were drenched by the time we made it there and got the windows up. It was a typical Spring storm. The air was thick and humid and the rain was warm on our skin.

We ran back to the boat, not pausing until we were on the deck, under the canvas awning. We looked at each other and started laughing. We were the proverbial drowned rats, our hair plastered to our heads, our clothes saturated, water filling our shoes like little boats. The rain continued to pound around us as we huddled together under the protection of the awning. I know we intended to go inside and get dry, but somehow it never happened.

The soft glow from the lamps in the salon were just enough to light us, and the raindrops falling only a few feet to both sides of us reflected the light like little fireflies flying kamikaze to the deck. That's when I kissed her.

And she kissed me back. So warm and welcoming. So right a place for me to be. At that moment I felt she was all mine, like Brogan was leaving her. Not all the way, but enough to let me in, the torch honorably passed between two men who loved her. I wasn't sure if the wetness on her face were tears or rain. But there was no stopping the kiss. I don't know when our hands started moving, but with no conscious thought of doing so, I was peeling off her clothes, and she mine.

There was no rush to be naked, but suddenly we were. We sank to the deck, lying on our discarded clothes, side by side. We touched and stroked and kissed. Time was standing still. I'd found my day with no sense of time.

I couldn't wait to kiss the tiny scar under her chin. She'd fallen off her bike when we were in grade school and needed eight stitches to close the gash. You could only see it if you knew it was there. I'd wanted to kiss it for ages. Her breasts were small and perfect. I'd never in my life touched something so arousing. My hands and mouth simply couldn't move past them, except to return to her lips.

When I moved on top of her at first I just lay there, relishing the full contact of our bodies, all the way down to our feet. I knew she'd bring me inside when she was ready. And she did.

Even if we'd wanted to talk, the rain hitting the deck would have drowned out any sound. Somehow that was appropriate, because there were no words for this moment. Some of the raindrops bounced off the deck and bounded into us, drenching us in their warmth. As I moved inside her I didn't kiss her. I had to stare into her eyes. Bring her into my soul. Tell her through them that she'd always been the only woman for me. The only one there ever would be. That I'd give my life, my soul, for her. I was here for a lifetime if she wanted me.

The almost peaceful sway of lovemaking turned more intense at some point, an unspoken change, pounding together as if doing so could merge two bodies into one. A life force. A creation. I was taking precautions against that tonight, but for the first time in my life, making love and the act of conception all of a sudden seemed to make sense. An act so incredible that a new life could spring from it, a door to heaven opened. Suddenly I could see how one could love the product of that creation more than they loved themselves.

When we were finally done I wrapped my arms around her and rolled her over on top of me. For the longest time we just kissed. When we stopped, suddenly we both burst out laughing at the same moment, like a great release of tension. Or maybe it was the vision of us soaking wet, buck naked on the deck of a dry-docked boat, in the middle of an orchard.

The rain had slowed to a drizzle, but it stayed warm, and sinfully and blissfully wonderful to be outside. And naked. I gently rolled Rita off me.

"Lie on your stomach," I said.

"Hmm. What do you have in mind?"

I started on her neck and worked down. Tiny kisses on every inch of her body, down her shoulders and back, extra time on her butt where some kisses became tiny bites, down to her feet. I'd worshipped every inch of the front side of her, and I wasn't about to be denied the back.

Finally, I laid down beside her. She seemed to barely have the strength to turn her head to face me, but she did. My eyes were inches from hers.

"I love you, Rita. I love you with all my heart and soul. I love you."

It felt so good to say it. She didn't say anything back and she didn't need to. Not every "I love you" needed it mirrored back in reply. Her look told me, and the tears which flowed from her eyes.

As suddenly as the storm had come it was gone, and to the side of the awning we could look up to see a sky full of stars and a crescent moon. I'm not sure how long we lay there, but finally Rita sat up.

"I'm going to check on the girls. Don't go anywhere."

She got up and as she walked through the salon toward the stairway I sat up to watch her, illuminated inside the boat. Although I'd just made love to her, watching her stride through the room naked was as erotic a scene as I may ever see.

Everything was perfect until a moment later, when Rita's scream filled the night.

24

I WAS ON my feet and flying through the boat before her scream ended, turning into a tortured wail. At first I could only see her back filling the doorway of the kids' stateroom, rigid with shock. When she moved toward her children I could see more, and what had made her scream.

My first fear was that Remy and Emma were dead.

They weren't.

They were alive. They had probably been asleep and Rita unintentionally woke them when she screamed. Startled, they began to cry. Rita quickly reached for them and somehow managed to pick them both up and embrace them to her body at the same time.

In the playpen was a sharp pair of scissors, stabbed forcefully into and through the bottom of the playpen. I looked at the girls.

Neither were cut, or appeared to have been physically harmed. But someone had crudely chopped off all their hair.

25

THE THOUGHT STRUCK suddenly. Was whoever did this still on the boat? Were the scissors left there because they heard Rita coming? Or had they been left on purpose? Rita was doing her job, calming the girls. Mine was to make sure they stayed safe.

I squeezed past her and grabbed the scissors. I needed a weapon in case I found someone. I opened the scissors all the way so one blade stuck out like a knife. One good thing about a boat was there was virtually no place to hide. We'd already run through the cabin, leaving only the master stateroom, the head and the storage room to search. The doors to the stateroom and head were open. No one. As I approached the door to the storage room, I noticed wet footprints heading up to it.

I edged the door open just enough to see the room was dark, then slipped my fingers through to reach the light switch by the door. If someone kicked the door back at me at that moment, I'd be minus a few fingers.

Switching on the light didn't produce a kick to the door. A quick scan of the room told me it was empty, but I saw where the intruder had come in. The small access door in the stern was ajar. I'd closed it when I heard Rita drive up. I hadn't locked it, though. Now I did, then went upstairs and did the same with the door to the salon.

Whoever it had been, he was gone, passing within fifteen feet of where Rita and I had been making love above him. Did he stop to watch, hidden in the rain's sound and fury? I felt sick.

When I got back to Rita, she was sitting on one of the bunks, both kids back asleep, securely clutched to her chest. She wasn't about to put them down; they were fixed to her body. I grabbed a robe from my closet and wrapped it around her shoulders. She was still naked and her previously confident, nubile body now looked frail and vulnerable.

I sat on the bunk opposite her and took a closer look at the girls. The only hair left on their heads was in uneven, harshly clipped patches. In some areas it was cut right to the scalp while in others it was about half an inch long.

It suddenly occurred to me I didn't see the hair which had been cut off. Not only did someone hack off their hair, they took it with them.

26

"WHO WOULD DO this, Toby?" Rita's face began to fall in on itself. "I can't take it. Not again."

It had only been last year when one of the girls had been taken, gone for a full month, each day all of us wondering if news would come she'd been found dead. Then, it had been Rita's and Brogan's celebrity to blame, one of the perils of fame. This time it was me. My job. It had to be. A warning. To me. As if to say, *Look what we did. . . and we could just as easily have hacked them to pieces.*

"Are they. . . okay?" I asked.

God, how I hated the need for the question. But an animal who could break into a home, hack off babies' hair, then leave the scissors inches from their sleeping bodies, may not have stopped there.

Rita closed her eyes, unable to keep her mind from imagining what could have occurred. It's a strange world when you are thinking, *Please God, let someone only have broken in and slashed off my babies' hair and scared me to death. Please, only that.*

She laid their sleeping bodies on the bunk next to her and undressed them, looking for any sign of an alien hand. Under their pajamas they wore diapers, the old fashioned cloth kind. Rita was a traditionalist.

When Rita saw the diapers she sighed with relief.

"No one's taken these off. I could tell if they did."

I knew what she was referring to. To me, a diaper was a diaper, but evidently to a mom an applied diaper was like a fingerprint, no two people folding and pinning one exactly the same.

Still, she undressed them fully. I was so glad they were asleep. No child should ever see the look on their mother's face that was there now. At this moment, she was hollow, filled with dark terror. She dressed them again and gently laid them back down in the playpen. She looked at me and asked the same question I'd left unanswered the first time she asked it.

"Why would someone do this, Toby? Do you know?"

The night of my life was over, ending with such tragedy that at the moment I couldn't even recall the joy preceding it. I was afraid the risk I'd evidently now brought to her family might end our new beginning before it ever got started.

Technically, the attorney-client privilege barred me from talking about my cases, but at the moment I felt my biggest obligation was to Rita. So I told her. All of it. The blackmail notes. Nevin's murder and his tie to organized crime. Julian Toscano. A missing birth father no one would name. And the complete version of Zuley and Fistmaker, including the meth lab and the hood over my head which I'd left out of my previous telling.

I hadn't quite realized what a roller coaster I'd been riding until I described it all. Knowing Rita, it should have been no great shock that she still had some compassion left over for me. She got up from her bunk and moved to mine, her hand touching the side of my nose where the faintest of bruises remained. She kissed me there gently then stretched out on the bunk. She put her head on my lap and looked up at me. She could read my mind.

"It's not your fault, Toby. Don't put this on yourself. Okay?"

I appreciated that she wanted to free me of my guilt, but it wasn't going to work. True, I had no way of knowing there was any risk to Rita or her children, but that didn't change the fact that I'd brought that person here. The warning had been for me.

"I think I should take you home now," I said.

I knew we wouldn't be getting any sleep here, and she'd feel safer at home. It hurt to see her face show its relief when I said it. The truth was she didn't want to stay, but didn't want to abandon me.

Rita usually ignored the perks of stardom, but on the drive home she took advantage of them. She arranged for the girls' pediatrician to make a house call and check out the girls, just to put her mind at ease, and a call to Paramount's studio chief resulted in a promise to have some private security people sent out as well. She'd take no chances when it came to her children.

She asked me to stay with her but I felt contaminated. I was dangerous goods at the moment, so I declined. Besides, I had to decide what to do. I'd never run away from anything. I could handle threats to me. But to Rita's children?

The next morning I wasn't in the mood for tennis, so after blowing off the courts I went to my office. When I passed through the Pro Shop, Hilary waved to me from behind the counter.

"Hey, Toby. Got something for you."

She looked under the counter and came up with an elegant envelope.

"Somebody dropped this off just before closing yesterday. Said to give it to you ASAP."

"Okay, thanks."

I took it from her and brought it into my office. Inside was an invitation. From Julian Toscano.

27

THE PARTY WAS tomorrow. Clearly I was a last minute addition. The invitation billed the gathering as a charity affair, to be
held at Toscano's home. I knew enough to know he held the kind
of charity events I didn't go to, where most of the money intended for the charity goes into paying the orchestra and caterers
to put on the event. But it got his face in the society pages of the
newspaper, and fostered the impression of a loveable rogue.

I knew this was no invitation, however. It was a summons. If I
had any doubt who last night's warning was from, this seemed to
clinch it. He knew I wouldn't ignore the invitation now.

I owed it to Rita to tell her. She picked up on the first ring and
I told her about the invitation, and what I thought it meant.

"I'm going," she said.

"What?"

"I'm going with you."

"Rita, no, let me—"

"These are *my* kids, Toby. My *babies.* This bastard's going to know he can't touch them again. Never again."

And with that she hung up, effectively cutting off any argument about it. When I called back she didn't pick up. She'd even unplugged the answering machine.

Toscano lived in Rancho Santa Fe, the most expensive enclave of homes in San Diego County, perhaps the entire nation. The house was a monstrosity of excess, more like an office building than a home. There were valets waiting for the cars. With the row of Bentleys, Benzes, Lamborghinis and the like, my Falcon fit right in. At least my fear that the Hawaiian theme stated in the invitation was a cruel joke proved to be unfounded. Everyone was getting out of their cars in their flowered shirts and muumuus. Lotta jewelry for a luau, though. Get all those ladies out in the sun and I'd go blind looking into the glare of diamonds. Thanks to Gil I'd learned that one lady who wouldn't be attending was Bodacious Pumpkins. The two were recently separated. Evidently California's high divorce rate was even higher in mobster-stripper marriages.

We were ushered through the house and into the back yard. *Yard* didn't describe it, though. Maybe *jungle.* It was like one of those Vegas hotels with the tropical pool serpentining through lush little forests of ferns, palm trees and brightly flowering plants too exotic for me to identify. In the center island there was an enormous aviary with giant parrots and macaws. I wondered if the yard was always like this, or if he built it just for the event, using most of the proceeds to write it off as a deductible expense.

Normally Rita managed to blend in, but the minute we walked inside she started catching some people's attention. The attraction to the famous is amazing. She'd been my friend since we were in kindergarten, and to me she'd always be the girl with the goofy grin and the long, skinny legs. I'd rather she was a grocery store clerk than a rising movie star, but life is what it is. Most people don't expect to bump into film stars at their local 7-11, so what Rita usually heard was "Anyone told you that you look like Rita MacGilroy?"

But that wasn't going to happen here. I had a hundred things to feel insecure about, and the looks I got of "what's she doing with him," reminded me of all of them. But if Rita was blind to my overwhelming mediocrity, I'd try to be too.

After twenty minutes I still hadn't seen Toscano, and that was the only reason we were here. I knew Rita wanted to be with me for my meeting with him, but I felt it'd go better if I were alone. He didn't deserve to even be in her presence if he was responsible for what I thought he was. When Rita was pulled away by a group of fans I slipped away. Besides, I don't think I really wanted to hear what it was like to kiss Brad Pitt, and were they really naked together in that waterfall scene.

After fruitlessly asking the waiters where I could find Toscano, I noticed a few guys standing around the property, looking more like hired muscle than guests, trying to blend in with their Tommy Bahama shirts. As expected, they knew. One pulled a walkie talkie from his pocket and passed on my request. I was told to go back inside and up the stairs. Someone would meet me at the top.

Another muscle man did indeed meet me and walked me to a pair of massive double doors. Before he opened them he frisked me. I'm not sure if it was for weapons or listening devices, but I had the feeling it was routine for everyone before seeing Toscano. Muscle Man knocked once, apparently just as an announcement, since he didn't wait for a reply, then closed the door behind me.

The room was as big as Nevin's study. Toscano was sitting behind an aircraft carrier-sized desk, smiling smugly and saying nothing. It was easy for me to match the silence since I had no idea how to start the conversation. *Did you kill Nevin Handley?* Or *Did you have someone chop off Rita's kids' hair as a warning? A warning for what?* But none of them were great opening lines, or sufficiently tricky to induce a signed confession.

My eyes were drawn to the center of the room where there was a huge circular aquarium. It rose from the floor to above my head, filled with some large and unattractive fish, and a pirate theme complete with a miniature sunken ship and spilled plunder.

"Piranhas," Toscano said. "Eat the flesh right off your hand if you dip one in."

Great. A room full of killers.

"No thanks," I said, turning from the fish to him.

He was reclined in his chair, all the way back, his feet up on the desk. Any further and he'd be ready for a rinse and a shampoo. If he wanted to show how unconcerned he was about our meeting, his body language made it clear. It wasn't an act, though. Some people had power and knew it.

He didn't stand up, shake hands or ask me to sit down. In fact, he actually closed his eyes like he was on the verge of a nap. That's how boring and insignificant I was. That was the message. When he did look at me, his eyes burned evil. I had to fight not to take a step back. For the first time, I was scared.

"So, where's the movie star?" he asked.

I took a slow breath. "Downstairs, at the party."

"Too bad. I'd enjoy meeting her. Pretty lady. I've heard her little girls are even cuter."

So there it was. The guy didn't waste any time. He cracked

his eyes open a sliver only to close them again.

"So," he went on. "I hear you been pokin' around, asking about me."

Good. He was getting right to it. I could get this over, get Rita, and leave. "I—"

"All I'm hearing about is Toby Dillon. I'm talking to Handley on the phone and who does he stop to talk to? *Toby*. I ask, 'Who's Toby, listening to our phone call?' 'Nobody, some tennis coach,' he says. Then in the paper I see your picture with him, some protest in front of his house about one of my developments. Find out it was you over there. 'Toby Dillon, Fallbrook attorney,' it says. Then I start getting calls about you. You're calling the state. You're calling overseas. Then with the cop. All the time, people seeing you with the cop."

He fully opened his eyes and fixed them at me.

"So I'm wondering, why the hard-on for me, kid? Thought we should have a talk about it."

I could guess what was next. How much did I know? Had I told anyone? All that changed though, when I looked past him, behind his desk, on the credenza a few feet behind his chair. A snapshot. I could recognize the setting from where I stood; it was the crew cabin on my boat.

Without even thinking, I walked right past him and picked up the photograph. It was of Remy and Emma, the night their hair had been chopped off. The picture showed them sleeping peacefully in the playpen, like two blond angels, their long hair fanned out too perfectly to have been by chance. It had been arranged for the picture before the hair had come off. I almost gagged at the image of someone touching and caressing them.

Toscano didn't move anything but his eyes as I went around behind him. He did move his lips though, to laugh.

"I wondered how long it'd take you to notice it. Nice picture, isn't it?"

The bastard contently closed his eyes again, a peaceful smile crossing his face, his hands moving behind his head as if he were relaxing in bed. The bear who knows he can sleep in the presence of the terrified deer. Evil filled the room like a stench.

"The thing is, Toby," he said, using my name as he would a child's. "Sometimes messages must be sent. You got my message, right?"

Some message. Disfiguring two sleeping babies.

"Yes, I got your message."

"So now you're thinking, can you prove any of this? And you've already realized the answer is no, cause you're a bright guy." He paused to yawn. "I know you're not wired. And if you wanted to share this little story, my guys would testify they were in the room the whole time and you made up the whole thing. And I sue you for slander and take what miserable little life you have. Goodbye law practice. Goodbye everything."

The bastard still didn't even open his eyes, despite the fact I was standing right behind him, above him even, his power making him bullet proof, mocking me.

"So what do you want from me?" I asked.

"What do I want? What do I want? Well, for one thing, I never want to hear your name again. From anybody. The cops I don't worry about. They got nothing on me. They can be as suspicious as they want, but they'll still end up with nothin'. But crusaders like you that think they can make a difference. . . that don't play by the rules the cops gotta. That I don't need."

"So why didn't you just kill me?"

He laughed softly.

"Careful what you wish for, kid. Actually, I'm guessing you

already told your lady friend, maybe the cop too. You, nobody'd miss, but taking down a cop or a movie star, that's a lot of heat. So it's not really the easy way. Talkin's better. Lucky for you."

He wasn't done. "But this is the real reason you're going to forget what you've put together. . . it's your two little cuties. You ever think about all those missing boys and girls you read about? Where they are? How they got there? Well, let me tell you . . . they're a cash crop, my friend. Used to be we went with teenagers. Runaways mostly. Nobody missed 'em. But nowadays, it's the little ones the pervs want. Train 'em early so they grow assuming it's the way everybody lives. Ya know? Ship 'em out of the country and they never see the light of day again."

He opened his eyes halfway, just long enough to make sure he still had my full attention, then closed them again.

"You have any idea what those two girls would bring? With the movie star connection? Christ, there'd be a *bidding* war. Probably get a million, easy. . . So that's why you're going to forget what you know, because no matter how careful you are, you can't guard those kids forever. And one day, maybe, years from now, poof! Gone. Maybe when that pretty hair grows back."

I'm not sure when I noticed the fancy letter opener on his credenza, or how it got in my hand. It was beautifully ornate with colored gems on the handle, but with a lethal blade. It was a veritable ice pick, a killer's tool more than a letter opener, belied by its deceptive beauty. It occurred to me, with him reclined and his eyes shut in their conceit, I could drive the knife straight into his heart and send him to the hell he deserved.

He spoke again, this time sounding so bored he was half-asleep.

"You can go now, but leave the picture. I'll need it for the buyers in case you give me any trouble."

I'd been dismissed, and he didn't even open his eyes to do it, mocking my impotence, my inability to do anything to stop him—to protect Rita's children, or the faceless children who'd take their place. I willed the hand clutching the knife to do its duty, to remove an evil the law couldn't touch. To drive it into his heart, and deliver him to hell. I willed him to rise up and strike out at me, giving me the excuse to what had to be done. But he stayed inert, defenseless.

I watched as my hand haltingly put the letter opener down on the corner of his desk, obeying my soul, but betraying my desire. A body a war with itself.

I managed to get some words out. "I'm keeping the picture." I clutched it like doing so somehow protected the people who meant so much to me in it.

He opened his eyes.

"Fine. Keep the picture. I'll just send someone to take another one." His mouth bent into a sick smile. "And who knows what might happen then."

I realized I couldn't win. At least not today. I watched as my body betrayed me a second time and put down the picture. Strangely though, I no longer felt defeated. Just the opposite. I'm not sure how it happened, but with all my heart I knew at that moment that I had one quest in my life: to beat this man, to take him down. And I'd do it when he was standing up and his eyes were open, just so he could see me coming.

The Muscle Man guard was still outside the door. He said nothing as I passed and neither did I. I had the feeling Toscano left many visitors speechless.

I moved away from the house through the crowd below, looking for Rita. Instead I found someone I least expected to see.

"What are you doing here?" I asked.

Coming toward me, just as surprised to see me, was Hawkes. With his Hawaiian shirt he blended right in.

He didn't look happy to see me. "That should be my question for you. What are *you* doing here?"

"I asked you first." *Nanny nanny nanny goats* I could have added.

When his stare-down didn't work he pulled me outside the hearing of the partiers. "I went to my lieutenant with what you told me about Toscano's possible financial connection to Handley. Sent me straight to the chief, and from him to the mayor."

I could guess where this was going from the expression on Hawkes' face.

"They gave me the message loud and clear, Toby. Do *not* touch Toscano. Do *not* pass go. He's golden as far as they're concerned."

San Diego politics. Figures. "Then why are you here?" I persisted.

He grinned. "Punishment. All the top guns from the department were invited. They made me come too, maybe to see the charity work the great man does. Supposed to change my mind about him I guess."

"And?" I asked, wondering if I was about to lose an ally.

Instead of answering me, he unobtrusively touched his shirt pocket and said, "Smile."

I hadn't noticed the top of an ultra thin digital camera protruding from his pocket, a natural enough thing to have at an event like this.

"I've got pictures of three of his guys so far," he said. "You never know. I may ID 'em later and find an outstanding warrant. Wouldn't it be a shame if I had to come back and arrest one of them here? Maybe get an excuse to search the premises? Of course, it wouldn't be *Toscano* I'd be after. Be a shame to turn up something on *him*."

I smiled. With Hawkes on our side, we had a shot, even if he didn't know the full battle.

The hint of a smile on Hawkes face dropped away. "You haven't told me why *you're* here."

"Hey, I got an invite too. Just looking around like you."

He didn't look like he bought it, but he wasn't exactly in a position to challenge me. When he spoke again it was more like the friend I knew he was.

"Listen to me, Toby. I'm hearing whispers of some really bad stuff about this guy. Trust me. You shouldn't be here. Leave. Now. Please."

I appreciated him wanting to watch out for me, but I had a private war he didn't know about. There was nothing left for me to accomplish though, so I let Hawkes think he convinced me.

"Okay, you're right. I'll find Rita and take off."

He looked mad. No, he *was* mad. "You brought Rita?"

There was no way to prove the threat to Rita's children. Better to just let him think I was an idiot and was here due to Nevin's murder, putting Rita at risk in one of my adoption cases.

So I gave him a sheepish shrug and turned toward the crowd to find Rita, feeling his eyes watch me until I was lost amidst the other flowered shirts and dresses. Human flora. Actually, leaving had been my plan the minute I'd left Toscano's office. The one thing I didn't want was for Rita to be face to face with him. I couldn't image how she would have reacted if she'd seen the snapshot and heard his threats.

There were more than two hundred people milling around, and after ten minutes of circling around the jungle I still hadn't found her. After my third loop, a woman waved me over.

"You looking for Rita?" It was the Brad Pitt kissing questioner.

"Yes."

"Oh, she just left to look for Julie."

Damn it.

Then, a scream.

It came from the direction of the pool and was loud enough for even the neighbors to hear. My first thought was of Rita and I started running toward the sound, but then so did everyone else, all two hundred of them. I tried to push through, only to hear more screams, then shouts. When I finally made it through I saw a half dozen people in the pool. I got the story from a poolsider. One of the guests had fallen into the pool, maybe too much to drink. An equally drunk guy tried to play the hero and jumped in after her. She panicked and clawed at him and they both started sinking to the bottom. More jumped in. Anarchy, but it was finally under control. Several of Toscano's hulks were in evidence, smoothing things over, avoiding mini-lawsuits.

But there was still no sign of Rita, meaning she was on her way to see Toscano. Hopefully Muscle Man would stop her, as the last thing I wanted was Rita alone in the room with him. It was then I saw Muscle Man calming the nearly drowned guests, meaning Rita's path to Toscano was clear. I moved toward the house as fast as I could without calling attention to myself.

There was no one inside the house. Everyone must have been drawn outside by the screams and ensuing panic. The doors to Toscano's office were closed and I burst in without knocking. But I was too late. Rita turned from the desk, panic in her eyes. She had the letter opener in her hand, clutched like a dagger. Behind her I could Toscano, unmoving, his chest covered with blood. The ice pick of a blade had cleanly pierced the shirt right over his heart, and the blood was neatly contained within the shirt, like subcutaneous bleeding.

I imagined Toscano's act, lying back in his chair, eyes closed, uttering his threats with impunity, considering himself protected by the aura of his power. But where I had faltered, Rita had not. The lioness that would die protecting her cubs. The one thing Toscano did not anticipate; the fighting heart of a mother.

I tore my eyes off Rita and took a closer look at Toscano. There was no doubt. He was dead.

28

RITA'S EYES WERE wild and unfocused, her voice quaking like she was freezing. She wasn't built for dealing with murder. Neither of us were.

"My God, Rita. What have you done?"

I regretted it the moment it left my mouth.

The barest flick of anger, something primal, flared in the back of her eyes.

"Toby, how could—"

There was the sound of voices at the bottom of the stairs. Loud and male. Toscano's guys. At least it forestalled what Rita was going to say, and what my ego could not face hearing. . . *How could you have brought this monster into our lives? How could you have heard his threats yet left him alive? . . . Left him for me to deal with.* She was right on each count and I was filled with shame.

The voices were now at the top of the stairs, only seconds

away. Rita looked again at the knife in her hand and in a moment of genius walked to the aquarium and dropped it in.

The combination of the water and the blood-thirsty piranhas ensured the blade was clean before it hit the gravel. Its weight forced much of it below the surface, only its jeweled handle sticking out. Now it was just one more piece of the pirate plunder theme. Invisible in plain sight. My eyes quickly went to Rita's hands. Good, no blood.

She was at my side when the two goons walked in, one of them Muscle Man. We didn't have to fake our shock at Toscano dead in front of us as their eyes moved from us to Toscano.

"Jesus!" Thug One ran to Toscano with Muscle Man a step behind. Why those destined for hell liked to call on Jesus at moments like there, I'll never know. At least I assumed if he worked for Toscano he shared his destination.

Their backs were to us, ministering to Toscano, when I noticed the girls' picture lying on the corner of his desk. But Rita was a step closer and grabbed it before me. Just as quickly I snatched it from her. If one of us had to be caught with proof of motive, I'd rather it was me. I'd failed Rita before; I was not going to do it again.

I'd just slipped the picture into my pocket when Toscano's men gave up on reviving him and turned back to us. I didn't like the look in Muscle Man's eyes. He'd been guarding the door earlier and he would see Toscano's murder as his failing, as would Toscano's other men. He'd want some quick redemption, and the two people standing in front of the corpse were fairly natural suspects.

I could see them thinking. Who do the bad guys call when one of their own has been murdered? More bad guys, or the cops? Maybe thanks to the hundreds of guests just a wall away, they went with the cops.

"Don't let 'em move one inch," Muscle Man said, then dialed three digits, obviously 9-1-1. With the efficiency of a cop he reported the murder, then walked over to us.

"Put your arms out."

I started to comply then remembered we had to act innocent, for Rita's sake. I needed to get into lawyer mode quick, even if I was just an adoption attorney who learned what little he knew about criminal law from watching *Law and Order*.

"You're not touching us!" I said. "We just walked in and found him like that."

I thought the "we" was a good touch. *We* didn't find him, but if I could shelter Rita by covering for the fact she'd been alone with Toscano, I'd risk everything to do it. What's a little perjury for the woman you love.

My outburst didn't impress them. Their only concern was not to do something that would put them in hot water with the cops. Thug One and Muscle Man shared a look.

Thug One pointed a finger at me. "I only saw him going up the stairs. Maybe half a minute ahead of us." He looked toward Toscano. "Not enough time to do that."

Muscle Man nodded at Rita. "What about her?"

"Dunno. Didn't see her. She musta already been here." His eyes hardened. "Had to be her."

Great, my alibi for Rita already quashed. Worse, if I kept covering for her and screwed it up, it'd be seen for what it was and put her in more jeopardy. I told myself to think. The key was the murder weapon, and as of this moment it wasn't here. At least, not on us. No way they could pin it on Rita without the murder weapon when there'd been no time to leave the room. No one would think she'd kill someone, leave to hide the murder weapon, then run back to stand next to the victim to be found.

With this germ of a strategy I reconsidered my mock outrage at the planned search. The sooner we established we didn't have a weapon, the better. It was the first step in clearing Rita.

"Go ahead," I said, putting my arms out and nodding to Rita. "Search us. We've got nothing to hide. Let's just get it over with."

Muscle Man gave a look to his cohort then moved behind us, forcing us to turn to face him, which put our backs to the desk. The reason became clear as I could hear some drawers being quietly opened. They were cleaning house before the cops arrived.

He slowly and carefully patted me down. He was looking for a weapon and his hand passed right over the flat picture in my pocket. He turned to Rita. "Now you." At least when he searched her, he was all business.

"No weapon," he said when he was done, sounding disappointed.

Out of the corner of my eye I could see Thug One leave the room, trying to walk casually but clearly holding something on his far side out of view. Good, I could alert the cops to files being removed, maybe giving them grounds to search the entire house and bust up Toscano's criminal enterprise.

No, damn it. Cancel that. For all I knew, Rita's and my names were in those files, or Remy and Emma's. If so, presto—a motive for Rita to kill. Suddenly I realized I was forced into being a silent accomplice in a cover up with Toscano's men. I briefly wondered how Rita and I could be on the side of right if our interests were even temporarily aligned with theirs.

There was a sofa against the far wall and Muscle Man nodded toward it. "Sit over there. Both of you."

We did as we were told, then watched him return to the desk, searching for the weapon. Most people don't look for what is *missing*, so hopefully the absence of the letter opener wouldn't even be noticed. Few would think of it as a weapon anyway. Likely they were assuming the killer had brought his own weapon. At least, that was what I was hoping, as it would keep anyone from looking closely at deep-sixed treasure.

Thug One returned in a moment and joined him in the search, being careful not to touch anything. I guessed they'd both been around their share of crime scenes, likely as the accused. They didn't seem broken up that Toscano was dead. Maybe each one was less concerned with catching a killer than taking over Toscano's spot and occupying his chair, and the sooner they gave the evidence to the cops, the sooner everyone was out of their hair. I wondered if either of them was the one who broke into my boat and cut off Remy and Emma's hair. Or killed Nevin.

I leaned close to Rita. At this moment I should have been thinking of nothing but what she was facing, but the truth was I was worried about *us*, as in everlasting bliss, and how much she blamed me for her being forced to do what she'd felt had to be done—because I hadn't. No man wants to be seen as a coward, yet somehow in electing to not kill a man, I had become one. In my mind, at least. But in Rita's?

I leaned close and whispered, "I would have handled it, Rita. I swear. You didn't have to kill him. I'd have made sure Remy and Emma were safe."

I wasn't sure which was more pitiful, the fact I felt I had to defend myself in her eyes at that moment, or the look she gave me for doing so. Tears were a slow river of pain down her face, wetting her blouse where they fell. But her eyes, when they looked up at me, were losing their fear. The pinprick of anger I'd seen earlier seemed to grow and reach out. To me.

I moved my mouth even closer to her ear and spoke urgently.

"Rita, listen to me. If they find your fingerprints on the knife, say you found him dead and just picked up the knife. I'll tell them I did it when I was up here before you. Let me say that."

Thug One must have heard my whispers as he looked up.

"You two. No talking."

It hadn't been the fear of prison which had kept me from wiping Toscano off the planet. Prison I could do for Rita, or her kids. But kill a helpless man, even though a terrible one? No. That I couldn't do. I could do the time but not the crime.

I had no sooner offered to confess for her when I realized it may not work. My alibi for her would only fly if Muscle Man hadn't gone in to see Toscano after I'd left the room the first time I was there. If he had, he'd know Toscano was alive when I left him.

The first cops arrived within just a few minutes, a pair of uniforms. They got the basic facts from Toscano's men, including a lot of emphatic finger pointing our way. The cops moved them away from Toscano's desk, protecting the crime scene, then came over to us. Initially, their manner was severe, then they saw Rita and their faces went kind of slack for a second.

"Aren't you Rita MacGilroy?" The younger of the two asked.

"Yes."

I watched as he forced his mind from Hollywood to homicide.

"Tell me what happened."

The older cop spoke up.

"You got to Mirandize them, Mark."

I may not practice criminal law, but I knew the basics of Miranda. Talking to witnesses did not require a Miranda warning, but once they were considered a suspect, the advisement was required or any statements after that couldn't be used as evidence against them. So in the first minute anyway, one saw us as suspects and one didn't.

Young Cop looked pained and instead said, "The detectives will be here soon. I'd like you not to talk to each other until they arrive. Okay?"

We nodded, but then he seemed to reconsider.

"Tell you what. Ms. MacGilroy, please stay where you are." He looked to me. "Sir, I'd like you to please have a seat there." He pointed to a chair about ten feet away. Not a bad move. Keep the suspects from conspiring a tale, but not risk offending a celebrity. They were going to tread very carefully with Rita.

Rancho Santa Fe, like Fallbrook and most of the smaller towns outside San Diego's city limits, was covered by the Sheriff's Department. The good and bad news of that was that Hawkes would be involved. Good to have a friend on board, but bad as he'd be one very pissed friend. He'd told me to amscray, and instead here we sat, prime murder suspects. That got me thinking why, with all the top cop brass just a cocktail away, they weren't up here. Then I realized the political repercussions. Top level cops are more politicians than crime fighters. With his murder, Toscano had gone from a powerful ally to a political liability. The house had suddenly become the Titanic, and they were likely looking to bail before some enterprising reporter spotted them and listed their names under "guests attending at the time of the murder." Hawkes didn't care about the politics, however, so they must have him busy downstairs.

Rita was still avoiding my eyes, and my eyes were avoiding Toscano's body, so I studied the room. His office was big enough to have a good twenty feet of clear space to the walls on all four sides of his mammoth desk. He kept it uncluttered, with only a telephone positioned in the middle. The room was surprisingly tasteful compared to the rest of the house, one wall filled with louvered doors letting in razor thin bars of light from the small balcony outside, with a few matching doors along the wall, probably for closets or side rooms. I didn't know much about art, but the paintings looked original and expensive, set off nicely by the walnut paneled walls. Money can't buy class, but I guess it could buy taste. The room was filling up quickly with more of both Toscano's men and cops. I didn't even see Hawkes until he cleared his throat next to me to get my attention.

"So, what part of '*leave now*,' didn't you understand?" He looked as angry at me as Rita was. At least he wasn't using his cop voice, so it wouldn't carry to the others in the room. His body language was all cop though, so anyone looking over would see only a cop and a suspect.

"I went looking for Rita. I—"

I cut myself off. Hawkes was a friend. In fact, Emma's kidnapping could have ended in a child-sized casket if not for his help. It had made him an unofficial part of Rita's family, even if he refused to acknowledge it with his "just part of the job" self-deprecation. Still, that friendship would not make him look past a murder, no matter what his history with Rita. Or would it? I watched as Hawkes' eyes left mine and found Rita's. His eyes seemed to tell her, *Don't worry, it'll be alright.* Then just as quickly, it was gone. Maybe it was never there.

I needed the world to slow down and give me time to play the angles right. Say the right thing and it may go a long way to getting Rita off; the wrong thing and she was going to prison.

Option one: bluff if out. Murder convictions came from proving motive, means and opportunity. If they didn't know about the threat to Remy and Emma, there was no motive. And even if they found the picture, by itself it proved nothing. It was just a picture of them sleeping. Anyone could have taken it. Toscano's guys sure couldn't come forward and identify it for what it really was, evidence of their threat to sell them as human cargo. Once again, Toscano's men were indirectly in league with us. My skin crawled.

They also couldn't prove means, as without the knife, there was no murder weapon. And if they did find it, unless Rita's prints were on it, there was still no proof she used the knife. We were upstanding citizens, simply guests at a party who walked in on a murder victim. And opportunity? Not that either, as I could explain away Toscano's guys seeing only me on the stairs by saying Rita was just ahead of me, and I caught up before she even got to the desk. I'd be her alibi.

Option two: come clean right now. What if Rita's prints *were* on the knife, or there was evidence in the house showing Toscano's threat to the girls? Hello, motive and means. And as for opportunity, suddenly standing before the body became damning. So what did that leave us? Convince Rita to admit she did it? There would be sympathy from the cops—and a jury if it got that far—as the man she'd killed was a monster. An animal, stealing children and sending them to living deaths. What parent wouldn't do what she'd done? Some would hail her a hero.

But what if we couldn't prove it? What evidence did we have against him? A picture anyone could have taken? Two little girls with really bad haircuts? My testimony of Toscano's threats which would clearly be seen as biased, especially after we had initially lied and tried to get away with it? Worse, what about the fact that Toscano was found lying back in his chair, his feet up on his desk? Not exactly the stuff self-defense claims are made of. And even if Rita were acquitted, for years the tabloids would label her the "killer mom." Remy and Emma's lives would never the same again. The more I thought about it, the more confused I got. The key was Rita's prints on the knife, assuming they even found it. I suddenly wished I watched *CSI* so I'd know if finger-prints survived water.

"Well?" Hawkes voice was firm.

I wondered how long I had been blankly staring at him. Five seconds? Ten? I was saved answering by the arrival of who must have been the lead detective, based on the deference he was get-ting from the other cops. Hawkes left me and joined him and they conferred with the first two cops on the scene. More of Toscano's men had arrived and there were now four of them, huddled in a far corner. So far, no one resembling a family member or friend had come in. Maybe Toscano had neither.

It was a good fifteen minutes before the detective made his way to our side of the room. He was in his mid-40's, built like a fullback but wearing a well tailored suit. His neck was as big as my thighs and the eyes which filled his squarish face were filled with an intelligence which belied his physique. He walked toward Rita then waved me over.

"I'm Lieutenant Allan Orcutt of the San Diego County Sher-iff's Department. I'm going to advise you both of your rights before I ask you any questions. This is a formality, but I need you to listen."

I'd never been advised of my rights, although I'd heard them given, once in person and a million times on TV. When they are addressed to you, however, you tend to pay more attention. Sud-denly the words mean something when the choices you make can mean your incarceration or freedom, particularly when you were actually guilty as we were, a murderer and an accomplice after the fact.

"You have the right to remain silent," he began, and pro-ceeded to tell us the many rights our great Constitution gave us.

At the moment, I felt unworthy of its protections.

"Do you understand these rights as I've explained them to you?"

"Yes," we said in unison.

"Having heard these rights would you like to talk to me?"

Man, was this guy by the book or what?

"Yes."

He nodded. "Good."

He seemed pleased. Either agreeing to speak without counsel pleased him because it gave us the appearance of cooperation and innocence, or because we were stupid in agreeing to talk, and we were going to make his case for him. But I was even more pleased, as it looked like he was going to question us together. Something he'd seen or heard, or maybe a good word from Hawkes, had him slanting more toward seeing us as witnesses than suspects.

We formally gave him our names, which seemed safe enough. He either didn't know who Rita was, or he was one of those guys who like to pretend they don't recognize famous people.

"Let me start with you, Mr. Dillon. I understand you were an invited guest today, and you brought Ms. MacGilroy. Is that correct?"

"Yes, I asked her to come with me."

Still to me. "And you were a friend of Mr. Toscano?"

"No. Actually I'd never met him until today. I guess I was invited since it was a charity event."

"He called you personally?"

"No, I'd never even spoken to him until today. I just got an invitation."

"Uh huh." He turned to Rita. "And you, miss, did you know him?"

"No. This was my first time too."

Back to me.

"Okay. Tell me exactly what you did when you arrived, and when you came to see Mr. Toscano."

I noticed how formal and precise he was. He didn't refer to him simply as Toscano, or *the victim.* He was as proper as he'd be if he knew every word was being recorded for later examination.

"We got here around one," I said. "We walked around downstairs, talked to people. You know, the usual. Then I asked where to find Mr. Toscano since I hadn't seen him yet."

"You asked where he was? Who specifically did you ask?"

"Some of the food service people, but they didn't know. Eventually I asked one of those guys." I nodded to the four thugs now being questioned by Hawkes. "And he told me to come up here."

He turned his head to look. "Which one?"

I told him and he nodded, as if he'd already heard the same thing.

"So, what happened when you came up?"

I nodded again to the cluster o' thugs across the room. "That guy, the one in the blue shirt with the parrots, he was at the door and let me in." I could have said "The one with the big muscles," but that'd make me sound a bit light in my loafers.

"I was told he patted you down first. Is that true?"

"Yes."

"Did that strike you as odd?"

Good question. If Rita and I were naive invited guests, like everyone else downstairs, we wouldn't know Toscano was a mobster so it would have been a shock.

"Yeah, real surprised," I said. "It seemed strange, but. . . I don't know, that's just what he did."

"Okay, so he searched you. You went inside. Then what?"

He had to be thinking I couldn't have brought a weapon into the room since I'd been frisked. Good for me, but that didn't help Rita.

"Well, he was sitting at his desk," I said. "And we just talked for awhile. I thanked him for inviting us, and that was about it."

"And you were with him how long?"

I spread my hands. "I don't know. Maybe five minutes?"

"A five minute thank you? Seems kind of long."

"I don't mean all I said was 'thank you.' We were here for a charity event and I do some charity stuff too. So we talked about that kind of thing. Charity stuff."

"And you sat. . . where?"

"Actually, I stood the whole time."

"Stood?" He seemed surprised I didn't sit down if I was there for so long. "Stood where? In front of the desk?"

Did I touch anything when I went around the back of his desk? The letter opener, but Rita handled it after me, likely removing my prints. And Remy and Emma's picture, now resting in my pocket. It looked like "yes" was the safest answer.

"Yes, in front," I said.

"Okay. Do you recall touching anything in here?"

"No, not that I can think of."

"So then you did what after that?"

"Just went back downstairs where the other guests were."

"And was anyone outside the door when you left?"

"Yes, the parrot shirt guy. Guarding the door like before."

"Fine. Then you immediately found Ms. MacGilroy outside?"

How I'd like to say yes and give her an alibi, but too many people outside could say otherwise. Get too cute and clever and I'd blow it. Stick with the truth except for the killing itself.

"Actually, no. I was looking for her and then someone fell in the pool and someone jumped in to save her. A bunch of people ended up in there. It was kind of a big mess down there and I never found her."

His head swiveled to Rita.

"How about you pick it up here now, Ms. MacGilroy. You stayed downstairs at the party until when?"

Rita's previous emotions were under control and she spoke calmly.

"Well, I don't know the time exactly, but we'd probably been here for about half an hour before I went upstairs. I didn't see Toby so I assumed he went up to thank Mr. Toscano. I wanted to join him and do the same."

"Alright. And you knew where to go. . . how?"

"Just like Toby, I just asked a few people until someone knew."

I felt like we were scoring points. He hadn't got to the punch line yet, where we had to answer why we were in a room together with a dead body, but neither of us hid the fact we were headed up to see Toscano. It all sounded innocent.

"So when you came up, was there anyone guarding the door, like Mr. Dillon mentioned?"

"No, not when I got here."

I hadn't had a chance to talk to Rita about anything after the cop had separated us. I had to guess that she came up the stairs just after someone fell into the pool. When the screaming started, Muscle Man had probably run downstairs. A charity party probably wasn't considered a high security event.

"Had the incident which Mr. Dillon described. . . the people in the pool, occurred yet when you headed upstairs?"

He was looking for a time line. How much time had elapsed

between my departure from Toscano's office, and her arrival. The killing time.

I cringed when she said "no," but then she saved it with "but when I got to the house I used the restroom downstairs before I went up."

Perfect. Time for an imaginary person to have done the deed, and Muscle Man could have run right past her toward the pool and not seen her.

"And you were in the restroom how long?"

I caught a flash of chauvinistic defeat in his eyes, likely imagining his wife saying "be out in one minute," then exiting the bathroom twenty minutes later, swearing she'd only been in there a minute or two. Women's estimation of bathroom time was a joke among the male gender. Rita must have caught it too, as she gave a vague answer that couldn't hurt her, only help.

"Oh, it's so hard to say. A few minutes, or maybe ten. I just don't know."

Orcutt had to be thinking the same thing I was. If the door to Toscano's office was unguarded somewhere between when I left and Rita arrived, anyone could have come and killed Toscano, even one of Toscano's own men. Perhaps even Muscle Man, who could have done it himself, then run downstairs to give himself an alibi, returning with an associate to *find* the body. Of course, none of those scenarios were true, but Orcutt didn't know that. I suddenly realized that unless something went wrong, Rita was going to walk out of here.

"Did you pass anyone leaving the house, or coming down the stairs on your way up?"

"No."

"Alright," Orcutt said. "So, you what? Went upstairs and walked right in to his office?"

"Well, I knocked, of course, but the door was already ajar. So I walked in. . . and saw him."

"Mr. Toscano? At his desk?"

Rita nodded and he went on. "And could you tell he was deceased at that point?"

"I could see the blood, and he wasn't moving, so yes, I assumed he was dead."

"And how long was it before Mr. Dillon joined you?"

There'd been no chance for me to tell Rita how I could give her an alibi, indirectly supported by Toscano's men, so I cut in quickly.

"It must have been just a few seconds," I said. "She was at the top of the stairs just as I started going up. She wasn't even to his desk when I walked in right behind her."

If he was annoyed that I had answered a question meant for her he didn't show it, just looked to Rita for confirmation.

"It's hard to say," she said. "I'd guess maybe a few seconds, however long it took me to walk in about twenty feet. Then Toby was right behind me."

Man she was good. Why should I be surprised, though? She was an actress after all, and a damned good one. I guessed she'd had a good lead of at least a few minutes on me, alone with Toscano, but it had just turned into a few seconds in Orcutt's notebook. I felt just the slightest chill that she could kill, then lie so effectively about it, but I pushed the discomfort aside.

Orcutt nodded, still focused on Rita. "And did you touch anything?"

"No. I just stood there. I guess I was just frozen. Then Toby walked in, then two of those men." She nodded toward where Hawkes was finishing up with Toscano's guys, and was now heading our way. He took up a position next to Orcutt, watching us carefully, but saying nothing.

As she spoke I flashed on the memory of her hand reaching out for the girls' picture. It had laid flat on the desk and her fingers had to drag on the desk top just outside the edges of the picture to pick it up. At least, I think they did.

Fingerprints. Evidence.

"Well…" I let myself sound uncertain.

"What?" Orcutt asked.

"Rita may not remember," I went on, "but she sort of fainted a little bit and fell toward the desk. I caught her, but I think she might of tried to steady herself on the corner of the desk. I'm not sure."

Now who was the chauvinist? I was more likely to faint than her, but I needed to explain any prints. Rita caught on right away, obviously remembering picking up the picture.

"Yes, Toby's right. I did kind of lose it for a second. But I'm not sure if I touched the desk."

Everything was going perfectly. Our uncertainty of what happened made her look innocent. It's usually the guilty who have every detail covered. I could only hope she didn't touch anything besides the letter opener when she was alone with Toscano.

Orcutt seemed to buy everything we were spinning. Over his shoulder I could see some tech people start to set up their equipment. Hawkes walked over to one of them and pointed to the corner of the desk and then at Rita. Good for him. Making sure her prints were expected to be there, fully innocent. Orcutt turned to me.

"Okay, then. Back to you, Mr. Dillon. You're downstairs, just back from seeing Mr. Toscano. How long were you downstairs?"

He was no dummy. I noticed he was now doubling back over what we'd covered before, looking for more details, and maybe a contradiction.

"I don't know. Maybe fifteen minutes. However long it takes to make a few loops around the pools, pushing through the crowd, then those people falling in the pool. Maybe more like twenty."

"So you eventually came back up to see Mr. Toscano again?"

"Yes."

"Why?"

Good question. I knew it was coming, but my mind had been working overtime just to keep up with the ones being thrown in our faces. I couldn't risk jumping ahead or risk screwing up. Landmines everywhere.

"Well, I didn't really need to see him again, but I couldn't find Rita outside, and someone said she'd gone looking for me up here. I was just trying to find her."

"So you'd told Ms. MacGilroy you were going up to see him? The first time, I mean?"

Keep it simple. Lie only when you have to. There'd been people talking to Rita when I slipped away, so if questioned they would say I hadn't told her where I was going.

"No, not at that moment, but on the drive over we talked about making it a point to see him and thank him for the invitation."

"Alright, now on your way upstairs the second time, did you pass anyone coming down?"

"No." Wish I had. Maybe someone with Remy and Emma's chopped off hair clutched in one hand. Nice to pin Toscano's murder on him.

Orcutt had circled right around to where he had started. He gave us each a quick look then excused himself to join a cop questioning Toscano's men with a second round of questions, maybe running Rita's and my version past them. He was back after a short discussion. He looked at me.

"I'm going to have to insist that before you leave the premises you both agree to a complete search. You can decline, but if you do I'm going to request that you be transported to the station and have the search made there. And obviously you can confer with counsel if you wish prior to agreeing."

Given the fact we were found with a recently murdered body, even absent a murder weapon, the request seemed reasonable. Besides, I think he had to be thinking there was no reason a film star and an adoption lawyer would come to a charity fundraiser and stab a stranger in the heart. As long as we gave him nothing to be suspicious about, we were home free. At least for now.

I looked at Rita and she nodded assent. Why not? The murder weapon was in the aquarium.

"Okay, " I said. "If that will help, that's fine. We just want to go home."

"And you'll need to be printed too, to identify any prints we find here."

We nodded our assent again. What else could we do? Then I had a thought.

"What about them?" I nodded towards Toscano's crew. "Are you searching and fingerprinting them too?"

"Of course." He didn't seem put off by the question, just happy we were cooperating.

He looked to two uniformed cops who were waiting for his signal, a man and a woman, and they came over. "If you'll each go with these officers we'll get this taken care of."

Rita and I were at the door when Orcutt's voice stopped us. His tone was disturbingly casual, Colombo without the rumpled raincoat.

"Oh, Ms. MacGilroy. When you went to the restroom, do you

remember what color the towels were?"

The breath went out of my lungs. If she was smart she'd say she didn't notice. Who would? But she looked him in the eye.

"Burgundy," she said. "With a stripe. White or tan. I can't remember."

He smiled and nodded to our escorts, who then took us into separate rooms. Somewhere on the way I started to breathe again, wondering how she knew the answer. One of a hundred questions I was dying to ask her.

My escort toted a clipboard with a preprinted itemization list.

"Okay, so you want me to empty my pockets?" I asked.

He looked embarrassed.

"Well, yes, sir. But didn't Lieutenant Orcutt tell you? He requested a complete search. That means disrobing, sir. We have to ascertain if any evidence is secreted on anyone's body and trying to leave the scene with it."

So I started emptying my pockets. I had my wallet, car keys, and cell phone on the bed when Hawkes walked in. Normally, I'd be worried about two guys staring at me undressing, but at the moment I only thought about Remy and Emma's picture in my shirt pocket. I took a chance and left it inside and casually tossed the shirt on the bed. As I'd hoped, it landed slack, the picture not distorting the shape of the pocket to give its presence away. Next I threw down my pants and underwear. The clipboard cop picked up the pants and slowly went through every pocket, then turned the pants inside out. Any hopes I had of the picture going undiscovered disappeared. In fact, it was Hawkes who reached for the shirt while the other cop finished with my pants.

He came out with the photograph and gave me a look.

"Oh, sorry," I said casually. "I forgot I had that."

Hawkes initially had the picture upside down because he

turned it around and his face relaxed as he handed it to the other cop. "It's just a picture of his girlfriend's kids."

I wanted to kiss him, but that probably wasn't a good idea, especially considering I was naked. But then he added, "Make a note of it in your inventory, though." I bit back a grimace. Still, it could have been worse.

The young cop nodded as Hawkes left the room, then dutifully wrote down every item in my possession, including everything in my wallet. When he got to the picture Hawkes had given him he said, "Cute kids," then handed me back my things.

"Thanks."

"You can get dressed now," he said. "I'll be waiting outside to bring you back to the lieutenant."

Within a few minutes I was escorted back to Toscano's office. Orcutt was in the process of looking under the cushions where Rita and I had been sitting. Then he tilted the whole sofa onto its back to look underneath. Not a bad thought: stash a weapon where we were sitting before the police searched us. Behind him I could see the louvered doors open, closets being searched and inventoried.

Rita joined me a minute later. Now that we were done, Toscano's men were getting the same treatment. At least the suspicion was divided up among a large group, and I'd bet that bunch didn't have the squeaky clean records Rita and I did. It seemed to me there was only one way we were at risk, if Rita's prints remained on the letter opener. But they'd have to find it first, and I didn't think they would. The cops had never seen it to even know what they were looking for, and likely they weren't looking for pirate plunder.

Orcutt walked over to us after he put the sofa down.

"Thank you for your cooperation." He nodded to both of us.

"Mr. Dillon. Ms. MacGilroy. I've got your contact information. I might be contacting you in a day or two with some further questions. If you think of anything before then, please let me know."

We agreed and left the room, counting our blessings. Not once did our eyes go anywhere near the aquarium.

29

RITA DIDN'T PUT her hand in mind as we drove home, and I tried not to put any meaning into it. She seemed resigned, but to what I wasn't sure. When we'd left Toscano's I was surprised by the activity downstairs. I'd forgotten the other guests, so that meant there were a couple hundred suspects. All the better.

For the first few minutes neither of us spoke, hiding from each other in the anonymity of the early evening darkness. It wasn't until we hit the freeway that Rita broke the silence.

"So they think someone came in after you and before me."

"Yeah."

Silence.

"And you didn't see me ahead of you at all, did you?"

I shook my head in the darkness. She already knew the answer.

More silence.

Finally she said, "Remy and Emma's picture. . . Toscano admitted everything to you, didn't he? And you didn't do anything. You left him alive."

She said it dully, but to me if felt like an accusation.

"Yes." I choked it out. "I had the knife right in my hand. I just, I just couldn't do it. I'm sorry."

My words hung in the air.

"Toby?"

She waited until I looked at her before she continued. "You did the right thing."

If I'd been right, then why did I feel only shame?

Then she added softly, "I just wish you thought I did the right thing too."

It was me who had let her down, yet she was trying to give me absolution.

"Rita, I—"

"No, please. Leave it alone. We both did what we did, okay?"

I wanted to talk. Needed to talk. But I wasn't going to force her. "Okay."

"Toby, should. . . should I get a lawyer? Or will that make me look. . . guilty?"

She knew criminal law wasn't my area and I'd be of little help defending her if necessary, other than providing an alibi. I told her it was a good idea to talk to someone—and she could afford the best—but recommended the attorney not contact the police on her behalf. They didn't need to know she was getting the advice of counsel, perhaps making them look at her as more than a witness. Witnesses didn't think they needed lawyers.

Suddenly I thought of Orcutt's question.

"When he asked you about the towels. . . did you really use the bathroom?" Part of her alibi. Alone in the bathroom for critical minutes.

"No."

"Then how'd you know?"

"The door was open when I walked by."

"And. . . and you noticed the color of the towels?"

Her voice was fading from fatigue and I had to strain to hear her. "It was hard not to. The walls were pale blue. They didn't match at all."

Unbelievable, the things women notice. Their sensory input is so far superior to men, I'm often amazed every cop, judge and doctor isn't a woman.

She sighed. "What's going to happen if they find the knife, Toby. . . and my fingerprints are on it?"

I didn't want to think about it. "Maybe they won't find it. And if they do, maybe the water washed them away. I think you're going to be okay."

Somehow I'd find out if water removed fingerprints, and then hopefully clear her mind. I reached out and put my hand over hers.

"Don't worry," I said. "If that happens, I'll say it was me. Okay? You don't have to be afraid. If your prints are still on there, probably some of mine are too. I mean it. I'll say it was me."

I didn't expect gratitude. It was my fault she was even there. But I also didn't expect the silence that answered my offer. She still hadn't spoken by the time we pulled into my carport a half hour later. I knew Remy and Emma were secure at home with Rita's longtime live-in, Lettie, so she could stay the night if she wanted. I desperately wanted her in my bed. Just to talk. To hold. To forgive and be forgiven. Heads under the blanket in a universe of our own making. But she quashed my hopes as we got out of my car.

"I'm not coming in, Toby. I need to go home."

"Rita, please—"

But she had already turned and was walking slowly to her car, her head down. I ached to run after her, hold her in my arms and take away every ounce of pain, but I knew she didn't want that. Not from me. Not tonight.

30

TENNIS NEVER LET me down. It was the one thing that was always there for me, and I'd rarely needed it more than the next morning. I owed it to Rita to put on a strong face and act normal. That's what I kept telling myself anyway.

Lars was back to handle the morning clinic but I showed up to help him. No matter how bad my pain, the courts were an aspirin to take them away. Tennis therapy.

To be a great tennis player you have to focus every ounce of your energy on the ball. I tell my students to watch it so intently they could read the brand name stamped on the side as it flies toward them. Impossible to do, but that's the focus needed to react quickly to a ball, its speed and spin, and to make sure it finds the sweet spot on your racquet. It was that intense focus that drove everything from your mind. Yes, even Rita. And murder. Those thoughts would be back the second I stepped off the courts, but for now I was free.

My freedom was short lived, however. As we finished a ground stroke drill I saw Hawkes leaning against the fence just inside the gate. He wasn't waving handcuffs at me, so I assumed Rita's and my stories were holding up. While everyone else went for some water I trotted over to him.

"I'm impressed," he said. "You're some tennis player."

"I have to be decent at something," I said.

"Hey, it's a compliment. Take it."

I shrugged. The thoughts of the two murders were flooding back into my mind. Tennis therapy was over.

"Okay, thanks. What's up?"

"We need to talk," he said. "How long before you're done?"

The clinic had another half hour to go, too long to make Hawkes wait, so I gave a wave to Lars and turned back to Hawkes.

"I can stop now. Let's go up to my place."

He'd been there before to hang out and watch more than a few weekend ball games over the last year. He knew the way and walked next to me without saying anything. When we got inside I grabbed two glasses of ice water and we headed out to my little balcony.

"Fixing up the place a bit, huh?" Hawkes said, collapsing into one of the canvas chairs and eyeing the new potted plants and Boston ferns hanging from the eaves.

"Rita brings a plant every other week or so. I think she's trying to dress up the place a bit."

He laughed. "She can't do that. Not as long as you're here."

I knew he was going for the standard male humor we insulted each other with, but I wasn't in the mood for it right now, at least not about Rita and me.

"So what's up?" I asked. I couldn't very well ask if they'd

found the letter opener, and if so, if Rita's prints were on it. But I knew if that were the case, he'd have opened with that.

The idle chatter mode fell from his face. That was fine. I knew he was here as a cop. The friendship in the middle was hard on both of us.

"I spent the last hour comparing notes with Orcutt." Good, I was likely going to get an up to the minute report, whatever he was willing to tell me anyway. But then he changed gears. "How's Rita doing? It must have been hard on her finding the body."

The honest answer was that I didn't really know. I had called her last night to make sure she got home okay. Lettie said she'd arrived but had already gone to bed and she'd have her call me in the morning. But she hadn't, and my calls to her cell went straight to voice mail. Then, before the tennis clinic I'd run to my office to squeeze in an hour's work. The last thing I expected was a message from Rita to be left there.

It was time-stamped last night. There was only one reason she'd leave a message there rather than at home: to avoid talking to me. Not that it was any secret after hearing her message: "Toby, I know you're worried about me, but I'm. . . okay. I just need some time alone. Will you try not to be hurt if I have some time to myself? I'll call you in a few days when I'm ready. I'm going to take the girls up to the mountains and just get away for awhile. I just need some space, okay? So, please, don't call. Not right now."

I may have lost some of my morality yesterday—covering up a murder—but at the moment my only fear was that I may be losing Rita. Was she pulling away because she was ashamed of herself for what she'd done? Or of me for what I didn't do? But I couldn't let Hawkes know what Rita was really going through.

"About what you'd expect," I said. "Finding Toscano like that, she's pretty shaken up. She's going to go up to Big Bear and spend a few days. You guys have her cell number if you need to reach her."

Hawkes knew she and Brogan had bought a small cabin a few years ago on the shores of Big Bear Lake, a rustic mountain town a few hours inland. Although I was going to miss her, with all the violence surrounding us lately, it was the best place for her and the girls. I should have recommended it myself.

Hawkes nodded agreement, then went on, "I had the feeling she was mad at you when Orcutt was questioning you. Everything okay between you two?"

The voice was that of a concerned friend who knew Rita's and my long history, but his eyes were a different story. They were cop eyes, watching me closely. I tried to make light of it.

"Oh, I don't know. Maybe. I mean, it was because of me we were there, and she wouldn't have even been there to find the body. And if I'd brought her up with me to begin with, she wouldn't have had to go looking for me and find him. I think mainly she was just in shock though."

"Hmm," was his only comment, but it was enough to make it clear he wasn't quite buying it. We sat without saying anything for a few minutes, then he broke the silence with what sounded like regret.

"You made a big mistake yesterday, Toby."

Damn it. Here it came. So I'd misread his approach after all. Was he here for me, and another cop on the way to arrest Rita? I forced the tension out of my body.

"What are you talking about?"

"Last night Orcutt and I went over everyone's statements. I wasn't aware until then you hadn't told him about Toscano's ties to Nevin Handley. You weren't there on just some charity crap like you told him."

I'm such a moron. I had been so intent on protecting Rita that I'd forgotten Hawkes knew about Toscano's relationship to Nevin. Now, with me at Toscano's, I was suddenly the common point in two murder cases. Not a good place to be. Hawkes paused to let me explain myself, and when I didn't, he continued.

"I'm the lead on Handley's murder so Orcutt didn't know anything about Toscano's possible role in that until I told him. If he'd had his way, your ass would have been in a squad car going down to the station for a formal statement."

I told myself the damage was minimal. It wasn't Rita they were scrutinizing. It was me. That I could handle.

"So why didn't he? Should I be thanking you?"

"Nothing to thank me for. I just had to point out you had those two magic words going for you: *attorney-client.* I told him the Handleys were your clients and you'd reluctantly had to cite the privilege when I spoke to you before. But I told him it was you who came to me with Toscano's tie-in to Handley. And it didn't hurt that the guy who let you in to Toscano's office confirmed he was alive when you left. Put you in the clear."

It was the first I'd heard of that. Good for me, but it took away any chance to cover for Rita and claim I'd killed him. At least my alibi for her that I'd been just behind her on the stairs wasn't compromised. Now I only had to talk my way out of this little jam. I didn't think it would be a problem.

"I don't see what Orcutt's got to be mad about," I said. "I told *him* everything that happened there. And I told *you* about Toscano when we talked about Nevin. What more do you want from me?"

Hawkes gave me his best glower. "Toby, get real. You told him you were up there for five minutes and only chatted socially and talked about charities. You expect him to believe that, when you went there knowing he may have been involved in the murder of your client? You expect *me* to believe it?"

I had two ways to go. I could cite attorney-client privilege and say Toscano and I had spoken, but the discussion was related to my representation of the Handleys and was not connected to his murder, so couldn't be revealed. That would drag in Catherine and Lynn, however. The other option was to stick to my story. All I knew for sure was that I couldn't tell the truth. Knowledge of Toscano's threats to Remy and Emma would put Rita in the cops' bulls-eye, even with no murder weapon.

"Hey, be a smart ass if you want," I said. "But who was it that found Toscano's name as Nevin's investor? Me. The truth is I don't know what I had in mind. When I got his invitation to come I thought maybe he wanted to tell me something, maybe knowing I represented the family. I don't know. So when I went up there I just played dumb and left it to him to see if he'd say something. But he didn't. Or maybe *he* was waiting to see if *I'd* bring it up. I'm sorry the truth is so boring, but I can't make up something to make you and Orcutt happy."

I thought it came out reasonably credible. Maybe if I moved on the offensive a bit he'd give up poking at it. "Your turn. Have you got any leads on who did it?"

I could see he was mulling over whether he wanted to share anything with me.

"C'mon," I prompted. "I've given you the only lead you've got so far."

He gave a tiny shrug. "Not much. Searched the house. Nothing. No evidence on the murder. No evidence of anything, actually. We're trying to get a subpoena compelling his attorney to give us his financial records now that he's deceased. No luck so far, though."

The disappointment in his voice was obvious. He was striking out twice, nothing to help him on Nevin's murder either. That meant Tocsano's guy who'd carried out some files from the desk either destroyed them or moved them out of the house.

"Two of his guys have records," he went on. "One for burglary a few years ago and another one for assault. We're going to bring them in again today and see if we can sweat something out of them."

He didn't sound optimistic.

"Oh," he added. "More bad news is that there's a second stairway in the back of the house. Someone could have gone up or down that way too."

I made my face look disappointed, but inside I was thinking: great, one more escape route for the imaginary killer. Rita was getting safer and safer by the minute. I wasn't going to let my guard down and feel overconfident, however. Hawkes and Orcutt were smart cops, working opposite ends of the same case. Both had to be looking for a scenario making sense for the hunter, Toscano, to become the victim. Little did they know he'd been done in by two little girls who could barely walk.

Hawkes and Orcutt were not all we had to worry about: the psycho that Toscano had sent to crop Remy and Emma's hair was still out there. I briefly wondered if at this very moment he was alone, running his hands through their sheared hair, unthinkably dark thoughts in his mind.

"You okay?" Hawkes asked, looking at me oddly.

"Yeah, why?"

"Your face. You looked like you were going to be sick."

I'd better watch it. Hawkes may be a friend, but I had to be careful around him.

"I'm fine. I just feel sick when I think about finding the body."

Finally, something I said to him that was true. He stayed a few more minutes, softening the cop visit with some personal talk before he left.

When he was gone I pulled my cell phone out of my pocket. I'd felt it vibrate twice during my time with Hawkes, but I hadn't wanted to interrupt our talk. The first message was from Aaron. Amanda was at the hospital, dilated to nine centimeters and counting. That meant a baby any minute. The second message was from Brent, returning my call. I realized I had to push Toscano out of my mind. I had work to do and people who needed me.

The sweat from the morning clinic had dried but I still needed a shower. Within fifteen minutes I was on the road to the hospital, and had Brent on the phone. I apologized for humbling him on the court and he let me know he'd rebound and would take me down next time. The usual brother crap going back and forth. Finally, we got to the point.

"So, what's up?" he asked.

"I forgot to ask you about something when I saw you."

I told him about the blackmail notes. What I got in return was a long silence.

"Brent, are you there?"

"Yeah, I'm here. What do you think it means, Toby? I didn't think anyone else knew about it. The adoption, I mean."

"That's what we all thought. So. . . Melanie didn't say anything to you about writing them?"

"Melanie?"

He wasn't just giving me a lawyer's outrage that his client would do anything wrong. His surprise seemed genuine.

"Hey, don't get me wrong," I said. "No one's trying to make trouble for your client. Catherine just wants the adoption to finally be done. She even understands that Melanie's probably bitter and sent those notes. Hell, even I'd have to admit Nevin and Catherine needed some prompting to get going on this. We just need to know if there's someone else out there sticking their nose in this."

I could practically hear Brent thinking through the phone line. I was doing the same. Either Melanie knew nothing about the notes, or she'd written them but not told Brent. Lawyers hate nothing more than clients who lie about things. After all, lying is the *lawyer's* job. Either way, Brent just saw his "easy adoption case" get a lot more complicated. But on the bright side, he'd have a lot more to bill for.

"I'll have to call you back on this," he said. "Better yet, how about we meet for tennis again and talk about it then?"

"Tennis?"

What was this guy, suicidal?

"Didn't I beat you bad enough last time?" I asked him.

"That's my game plan, man. Making you overconfident, then swooping in for the kill."

"Oh, and I thought your game was to run for the ball, hit it into the net, then stand there wheezing."

"Keep talking. I got your game figured out, little brother."

"Well, if I say *yes* to tennis, can you talk to Melanie right away and have an answer for me by the time I see you?"

"Yeah, should be no problem."

"And you won't forget about asking her about how soon we can get her started with the Adoption Services Provider? And about the birth father?"

"Already on my list of stuff to go over with her, don't worry.

You want to meet tonight?"

The sooner I could get answers the better, even if he meant he was padding his bill with all the unnecessary driving.

"Sure," I said. "I'm hitting with Lynn until six. Why don't you come about six-thirty. Give me a chance to eat in between."

"Lynn? Isn't that the girl this is all about?"

"She's the one."

He thought for a minute and I could imagine him figuring out how many hours he could get away with billing on the second meeting.

"Okay, then. Six-thirty."

We said our goodbyes and I pushed in a Beach Boys tape. By the last chorus of *Barbara Ann* I arrived at the hospital, not more than an hour from when Aaron had called.

Usually, I don't go to the hospital when my birth mothers delivered. My paperwork to release the baby to the adoptive parents was already there, so my work was done for the moment. But Aaron and Charlotte were my friends, and Amanda's family and I went back a few decades. Plus they asked me to come—that counted for a lot.

The front desk told me she was in Labor and Delivery room five. I checked in at the nursing station and was told I'd missed the delivery by fifteen minutes. That was fine with me. I only need to experience so much.

When I walked in Amanda was sitting up in bed, a baby cradled in her arms. She was beaming. There was a sad part to adoption for birth mothers—the saying of goodbyes yet to come. But there was also a happy part, knowing she created this life, and setting that life on a wonderful path.

"It's a boy," she said.

Aaron and Charlotte were by her side. I'm sure they were

aching to hold the baby, but they knew this was Amanda's time. They had a lifetime with him.

Charlotte came forward and gave me a hug.

"Thanks for coming, Toby."

She walked over to a chair where her purse sat and reached inside, coming out with a camera.

"Will you take our picture?"

The request would probably seem odd to anyone not schooled in adoption. Telling a child they were adopted is a part of their life story, just like other children hear about their mother's birth experience. A picture of Amanda, Charlotte, Aaron and the baby, all together at the moment he entered the world, said: Look, it took all these people, all loving you and wanting the best for you, working together to give you a wonderful life.

As they all crowded together, Amanda said, "Wait. His mother should be holding him."

And with that she handed Charlotte the baby. I could tell it was the first time she'd held him as her tears sprouted and fell freely. I took the picture, and no child could ever look at it and not feel unconditionally loved, and whole.

31

I MADE IT back to the courts just in time for Lynn's lesson. On the way from the hospital I'd swung by the library to use one of their computers with internet access. A Google search gave me ten thousand-plus listings when I typed "latent fingerprints after submersion in water." Most of the leads were worthless, but eventually I learned fingerprints were ninety-nine percent water, one percent of various oils, and that prolonged submersion in water was virtually guaranteed to eliminate latent prints. I left the library with my load lighter.

Nevin's service was tomorrow and I was surprised Lynn wanted to hit some balls, but like for me, tennis was her catharsis for many things. I wondered if her mom would have time to drive with her again, or if we were back to the usual limousine run.

I was glad to see the little Corolla pull up, Lynn at the wheel, Catherine by her side. I wondered if Smileyface was being escorted by limo when they were borrowing her car. Only Lynn got out of the car, though, and Catherine just waved at me and moved to the driver's seat and headed off.

Lynn wasn't herself though, and there was little conversation between us on changeovers. No doubt her father's funeral was on her mind, the finality of his death more real than before. She didn't even issue me a challenge to earn any driving time. Brent arrived a bit early and took one of the chairs against the fence. He'd gone through his youth taking his share of lessons and he knew not to interrupt, even to say hi. I wasn't happy that he was early, probably a strategy to get me to play without dinner. When I glanced at him though, his eyes were fixed on Lynn, likely fascinated with the person who was the center of all this mystery.

Lynn's mom arrived right at six but didn't get out of the car. I could see her through the windshield on her cell. Lynn had tossed her racquet into her gear bag and stopped on her way to the car.

"It's been hard on my mom," she said. "The police keep wanting to talk to her. Same with the lawyers from dad's office. They should leave her alone, at least until the funeral is over."

So like a kid. Worried about their parents.

"Is there anything I can be doing for her? For you?" I asked.

"You'll be at dad's service tomorrow, right?"

"I'll be there."

She gave me a smile much too wonderful for the likes of me. "That's enough," she said.

I couldn't tell her all I'd been doing was trying to help. She gave me a hug and headed for the car. I turned to see Brent's eyes riveted on her as she walked away.

I was annoyed and took it out on him.

"You scoping her out for your client?" I asked. "Give her a first hand report?"

Now it was his turn to get annoyed. More than I'd have expected.

"Man, Toby. Give it a rest. Okay? I can't help it if traffic's light and I got here early."

I realized I'd come on too strong.

"Yeah. Sorry."

He looked mollified, anxious to not have Lynn the center of a disagreement.

"She seems like a good kid," he said.

"She is. So, you get a hold of Melanie?"

"Yep."

"She answered everything?"

"Yep."

"Good deal. In that case, I can offer you a grilled cheese sandwich at my place. C'mon."

He followed me up to my apartment and buttered some wheat bread as I sliced the Cheddar. While I browned the sandwiches in a pan, I put him to work slicing a couple apples, and asked him to spread some peanut butter on each slice. Hey, tasted great as a kid. Why change?

"So, what do you want to start with?" he asked. "She's ready to meet the Adoption Services Provider you recommended. In fact, I already called her. . . what's her name?"

"Sherry Rosman."

"Yeah, Sherry. I gave Melanie her number and she's going to call tomorrow and set it up."

"What about meeting with me?"

She wasn't required to meet with me for any legal reason. I just wanted to help put everything in perspective for her. Give her some thoughts about meeting with Catherine after so many years, and seeing Lynn for the first time.

"She's not ready for that, Toby. And no offense, but she doesn't *have* to meet with you."

I shrugged. "I know. I just wanted to."

I assumed she was embarrassed about the notes.

"Is it the notes?" I asked. "Is she worried about them?"

"Toby, I asked her about them. I let her know there were no hard feelings if she wrote them. But she swears up and down she never sent them. In fact, she seemed pretty upset someone would do that. She said nobody else knows. Or at least, is supposed to know."

When the sandwiches were nicely browned I slid them from the pan. Brent had two plates ready, apple slices presented in symmetrical arcs. Not bad for a couple bachelors. I poured us some orange juice and we moved over to my little dining table, big enough for two chairs.

"And you believe her?" I asked.

"Yeah, I do. She's just as worried about it as you are. Finally the adoption is getting done right, and she's got to deal with this."

It was still possible she sent them but wasn't copping to it, despite the promises of no consequences. That was another reason I wanted to meet her in person. To look in her eyes when I asked her. Still, I tended to think she was being honest about not sending them. But who else would know? Who else would care? What would they have to gain? And did it mean anything that no notes had been received by Catherine since Nevin had been murdered?

The notes weren't the only unanswered question, though. There was the mystery surrounding the birth father. Would Brent have an answer for me there too?

"What did she say about the birth father?"

"Man," he said defensively. "How about if I get to ask a question."

"Sorry. Ask away."

"The birth father," he began. "Let's say she names him. When he signs the papers. . . the local judge is going to see it. Right?"

"Yes. The final report that Social Services will do not only approves the adoptive parents, but also confirms the birth parents have consented, or had their rights terminated."

"And if there was some. . . impropriety in him sleeping with her, what then?"

We were back to it. My belief had been that Nevin and Catherine knew who the birth father was, and had known all along, but were delaying the information until the last possible moment. And Melanie's mother challenging me that I also knew, implying I was in on a cover up—another example of the rich and powerful getting their way. Maybe finally, I was going to get some answers.

"You mean her being seventeen, if the birth father was legally an adult?" I asked.

"Exactly."

I shook my head.

"So many years have gone by, I can't imagine the court will really look at that. Even when it happens now, when it's voluntary and the birth mother is almost eighteen, it's so common no one does anything about it, even though it's technically stat rape. It's just when the girl is real young, and the guy's a lot older, then they'll go after him."

Brent didn't say anything so I kept going.

"You haven't asked me yet what happens if the birth father is dead."

"Dead?"

"Yeah." It was time to finally ask the question I didn't want to ask, but had been nibbling at my mind since it all started. Nevin's hesitation to start the adoption. The desire to keep everything

quiet. Melanie's mother's allegation someone was being protected, money and power having their way.

So I asked it. God, I hoped I was wrong.

"Is Nevin the birth father?"

32

"NEVIN?"

Brent seemed honestly surprised.

"God, you think Melanie slept with *Handley*?"

"Then tell me, Brent. Who is it?"

He looked me in the eye and sighed.

"It's me, Toby. *I'm* the birth father. That's why she called me. That's why I'm here."

I could only stare at my brother. After a minute he couldn't meet my eyes any longer and looked down.

"I'm sorry. This is. . . needless to say. . . embarrassing."

I could think of a lot more words that came to mind than embarrassing.

"Remember when dad transferred me down to St. Francis in my sophomore year?" he asked. "The quest for the great scholarship?"

I did. St. Francis was San Diego's powerhouse sports school in those days. Suddenly, I remembered Melanie's mom talking about Melanie and her friends from her Catholic school. So they'd been there together. And they were both two years older than me, so they would have been seniors at the same time.

"I'm not proud of the way I handled myself back then," he said. "Lots of girls. Melanie was just one more. And when she told me she was pregnant, all I saw was losing my scholarship. Maybe even going to jail. I was only a few months older than her, but she was still seventeen. Back then they took that stuff more seriously."

"So when did you find out about the adoption?"

"What do you mean? I knew the whole time."

"You mean—"

"I met the adoptive parents, and even met Melanie's mom. They kind of had me at their mercy. I was willing to do whatever they wanted, just to keep it quiet."

Now I knew why Melanie's mother was so angry when she met me. She assumed I knew the birth father was my brother. *He* was the rich and powerful person she railed about, the son of a wealthy lawyer. And when she said *your family has done enough*, she wasn't referring to my father and his lawsuit against her company, but my brother. She'd practically told me and I'd been blind to it.

"You met Nevin and Catherine? And they knew who you were? Your name and everything?"

"Yeah, I can't believe they didn't tell you."

Suddenly, I could.

They knew if they came to me and told me up front my brother was the birth father, I'd say the case would be a conflict of interest for me and decline it, no matter how much I wanted to help Lynn. So they'd let me stumble across it, likely when Melanie herself would tell me and it would be too late for me to back away. Now I could see why they wanted me. No doubt they were worried how Brent would react sixteen years later, an established attorney, dealing with an underaged pregnancy and adoption. Where Brent may have stonewalled some stranger, they assumed his own brother could approach him, be nonthreatening about it and find a way to make everything work.

"But why the sham adoption, Brent? Even sixteen years ago the age difference would have been no big thing."

"Toby, I was a senior in high school. Alright? What did I know? I never asked anyone to keep my name out of it. I just assumed since we weren't married they didn't need to have me sign anything. To be honest, back then I was just glad to see the whole thing go away. The first I knew it wasn't done right was when Melanie called me a few days ago. That's when I called you."

I told Brent about Nevin and Catherine telling me how they used their insurance for Melanie, something which they never would have gotten away with in the scrutiny of a real adoption.

"I don't know anything about all that," he said. "I do remember meeting them in their office. It was a dumpy little place back then, so I think they were being straight with you about not having any money. I wouldn't be surprised if dad had something to do with it though."

"You mean *dad* knows?"

"No. What I mean is that he was getting a lot of press even back then as a real aggressive attorney. Squash anyone in his way, and make them look bad in the press. I wonder if they thought if they did the adoption the right way, through the courts, that he'd find out and object or something, since it was his grandchild."

Even without trying, my father, making waves.

"Are you going to tell him? I asked.

"Dad? Are you kidding?"

We laughed, both of us teenagers again for a brief moment, fearing the wrath of our father. I was immune to it, but to my brothers he was not just dad, but the boss.

As much as I believed in kids knowing their extended birth families, I don't know that I'd want to throw my dad at Lynn. Not now anyway. Suddenly it hit me. This meant Lynn and I were related.

She was my niece.

No wonder she was such an ace on the court. My brother had been one of the county's top athletes in his youth. And maybe those matching strokes I shared with Lynn weren't just the lessons. Maybe there was a genetic thing going on too. People had often asked us if we were brother and sister. I'd attributed the question to just hanging around together on the courts, but maybe others had seen a similarity not apparent to us.

It had also seemed odd when I called Brent's secretary that she had me spell Dubravado. That'd be a normal question, but not if Melanie were one of their clients. Secretaries know how to spell their own clients' names. But Brent hadn't really been hired. There was no case at the office. He just got a call from a former flame. She called him as the birth father, not as an attorney, to let him know what was going on. No wonder he didn't know anything about adoption law. He'd come to see me as a birth father, but hid his status behind his lawyer front.

And now I understood why he'd asked several times which court would hear the adoption, and if the judge would see the document naming the birth father. He'd been worried if one of the judges he knew would be seeing his name appear in a way he'd like to avoid.

Brent and I never made it back to the courts to play. Instead we spent hours talking about Lynn. He insisted on seeing the pictures I had from some of the summer tennis camps she'd attended while growing up. He held each picture tenderly as she aged a year at a time, within seconds, before his eyes.

He was both excited and nervous about meeting her, but he knew it was Catherine's call first, then Lynn's. I told him I'd let Catherine know soon that I finally knew what she'd known all along, and that he'd cooperate. First though, she had a funeral to get through, and more grieving, but the time would come soon enough. I also had the good news for her that Melanie would be starting the consent process. We weren't done yet, but everything was finally in place to finish the job I was asked to do. I'd have to tell Catherine that Melanie denied sending the notes, though. I don't know what she'd make of that. I know I didn't.

I walked Brent outside and he led me to a new Lincoln Town Car.

"Nice car," I said. "But I thought you had to be over sixty to buy one."

"Shut up, wise ass."

But he was grinning. It was a good night for him. A secret no longer. The promise of a wonderful girl in his life. The chance to be one of many to nurture her, everyone with their unique gifts to offer, and send her through life the better for it. Of course, no one would benefit as much as him. The giving is always better.

33

SATURDAY BROKE CLEAR and beautiful. There were no clinics on weekends so my time was my own. Nevin's service was at eleven so I put on my blue sport coat then played *eenie, meenie, minee, moe* with my selection of slacks. I treated myself to breakfast at the club restaurant. Eggs I could manage at home, but I was in the mood for some hash browns and that was beyond my culinary skills.

The service was at Fallbrook Presbyterian, one of our town's largest churches. A forty foot stained glass Jesus stared down at me and the other three hundred attendees. It was my regular church, when I had the good graces to go. I believe in the Ten Commandments and that they give us the footprints to follow in life, but I'll admit to missing church when there happened to be a good football game on TV. Or baseball. Or basketball. At least no one could question my dedication. To sports anyway.

Despite its cavernous size, the church was packed. Nevin's

role as politician and business leader assured that. His murder was still news and a camera crew and some press photographers were there, at least being tasteful enough to shoot from across the street. Or maybe good taste had nothing to do with it and the church had barred them from the premises. Nevin was hailed as a wonderful civic leader, husband and father. I wondered when he'd lost his way.

There was a reception in the church's community hall after the service. I spoke briefly to Catherine and Lynn. For the first time it struck me they looked like mother and daughter. A lot of adopted kids and their parents look alike, either from learned mannerisms and expressions, or just others' wishful thinking. Still, they looked like they belonged together. If Nevin's death served a purpose, maybe this was it. To bring a mother and daughter together. It wasn't until I'd seen them sitting alone in the front pew that I remembered they had no other relatives. It was now just the two of them. Would they consider Lynn's bloodlines as part of their extended family? Or would they keep them at arm's length? If they were willing to accept it, I had the feeling there was a lot of love waiting for them.

I knew a few of the people present, but most were from downtown San Diego and were strangers to me. I recognized the mayor and several other county supervisors. The dirt hadn't come out yet about Nevin's business, so it was safe for them to show their faces. The one person I didn't expect to see was Melanie's mother. It had been a publicly announced service so she'd likely seen it in the newspaper, and also knew there'd be a large crowd so she wouldn't stand out. Of course, Catherine and Lynn had never set eyes on her, so she was safe from recognition. Still, she was hanging back, keeping a crowd between them. Was she there to look at Lynn, curious about her? Maybe trying to fill the void of an absent daughter and off-limits granddaughter? I made my way through the congested room to speak to her, but she saw me coming and eased toward the door. Rather than push my way through I just watched her leave.

After a few minutes I was ready to go myself and was just leaving the church's courtyard when Pastor Rick hollered from the narthex, on his way to the reception I'd just left. We were a pretty casual church and everyone called him by his first name.

"Hey, Toby. Not seeing you around here much lately."

"What do you mean? I'm here every week."

"Tuesday night basketball doesn't count. I mean church."

We had a weekly basketball game with the other local churches, and Rick had a pretty sweet jump shot from inside twenty feet. It was casual and co-ed, although I once heard the Mormons' power forward, big on brawn and short of smarts, term it *bisexual*. The Mormons were the powerhouse of the church league and rarely lost a game. We tended to play about even with the Catholics but beat up on the Baptists—great choir, but no defense.

"I'll try, Rick," I said lamely. "Hey, can I ask you a quick question?"

"Are we talking basketball or God?"

"God, as in an *everlasting soul* kind of question."

"Sure."

I hadn't planned on asking this, but my mind had been filled with the thought. I was guessing Rita's was too.

"I was just wondering. . . If someone kills a person, is that always a mortal sin?"

"That's a *quick* question?" He laughed. "I hope it's a hypothetical one."

I nodded. "Just give it your best shot, without a lot of scripture verses thrown in. The straight scoop."

"Worried about someone's soul, Toby?"

That was exactly what I was worried about, but I kept it to myself. I just shrugged.

"Okay, then," he said. "Well. . . it would not be considered murder in the eyes of God if it was in self-defense. To save your own life, or someone else's. Is that basic enough?"

"That much I can figure out. But what if it's not so clear? What if someone didn't have to do it that moment, but if they didn't, that person would harm other people? Kids. I mean *real* harm. They'd done it before and they'd do it again."

Rick let out a nervous chuckle.

"You're not planning to do someone in, are you? You're our only point guard, you know. Even the Baptists will take us if you're not there."

"No, no killings planned in my future. Just curious."

Rick looked skyward, evidently for guidance.

"Well, I guess I'd have to advise this person to pray."

"Pray?"

He grinned. "That's where the answers are."

"You're a big help," I said dryly.

"Okay, then I'll say this. Taking the law into your own hands is not the way to go. Follow Caesar's law and all that. But. . . God forgives *all* sin. Even murder. They just have to ask. God knows a pure heart when He sees one. Is that short and simple enough for you?"

"Like a fortune cookie, Rick. Thanks."

I may shoot hoops in God's house once a week, but I still had a fuzzy picture of heaven and hell. I just knew that I preferred the former. I thought of the old joke—if you got to heaven, great, but if you went to hell, at least all your friends would be there.

I'd just taken my first few steps into the parking lot when I saw it. The black Suburban. It was a good seventy yards away, in the most distant part of the church parking lot, right next to the road. As I started to walk toward it, I could see the whip antenna, the tinted windows. Had to be the same car. This time I'd get a plate number. I was still fifty yards away when its engine suddenly roared to life and the car shot forward, the sound of burned rubber hitting me a second before the smell. I knew that even if I broke into a run I couldn't get close enough to see the license plate before he turned onto the road. Had he been in the car the entire time, waiting to follow Lynn? Or had he been at the service, hidden in plain sight, one of hundreds. I'd told myself it was time to tell Hawkes about it and see if he had any ideas. Whoever it was had done nothing illegal yet, but why wait and give him the chance?

Instead of going home I headed out to the boat. I'd brought along a bag of work clothes and was ready for a day of labor. On my way I called my office answering machine and entered the code for messages. There were two, both good ones. Aaron had called; Amanda had been discharged and they were home with the baby. They named him Andy, and based upon their completely impartial observations of his lively eye and body movement, he and Charlotte were already convinced he was the smartest and most athletic child ever born. Parents.

The second was from Sherry Rosman, the Adoption Services Provider. She reported she'd had her first meeting with Melanie this morning and would be returning in ten days to witness the consent. She asked me to call her back and I didn't waste any time.

We exchanged a few pleasantries and got down to the subject of Melanie.

"So what's up with Melanie?" I asked. " Is everything okay?"

There had been a hint of worry in Sherry's tone of voice in the message.

"Yes and no, Toby. She's a very fragile person. I mean, I knew the history of the case from you so I was anticipating some buried emotions after so long, but she's so. . ."

"She's so, what?"

"Oh, I don't know. . . I guess the word I want to use is *damaged*. She's just made so many bad choices in life. There were some drugs in there when she was in college, and she fell into the wrong crowd. And the men she chose. Every one of them. . . not exactly using her, but. . . not coming through for her."

My brother being one. True, he was a kid himself, but he was part of it nonetheless. Followed by Nevin and Catherine's own manipulation, and a downward spiral since then. Who do you blame when that happens to a life? Or is blame even the right word?

"So," Sherry went on, "what she basically did was just drop out of society. But she's found a path back, and it's working for her. So she's not *un*happy now. . . she just can't face taking new chances yet."

"What are you saying? What does that mean for the adoption?"

"What it means is that she wants everything to go smoothly. She's committed to doing everything we need her to. So there should be no problem getting everything approved. She just can't face meeting Lynn or Catherine right now. Maybe someday, but not now."

It was a start. More than a start.

"Is that place she's at legit?" I asked. "They're not taking advantage of her or anything?"

"Actually, no." Sherry's tone brightened. "I was prepared for just the opposite. When I hear of a commune lately I think of some religious zealot pushing desperate people down some path no sane person would follow, you know? But this place is very nurturing. Anyone living there can invite guests in and I spent a few hours there. I didn't see any secrecy or hidden agenda. It reminds me of what communes were like when I was a little girl in Israel. They grow their own food, they build the houses they live in. Kind of southern California Amish."

"Well, just so she's doing okay."

"She is. Don't worry. This is going to work out. Just give it time."

In my simplistic view of life, I'd imagined myself getting Melanie and Lynn together and healing the wrongs of the past sixteen years, making them both whole again. Both had mothers who loved them, but the saying that "It takes a village to raise a child" was a true one, especially when it includes blood relatives. So Lynn had her village, and not only she, but the people in it— Melanie and her mom, Brent, Catherine, even me—would benefit.

Sherry promised to offer Melanie all the counseling she needed and would keep me up to date. We said goodbye just as I got to my grandfather's place. I changed into some work clothes, made a pitcher of iced tea, ready for needed refreshment after the pleasure of some good honest sweat.

Grandpa's grove was so large, more than two thousand trees, that I couldn't take care of it all myself. I had a grove manager keep the trees trimmed, the sprinklers working and the fruit picked. He got twenty percent of the crop for his work. That still left plenty of work for me. Besides the boat, there were shrubs to prune, weeds to pull, fences to repair.

I had two jobs for myself today. The first was to finish varnishing the wall in the salon. It would be nearly the last step in the renovation. While it was drying, I'd go outside and prune the bougainvilleas. They were abundant in Fallbrook, their vibrant red, orange and purple bracts erupting everywhere, even sprouting wild on hillsides. I'd planted a few at the base of the boat so their vines could snake up the stark whiteness of the hull. They were getting a bit too vigorous, though, and if I didn't trim them, in time they'd take over the boat. As beautiful as they were, it was a hated job to trim them. Their branches were covered with thorns, some of them a couple of inches long and sharper than any surgical instrument.

As usual, no matter how careful I was, I ended up with several scratches on my arms. I dragged the branches into a huge pile behind the boat. Later I'd bag them.

I worked until darkness fell then decided to spend the night on the boat. Tomorrow was Sunday and I could sleep in. After a hot shower, I gratefully fell into bed at just eight-thirty. I was out the minute my body hit the bed. It was still dark when the knife woke me up.

34

WHAT LITTLE LIGHT there was came from a slice of the night light through a crack in the door to the head. I could see the shape of a man above me. Arms twice as thick as mine. One of his hands had roughly grabbed my hair to hold my head in place, and the other held a knife under my chin. I could feel a small river of blood dripping down my neck, my skin straining, and failing, to keep the blade out. I couldn't talk for fear of pushing it straight into my throat.

I said nothing. I didn't even think about moving. At his whim, I knew I was dead.

"Recognize this?" he asked.

He kept the knife pushed into my throat, but angled its hilt toward my face. I saw a jeweled handle, its stones catching the tiny shaft of light. My eyes told him: Yes, I recognized it. And by now I recognized his shape and voice. Muscle Man. He'd have known that Toscano had a letter opener and that it was missing.

Unlike the cops, he was able to spot it for what it really was in the aquarium.

"Pretty smart, tossing it in the water, you or your movie star bitch."

He dragged the knife from under my chin to the side of my neck, as if he were slitting my throat, but just hard enough to scratch me without causing me to bleed out.

"So where is she?" He licked his lips. "Her and the babies."

So he was the guy who'd been here. Toscano's white slave hunter. He moved the knife so I could speak without lowering my jaw into the knife and impaling myself.

"I did it," I said. "I killed Toscano. Forget about her."

"Oh, big man, taking the fall." He laughed. "Who cares who did it. I just know they're going to find the knife with you. *In* you, actually. That should confuse the cops. And if it doesn't, at least I still had some fun."

I tried to think of something, anything, to reason with him, to delay the inevitable. Like how maybe it would be better for him to kill me a week from Thursday instead. Or even better, next month. The worst part of dying would be to know I was no longer here to protect Rita and the girls, and that they were his next stop. Despite the fact four people's survival depended on it, my brain wouldn't cooperate.

Then finally, something: money and greed. It was the language of people like Muscle Man. I had neither, but he didn't know that. There was nothing else I could have that he'd want.

"Please," I said, trying my best to turn it into an unmanly whimper, which wasn't too hard. "Don't kill me. If you let me go, I'll give you money. I've got cash. Lots of it, here on the boat. Money I can't put in the bank."

I thought the last was a nice touch. He probably assumed eve-

ryone was like him and the Toscanos of the world, with unre-
ported income to hide. Well, I *was* a lawyer, so maybe no big
stretch there after all. There was no doubt he was going to kill
me, but maybe he'd consider delaying it.

His eyes narrowed, maybe seeing it for the ploy it was.

"How much?"

"Twenty grand, maybe a little more. Some of my clients pay
me in cash. Can't put it in the bank."

Actually, if I added up all the money in my wallet, my change
jar, and any nickels which may have fallen under the bed, I could
probably scrape up eight dollars.

"Where?"

"In a hidden compartment in the main room. You'll never find
it unless I show it to you. There's little hidden areas all over the
boat."

I could see him thinking about it. Good. What followed
wasn't.

Without warning he took the knife from my neck and raised it
high above me then viciously stabbed it down into my thigh. I felt
the hilt of the handle strike my flesh, the entire seven-inch blade
in and through my leg. Strangely, it hurt less than I'd have
thought. Adrenaline, maybe. Or terror. Then the pain hit me.
When the scream left my mouth he didn't bother to stifle it. Like
in those slasher movies, where a dozen teenagers in a remote
cabin are hacked to pieces by some guy in a hockey mask, there
was no one to hear me.

I looked down at my leg. At least the blade must have missed
anything critical. I didn't see an artery squirting blood into the air.
Just as quickly, the knife was back at my throat.

"Just to keep you from getting any ideas," he said.

He pulled me up by the hair and marched me ahead of him.

The knife never left my throat as he pushed me up the stairway.

"Show me where," he said.

I was hoping this guy had never read Briar Rabbit. Since he seemed to lack any evidence of maternal nurturing, I was guessing it was a safe bet.

"You'd better let me get it out." I said it like I had a gun stashed and was using this as a trick to reach in and get it.

"No chance," he said. "Where? Or do you want one in the other leg?"

I tried to make a show of *damn, plan foiled.* I wasn't thinking Oscar, but he was swallowing it so far.

I sighed, a show of defeat. Not hard to fake.

"Right there, built into the wall behind the stairs going up. Just push it in on the right side."

He pushed me to the floor and took the few steps needed. He kept his eyes on me, his fingers reaching back to feel for the slight crack in the wood. He found it and the door sprung open. My hope was that he'd reach into the dark cavity and his fingers would spring the trap. In that moment of distraction, I'd need to find a weapon and use it. Running from the boat wouldn't help me. My leg wouldn't let me outrun anyone. The only possible weapon I could see was the antique fire extinguisher on the wall. Its steel canister would make a nice club. In my mind I choreographed the two steps to reach it, pull the strap that secured it to the wall with my left hand, and grab it with my right as it fell free. Then. . . swing like Babe Ruth.

He kept his eyes glued to me, his knife hand at the ready to strike again if I moved. With his other hand he reached blindly into the cavity. I was timing it, waiting for his arm to descend all the way in and reach the trap on the floor. But then, too soon, everything went crazy. Before his hand was barely through the opening, he jerked it out like a bolt of electricity had just run through his body, and yelled with a primal terror.

Clawing and biting its way up his arm was a rat. No, it was an opossum. It was huge, and attached to its two foot tail was the rat trap. Its eyes glowed with red anger. At least, the little I could see of it as it moved on Muscle Man like a demon. His tail must have sprung the trap, and he couldn't escape with the bulky wood base attached to him. So he'd been sitting there, one mad, mad dude.

The opossum was clawing its way up Muscle Man's body toward his face, leaving red slashes from claws and teeth. Like they do in the wild, he was going for the eyes of his enemy. The two were a dervish of motion, a rabid rodent terrifying the human killer more than any human could. He was trying to stab at the opossum but the animal moved like lightning. Muscle Man banged himself against the walls to rid himself of it, and finally ran out the door of the salon and jumped off the deck.

And right into the pile of bougainvillea.

The opossum smelled freedom and lit for the trees, with the trap bouncing from his tail behind him. Muscle Man wasn't moving. He gave a groan, then was still on his bed of nails. I'd seen too many movies where the bad guy was finally beaten, and everyone relaxes, only to have him rise up again—usually after being supposedly drowned in a bathtub. So I grabbed the fire extinguisher and hobbled down the steps to where he lay face down, unmoving. I raised the extinguisher above my head and gave him a good thunk on the head. Not a truly vicious one, just a go-to-sleep-for-awhile-asshole one. His back was rising and falling with shallow breaths, but I was fairly sure he wasn't going anywhere.

The knife was still in his hand. I pulled it from his fingers and grabbed a handful of dirt, rubbing it over the handle, removing any slight trace of Rita that could remain. Then I threw it out of his reach into yet more dirt. Surely the police would understand my not wanting to leave my attacker with a weapon.

The adrenaline my survival instincts had kicked in was gone and I could feel my leg give way beneath me. The boat seemed to blur, but I managed to find the stairs. On my knees I climbed them, my brain not processing the red marks left behind on the white steps. I got to the phone and couldn't remember if I was supposed to dial 411 or 911. The key pad was fuzzy and I'm not sure which one I dialed, but someone was talking to me. Usually in these emergencies the cops say "Officer down! Officer down!" So I thought it'd be hilarious to say "Attorney down! Attorney down!" So I did. I was still saying it when the cops got there and gently took the phone from my hand. I heard the words "He's in shock."

Then there was nothing.

35

AS AN ADOPTION attorney, I'd visited every hospital in San Diego County, so when I woke up I knew the two-tone light green and white walls meant I was at North County Regional. I was alone except for some flower arrangements.

It took me awhile to find the buzzer next to the bed, but once I found it I just held it in my hand. It was just nice to think about the fact I was alive. I looked down and saw two legs outlined under the blanket. That meant I could still play tennis and take walks with Rita and the kids. Anything else was gravy.

When I finally pushed the buzzer it only took half a minute for a nurse to come in. She was Korean, smiling and smelling of Pine Sol.

"Well, looks like our patient is awake."

"That I am. What day is it?"

Such a cliché question, but it really is one of the first things you think about when you've been out.

"Monday," she said. "They brought you in late Saturday night. You slept all day yesterday."

There was a clock on the wall, so I could see it was almost two o'clock. Sunshine through the window told me it was daytime.

"So, how am I doing?"

"I'll leave that to the doctor to discuss, but I think I can let it slip that you'll live. Let me tell her you're awake."

Evidently I fell asleep again because when I woke up the doctor was standing next to the bed. The clock said it was just shy of three. Had I just lost an hour, or another day?

"Please tell me it's still Monday," I said.

She smiled. "Yes, still Monday."

She bent over the bed and raised my eyelids, peered into my eyes with a penlight, then poked and prodded here and there. Finally, she took my blood pressure, then took a seat.

"You a runner?" she asked.

"No, lots of tennis though. Why?"

"The only thing abnormal is your heartbeat. It's a resting forty-eight. But that's normal if you do a ton of cardio."

Good to know at least one part of my body was healthy.

I reached up to scratch my neck and was surprised to find it all covered with bandages. I hadn't felt any. She saw the question in my eyes.

"You're still numbed up. You were pretty cut up. One even took a few stitches. They'll all heal though."

"What about my leg?"

"Let me tell you, you were one lucky guy there."

That's just what I was thinking when he stuck the knife through my leg. Lucky, lucky guy.

"How's that?" I asked.

"The knife blade was extremely narrow, so there was much less trauma than there could have been. It missed the femoral artery, as well as the bundle of nerves that runs down your leg."

"So my leg's going to be okay?"

Not much market for hobbling tennis pros. God save me if I had to practice law all day.

"Other than taking it easy for awhile and rehabbing it, I'd say you'll be one hundred percent in about six weeks.

"Will I be able to play the piano?"

"Of course," she said.

"That's funny, I couldn't play it before."

She looked at me strangely.

"Sorry," I said. "Old joke."

Damn that Gil. Now he had me doing it.

Perhaps afraid of another joke, the doctor moved to leave. She turned back to me at the door.

"There's been a police detective who's stopped by a few times and asked us to call him when you woke up."

"Hawkes?"

"Yes, I believe that was his name. I'll have the nurse call him."

"Has Rita. . . has anyone else been here?"

I'd been out for thirty plus hours. It was just a three hour drive from Big Bear.

"There was someone from your family. Your brother, I believe. But I've been on for only the last six hours, someone may have come by before then."

I nodded like it didn't matter. The nurse came back and brought me some food. I had nothing else to do so dragged the meal out as long as I could. I was still scraping the last of the chocolate pudding from the container when Hawkes came in. At first he just stood by the door and shook his head, a *whatta we gonna do with you* gesture.

"Having fun yet?" he asked.

He pulled up a chair and sat down.

"You got the guy, right?" I asked. When I'd last seen Muscle Man, he'd been unconscious. But then, soon after so was I.

"You first," he said. "You passed out before anyone could take a statement. Lost a lot of blood from what I heard. Give it to me from the start."

So that's what I did, leaving out only what I had to.

Hawkes confirmed Muscle Man was in custody, found lying unconscious in the bougainvillea where I left him. After his arrest he'd lawyered-up, refusing even to say anything about his injuries, so when I got to the part about the opossum, Hawkes almost had a seizure he was having so much fun.

"I love it," he said. "Capture by opossum."

I had a pleasant thought, imagining Muscle Man going through the rabies treatment. Daily anti-rabies injections in the stomach for six weeks.

"We hit the gold mine with that guy," Hawkes said. "Tony Simone is his name. You're not going to believe this, but one of Toscano's operations was selling *people*. Kids. You can guess for what."

I let shock show on my face. Letting on what Rita and I knew would only make us suspects, a motive to murder. He went on and described the trade of human trafficking.

"But I thought you said he wouldn't talk," I asked.

"He didn't. The moron kept records of every child he acquired for Toscano. Can you believe it? Looks like we can track where all those kids went. We've already got the Department of State involved. Some of those kids are on the other side of the world. This is big stuff, Toby. Big."

He was excited the way only a cop could be. Catching bad guys. Rescuing kids in danger. He wasn't in it for the headlines and promotions, but he'd be getting both.

"So, you think he'll talk now? Maybe looking for a deal?" What I really wanted to know was if he had said where he found the letter opener, maybe pointing suspicion at Rita.

"No way. Toscano's dead. There's no one higher for him to give up. Besides, he was in it up to his eyeballs. He'd target the kids. Take them. Deliver them. All of it. There's no deal he can make."

I nodded. "I hope one of your guys takes a rubber hose to him and beats the name of every scumbag he worked with out of him."

He gave me a look like, *don't worry, we know how to do it and not leave any marks.* As far as I was concerned, steal children and turn them over to predators, and you lose any rights. The Constitution should not exist for them. They should get the trap door straight to hell. And if their hell starts on earth, all the better.

Hawkes wasn't done. "It looks like we can make him for the Nevin Handley killing too. There were no prints, but we found a hair in his gym. Before, there was no one to try to match it to. But Simone's a perfect match."

I might be pushing my luck by asking, but it's not like the murder was going to go away if I pretended it didn't exist. "What about Toscano?" I asked. "Anything new there?"

"I haven't heard back from the tech guys, to confirm the comparison to the entry wound, but it's looking like the knife Simone used on you was the same weapon used to kill Toscano. A servant from the house already IDed it as Toscano's letter opener."

"I don't understand. What does that mean?"

"We're just guessing, but we know Simone was upstairs with Toscano until after you left, but was gone when Rita came up a few minutes later and found him dead. I'm thinking Simone did it, using the panic at the pool as a distraction. Then he stashed the weapon somewhere on the grounds. Probably figured with a couple hundred possible suspects in the house no one would suspect him, the bodyguard. I'm just guessing, but maybe he wanted to run the operation for himself, not for Toscano."

I nodded, thinking "keep believing that." Suddenly I was surprisingly tired. Maybe not surprisingly. Hawkes must have seen it on my face because he stood up. He seemed to have something he didn't particularly want to say. Finally, he did.

"Ah. . . I called Rita."

So she knew I was here.

"Yeah?"

He nodded. "She'll be here tomorrow."

Tomorrow. Three days from when I got here.

"When did you call her?"

He hesitated.

"Um, Saturday night. When we found you." He hurried to add, "But I told her you weren't in any danger, just needed to rest up a bit here. I assumed you wouldn't want her to worry."

"Oh yeah, yeah, you're right," I said. "No need for her to rush down."

"Yeah," he said, a worse liar than me.

I don't recall falling asleep but when I woke up Hawkes was gone. I was refreshed enough for what ended up being a string of visitors: Lynn and Catherine, Brent, a few tennis pals, even my mom and dad. Pastor Rick came by too, asking how I knew I was going to get attacked, evidently referring to my hypothetical question about defending myself against a murderous slimeball.

He left me with a wink and said, "I'm glad you didn't have to kill him after all." He also offered me his forgiveness. . . for leaving the team in the lurch for six weeks.

I just wanted the day to end, because tomorrow would bring Rita.

36

RITA CAME AT two-thirty the next afternoon. It's a long time when you're clock watching. Earlier in the day Hawkes had called to say Muscle Man was no more. A jailhouse fight and a shiv to the heart. Clearly it was an ordered hit, camouflaged as a jail brawl. You don't get caught with information putting your cohorts at risk, and Muscle Man had done that. Hawkes said he'd be by later and give me more details when he got them.

Rita was more beautiful than I'd ever seen her. The mountains and rest had been good to her. Some of her tension was washed away and she looked. . . resolute. Like she was seeking closure of an issue and had found it. I was glad for her. For us. We deserved a fresh start.

I told her about Hawkes' visit yesterday and call this morning. She'd heard about everything but Muscle Man's death earlier today.

"So it's over," I told her. "Toscano, all of it. They'll never know you killed him."

She just looked at me, something I couldn't identify filling her eyes.

"Toby, I didn't kill him."

"Exactly." I nodded my approval. No one would ever suspect it now.

"No, I'm telling you, *I didn't kill him.*"

I didn't know what to say. Was she in denial? The door to my room was closed. No one could hear from outside. Why was she doing this?

"But. . ."

"Toby, I tried to tell you when we drove home that night. I told you that you were right not to have killed him. That it wasn't the right way. I just asked for you to believe that I did the right thing, too. But you didn't. I kept waiting, but you didn't."

I thought back to the anger in her eyes that night. I'd assumed it had been for my *not* acting against Toscano, but it had been for believing that she *had.* For thinking she'd done what I refused to do. Hawkes had been right. It had been Muscle Man all along.

This was fantastic! I felt a giant weight come off my shoulders. I hadn't been able to admit how distressed I was that Rita had killed Toscano, but now that I was free of it, I could feel how I'd labored under the burden. Now there would be no shadow of a murder following us, tainting our lives. So why wasn't Rita smiling?

"Rita, I'm sorry. It's just. . . you had the knife, and you threw it in the aquarium—"

"I found the knife on the desk, Toby! I knew you'd just been up there. At first, I thought *you* did it. I admit it—I thought that, at least in that split second. Forgive me, but that's what I thought. So I picked it up, right before you came in. That's why I threw the knife in the aquarium. For you."

I struggled to keep up with my emotions. I thought I'd been protecting her, but it had been her trying to protect me. And I'd rewarded her by calling her a murderer. What I had thought was my alibi for Rita was actually close to the truth. She must have been just ahead of me after all, just far enough not to see her.

"Why didn't you say something?" I asked softly.

Her eyes had the same look as the night I'd asked her why she'd killed him.

"I shouldn't have had to, Toby. I shouldn't have had to. He was practically lying down. How could you believe I could do that? Stab a man in the heart? Take a knife and end his life." Her voice started to choke up. *"What do you think I am?"*

She started to cry, her tears a heartfelt accusation. I didn't kill him, despite what he was, and the threat he posed to Remy and Emma, because I'd known it was wrong. Yet I assumed she did it. And kept assuming, never even thinking to ask.

But this was just a little misunderstanding, right? Then why did I feel my life depended on what I said in the next few minutes. Rita's body seemed to get smaller and smaller before me, as if she were being pulled away. I put my hand on hers. The hand that had pulled her up into our treehouse when we were six. The hand that had held hers when we ran with abandon through the Fun Zone at the San Diego County Fair the first time our parents said we were old enough to go on our own. The hand that had held hers when the news came that her father died. And when Brogan was taken from us. The hand that touched her with more love than I'd ever thought it possible for me to give.

I willed my mind to say the words she needed to hear, if only I knew what they were. I'd beg for forgiveness. I'd do anything. But before I could say anything she stood up and pulled her hand from mine.

"Rita, please wait. I—"

But she shook her head.

"It's not just that, Toby. It's all this. . . violence. Last year it was the kidnapping. And Brogan was killed. . . now people attacking you. . . threatening Remy and Emma, and trying to kill you. I just can't. . ." Her head dropped and I could barely hear her. "I just can't live this way. . . And I can't let the girls live this way."

She stood up and backed toward the door, her eyes on me. I couldn't form words, and my mind only registered how salty my tears tasted.

"I love you, Toby," she said. "But I can't be with you. Can you forgive me?" Now she was openly sobbing. "Please."

All I could do was nod, granting her wish, her desire to leave me, and letting her do it with as little guilt and remorse as possible.

She came back to the bed and bent down and kissed me, sweetly on the lips, like a caress.

Then she walked out of my life.

37

HAWKES CHOSE THAT MOMENT to arrive. Rita walked past him without a word, and he took in our two broken bodies, one departing and one remaining. He stood wordlessly at the door, not sure if he should silently leave or come in. After a moment's decision he came in and took the chair Rita had just abandoned. He turned it so he wasn't facing me directly, offering me company and support when I was ready, but without the intrusion of eye contact. He seemed to intuitively know what had happened. Not that he needed more clues when Rita took days to even come to see me.

Finally, he spoke. "When my wife left me it was because of the job. The violence. The fear of it touching me. Our family. Not everyone can take it."

I knew he was trying to help, but the words fell hollow between us. Suddenly I wanted my picture of Rita and Remy and Emma in my hands. There was one in my wallet.

"Can you get my wallet for me?" I pointed to the small desk/dresser unit against the wall. "It's probably in there."

Hawkes got up and walked over.

"Which drawer?"

Everything tilted for a minute and I clutched the bed with both hands to steady myself. Suddenly I was back in Toscano's office, his desk in front of me.

"What?" I managed.

"I said, which drawer?"

I didn't know and shrugged to tell him so. He found my wallet in the second drawer.

"Got it."

"I just want the picture that's in there. Can you take it out for me?"

He did, and suddenly the room tilted again.

"Thanks," I managed.

"No problem."

I stared at the picture in my lap as Hawkes waited patiently to help. Just doing what friends do.

"How did you know what part of the desk?" I asked.

"What are you talking about?" He looked over to the desk. "You told me."

"No, Toscano's desk. . . when you pointed out to the technician where to find Rita's fingerprints, to eliminate her as a suspect."

He looked at me patiently. "You told me, Toby, on the corner, when she started to faint. Don't you remember?"

I did remember, exactly.

"Yeah, but how did you know which corner? A desk has four corners, and that desk was as big as an aircraft carrier. How'd you know which corner? Even if you eliminated the back half of the desk, since we were standing in front, that leaves two. And there was nothing on the desk but a phone in the middle. There's no way you could have known."

He sat patiently and I went on.

"Maybe you knew because you saw her put her hand down to pick up the picture. You saw it because you were already there. In one of the closets. With the louvered doors you'd be able to see out. You saw where she threw the letter opener too. You saw everything."

I looked down at Rita and the girls' picture and thought of Hawkes' hands on it just now, giving it to me.

"And when you came in when I was being searched. You'd seen me pick the picture up off the desk and put it in my pocket. I bet you touched it before you killed him. You heard Rita coming up the stairs, just like we heard Toscano's men. You had just enough time to hide. But your prints were still on the picture. You didn't know if the other cops would see it as evidence and take fingerprints off it—yours—and you needed an explanation why they were there. So you had to handle it again."

And more was coming back to me. "That's why it took you so long to show up. You were trapped in the closet. You had to wait until the room was filled with people and you had a chance to slip out unnoticed. That's why I didn't see you come in, and suddenly you were right next to me."

To his credit, Hawkes didn't say anything in denial. He glanced toward the door, making sure it was closed. What was he going to do that required no intruding eyes or ears? He stood up and towered above me, then reached out and picked up Rita and the girls' picture. I knew I was at his mercy. But he just sat back down with it, and when he spoke his voice was soft.

"You've got it about right, Toby. I thought I'd shake him up a little bit. Catch him alone and see what would happen. Saw an opening with the distraction at the pool. I thought, screw the politics. You never know what will happen with an angry cop in your face, one-on-one. And then I saw Remy and Emma's picture on his desk. I'd heard rumors about the pandering, and I knew there was only one reason why he'd have their picture. When I accused him of it, he just laughed and said it was a gift from you. Said it was proof of nothing, and he was right. Then he tells me to get lost, and tilts back like I'm not even there."

Just like he'd done with me.

"So I did what had to be done, Toby. If not Rita's girls, someone else's." He looked me in the eye. "I'm not ashamed of it and I'm not proud of it. It wasn't what I planned but it's what came down. I'm just sorry you guys walked in on it."

I didn't deserve an apology. He did what I didn't have the courage to do. I tried to understand how I felt. What a sacrifice he'd made for us, and for others, but as a cop, how wrong. Or was it all backwards and he did just what cops are supposed to: keep people safe and put down the bad guys. Were the rules valid if they kept someone like Toscano on the street?

"I'm sorry you suspected Rita," he said. "I tried to clear you both as soon as possible with Orcutt. In a way Rita saved my ass. If she hadn't tossed the knife in the water, they'd have found my prints on it."

He handed the picture back to me. "I'll tell Rita the truth if it'll help."

He meant it. He'd tell her and put his life in her hands, just as he'd done by admitting it to me. Maybe I shouldn't be surprised by the sacrifice. One reason he'd probably done this was because he felt responsible for Emma. If he hadn't helped solve her kidnapping as an infant, she'd still be gone. Was it true? Save someone's life and you are responsible for them forever?

"No," I said. "It wouldn't change anything. She's gone but. . . maybe she'll be back."

Hawkes nodded. He didn't ask me if I was going to tell anyone. He knew I wouldn't.

His secret was safe. Everyone's secrets were.

38

I CHECKED MYSELF out of the hospital ten minutes later. Actually, I didn't check out. I just left. Pulled out the IV, found my clothes, and walked out. The duty nurse didn't even look up from her desk to see me leaving.

It wasn't until I was outside that I realized I didn't have a car. I'd been taken here by ambulance. My cell phone was still charged, though. I thought of who to call to bring me home, then realized I didn't want to see anyone. I didn't want human contact. I called a taxi. Sitting alone in the backseat, it felt appropriate. Alone.

My Falcon was out at the boat, and I was less likely to see anyone there, so that's where I had the cab drop me off. I thought I'd find peace, but when I went aboard, all I could see were reminders of pain. The soft glow of the wood Rita and I had varnished together. The deck we'd made love on. The dried blood on the floor where I'd almost bled out.

Before I realized what I was doing, I was outside, walking down the picker's path through the grove. My pants felt sticky and I knew I'd popped my stitches. Fresh blood was quickly soaking through my pants leg. I didn't care. I deserved the pain.

I fell into one of the oversized Adirondack chairs that had been sitting in the grove since my grandfather and I would collapse into them after a hard day's labor. In homage to him I put on an annual coat of paint to keep them nice. They were under the tree my grandfather had nicknamed the Toby Tree, planted together when I was shorter than the baby tree. Even now, years after his death, it showed the result of his love, somehow surpassing every other tree in its size and production of fruit. Or maybe it was the magic tree he always joked it was.

When I opened my eyes, my grandfather was sitting next to me. He wasn't looking at me, just staring off into space. That was his way, slow and easy. He was dressed as always, tan khaki pants and a blue work shirt, his gardener's hat in his lap. It was how I remembered him from my early lifetime walking in his shadow, and it was how I saw him now.

Finally, he spoke.

"How ya doin' kiddo?"

"Not so good, grandpa. Not so good."

He'd always been there for me, in life and in death. There was a reason my feet led me here.

"You want to talk about it?" he asked. He was looking at me now but I couldn't meet his eyes.

"So," he said. "What hurts? Is it Rita? Or this Toscano thing?"

I could only shrug. I had no energy to speak. No desire to hear myself talk. I wasn't worthy of my grandfather's words. Besides, he knew the answer. Everything was Rita.

"Do you think I can get her back, Grandpa?"

He seemed to run the thought around in his head.

"Yeah, I'd guess you could. If you set your mind to it."

Suddenly he had all my attention.

He said, "I guess the question is, do you want to try?"

"Do I want to *try?* Of course I want to."

Then I thought of the look on her face when she said good-bye. Her pain so great. "I mean, don't I?"

He crossed his legs and absently twirled his hat on his knee.

"Love's a funny thing. What makes it work, what makes it right. The mystery of the world right there in that one word. I guess you need to decide if you want to convince her to love you."

Convince?

Is that what I'd be doing? And if I succeeded, what would I have?

"You mean, I should. . . let her go?"

"I can't decide that." He gave me a look. "Only you can."

"No," I said. "Actually, only she can."

And she already had.

Out of the corner of my eye I could see my grandpa nod. We sat in silence for awhile before he spoke again.

"And your friend, Hawkes. You okay with that?"

I didn't quite know the answer. Part of me still felt shame that I hadn't done what seemed to have been my duty. Then more shame that another man did what I failed to do, to protect the people I saw as my family. Yet as wrong as it would have been for me, I didn't blame Hawkes for doing it. The truth was, I felt he did the right thing, and was grateful for it. If he hadn't done it, lives would suffer. Innocent children. How can it be wrong for me and right for him?

"You and he, cut from the same cloth." Grandpa said.

That was a joke. I was the coward who'd left Toscano for him to deal with. Hawkes was a doer.

"How's that?" I asked.

His eyes drifted to the blood soaking through my pant leg, then the discoloration around my nose courtesy of Fistmaker.

"Seems like neither one of you cares for rules much, but you manage to do what's right. Sometimes rules and laws, courts and cops, lose sight of that. And you do it without any thought to yourself. You think any other lawyers would have gone to see someone like Zuley, knowing what could happen? But you did it, just to help someone else. And that's not the first time, or I'd guess the last time. It's just the way you are. Hawkes is a good man, but he took the easy way. You never take the easy way. You take the right way. And that takes the most courage of all."

His words washed over me. Strengthened me.

Grandpa stood up and held out a hand. "Time for you to get up."

But I didn't need a helping hand. Not any more.

"Thanks, grandpa, but I can do it myself."

He smiled. "Hmm. Why am I not surprised."

He walked with me under the canopy of shade, the lowest branches of the avocado trees a few feet over our heads.

"So," he asked. "Going to call Rita?"

I thought about it for a second, but I already knew the answer.

"No. I love her. I always will. Maybe one day she'll feel the same. Like before."

"And if she doesn't? You okay with that?"

I looked up to the boat, to the deck where she and I had made love in the rain. The night of my life. The woman I'd waited a lifetime for. Was it better to have loved and lost or. . .

"Yeah, I am. As long as she finds happiness. If she doesn't, she knows where I am, and I'll be waiting."

He'd been walking next to me and when he didn't answer I turned to him. I was just in time to see him fading away in the splashes of sunlight reaching the edge of the grove.

I could just see the last flash of a smile and could swear I heard him speak one last time.

"And I'll be here, waiting for you."

39

THEY SAID SIX weeks to get the leg back to normal, but because I'm stubborn and male, I was back on the court in five. After a couple of days my timing was back. My wind would take a bit longer, but I was almost whole. Physically, anyway.

As expected, the government came after Nevin's estate, built in large part on illicit income. Catherine hired the best at that kind of thing—my father—and for once I was glad to see his connections and manipulations benefit someone. If he'd have known Lynn was his biological granddaughter, he'd have probably offered a five percent discount, but that information was staying private.

Catherine had to give up the house and all assets. They agreed not to touch the funds Nevin had put in Lynn's name, a sizeable $225,000, which had been her college account. They'd use that to get a new start, a place to live, their very own used Corolla, and Lynn could go to junior college followed by Cal State, just like I did. She'd be the better for it.

The best part of my dad's deal was complete confidentiality. The human trafficking story was a national headline, with international overtones, but Toscano's ties to Nevin's business never saw the light of day, never touching Catherine and Lynn. If it had, they'd be forever tainted, no matter that even Nevin had never known the details of Toscano's operations.

Lynn seemed glad to be free of the weight of living in a castle and loved the condo they were renting at Coral Canyon. She also thought the idea of her mom working was *cool*. Just like other kids' moms.

I'd seen the black SUV one more time. It was parked in a distant corner of the parking lot facing the courts, during one of Lynn's lessons. I called the Pro Shop on my cell and asked them to send Gil over in one of the maintenance trucks, to park in front of the SUV and block him in. Leaving Lynn to practice her serves, I walked over once I saw Gil's truck in place. He was ready for bear with a crow bar, and I had my racquet and killer backhand swing ready. At first, whoever was inside wouldn't open the door, and we couldn't see inside with the dark tinting. Finally, the driver tired of the stalemate and lowered the window.

Staring at me with a face red with embarrassment was a kid Lynn's age. He had almost as many pimples as I'd suffered through at his age. He was mum until he saw Lynn looking over at the distant commotion, then in a rush came clean. His name was Robbie and he knew Lynn from school. He was "crazy about her," but couldn't quite get over the fear factor of asking her out. So he took to following her around at times, settling for that.

I thought about offering him some dating advice, then decided I didn't want to ruin his life. But I did sink to some extortion: Ask her out within twenty-four hours, or I'd spill the beans. The next day I heard from Lynn she had been asked out on her first date. She informed me it was with a boy she had always liked but was afraid to approach. A boy named Robbie.

Brent had become a part of Lynn's extended family. Slowly at first, but they were more trusting and accepting of him with every passing week. Not pushing, just available. No, he wasn't taking the place of Nevin. Nevin would keep his spot in Lynn's eyes as her father, but Brent was an important addition to their lives.

Sadly, Melanie still wasn't ready to meet Lynn, but not every adoption worked out perfectly. And given what we had to start with, I couldn't complain. She'd had her second meeting with the Adoption Service Provider and her thirty days to change her mind had passed, making her consent permanent. Now it was just a matter of time to finish the home study and legally make Lynn Catherine's daughter. Melanie's mother was there in abundance, and I finally got my homemade chocolate chip cookies. I had the feeling there were a lot more where they came from if I played my cards right.

I was set to meet Lynn for our usual three o'clock, and Brent and Catherine were going to come at six, after work, for some doubles. Catherine was a novice, but eager to learn, and we'd pound the ball among the three of us, then every few shots lob an easy one to her.

Lynn had her license now, although she didn't need it at the moment. She could just walk from their condo. We had a fierce few hours and I was glad to sit when Brent showed up, soon followed by Catherine. She and I sat and watched Brent and Lynn rally.

"So how's the new job?" I asked.

"Good! I really like it. The salary is only decent, but there's medical and dental." Ah, the concerns of the working man. And woman.

She touched my arm.

"Toby, I really want to thank you. For everything."

I hate being thanked but at the moment I couldn't think of one of my smart ass remarks to deflect the compliment.

"You're welcome."

I wanted to change the subject before another nice remark came my way.

"Lynn's doing so great with everything," I said. "I can't believe she's accepted everything so well, and in just a couple months. You've done a fantastic job, Catherine."

She looked amused.

"You think she's only known for two months?"

"Well, yeah. That's when we found Melanie, and Brent came forward. That's when you told her. Right?"

"Yeeesss. That's when I *told* her, but that's not when she knew."

I looked at her, not following.

She said, "I wasn't sure until I told her everything, but it turned out she'd known she was adopted for years."

I could only gape at her, waiting for more.

"For years she'd been nosy, always listening at doors and on the phone. We told you about that—it's why we met when she was at school. Typical teenager stuff, I guess. Anyway, that's how she must have heard us talking about the adoption at some point. . . and Nevin on the phone," she cringed, "doing *business*."

My body tingled as the last piece of the puzzle of the last few months fell into place.

"So *Lynn* wrote the notes," I said.

Catherine nodded.

"I had my suspicions," she said. "That's one reason I never

wanted you to mention them. It was Melanie or Lynn. I didn't want to see either of them hurt. Besides, it was the first time Nevin would budge on getting the adoption right. Whoever did them, they were working."

I thought of the first notes. *If you love her, you will tell her.*

"So," I said. "She wanted you to tell her, not have to bring it up to you."

Poor kid. She probably didn't know how to ask about such a thing.

Catherine nodded, her face saying: I failed her once. I'll never do it again.

And the second note: *Do you love your daughter? Do you keep secrets from the people you love?*

How sad she must have been to write the notes and still not have her parents tell her. And how confused. How could she know her father was so deep into lies and illegality that he wasn't sure which of his indiscretions were being referred to.

She'd addressed those notes to both her parents. When she overheard her father's manipulations on the phone, particularly over issues she cared about, like keeping Fallbrook green, she directed them to him, telling him, *Be good, not evil* and *Do the right thing.* A young girl simply wanting her dad to be worthy of her love, crying out, *Be good, daddy. Please, just be good.*

I said, "So the threats in the last two notes—"

"She was just desperate to get him to stop. This was *her father.* She thought she could make him do the right thing. When I saw her use his birthday as a deadline, I knew it had to be her. She was just so angry, that was the cruelest thing she could think of doing, spoiling his birthday worrying about it."

"So that's why she didn't handwrite the notes," I said. "She knew you'd recognize her handwriting. Easier to just grab a discarded newspaper and bury it in the trash. You'd never think to look in your own home."

Now I knew why Lynn's name had never been used. As the writer, she'd have felt funny writing about herself like another person.

I had one last thought.

"But how'd she mail them?"

I thought of her being escorted everywhere by limo. Asking for a detour to the post office wasn't possible.

Catherine smiled.

"I asked her that," she said. "Sometimes it's too easy. She just dropped them in the courtesy mail slot they have in the Pro Shop. She was here almost every day."

Sure. I'd put mail in there myself. And that explained why not every envelope was mailed in Fallbrook. Hilary, the Pro Shop counter girl, would just take the mail and drop it off at a post office on her way home, or wherever she was headed after work that day.

"Hey, you two!" It was Lynn. "Time for some doubles!"

Catherine and I got up and walked over. Lynn was beaming. She was here with some of her favorite people, three people who would do everything in their power to help her grow up right.

Lately she had a new name for me. I had to admit I liked it.

It was time to choose partners and Lynn grabbed me.

"I got dibs on Uncle Toby!"

About the Author

Randall Hicks is an attorney who has completed more than nine hundred adoptions, litigated cases as high as the U.S. Supreme Court, and hosted the PBS series, *Adoption Forum*. He is the author of *Adopting in America: How to Adopt Within One Year*. Printed in four editions from 1995-2005, it has been featured on *The Today Show, Sally Jessie Raphael, The Leeza Gibbons Show, Mike & Maty* and *The Home Show*. His newest how-to adoption book is *Adoption: The Essential Guide to Adopting Quickly and Safely* (October 2007, Penguin).

Randy's debut mystery, *The Baby Game*, won the Gumshoe Award for Best Debut Mystery, was a finalist for the Anthony, Macavity and Barry Awards, and was named a "killer book" by the Independent Mystery Booksellers Association.

In his youth, Randy was an actor, playing the lead role of imprisoned smuggler, Billy Hayes, in NBC's *Escape*, the TV version of the feature film, *Midnight Express*.

Married with two children, he lives in Fallbrook, California, where he pretends to be an avocado farmer and sheep rancher, and plays tennis whenever his knees will let him.

For more information please visit TobyDillon.com. You may email the author at randy@randall-hicks.com.